SCORCHED BY DARKNESS

BOOK TWO DRAGONS OF ETERNITY

ALEXANDRA IVY

Scorched by Darkness

Editor: Julia Ganis
– JuliaEdits.com

Formatting by
Sweet 'N Spicy Designs
– http://sweetnspicydesigns.com

http://alexandraivy.com

CHAPTER ONE

Torque was in the zone.

That perfect place where he was intimately connected to his inner dragon and capable of seeing the world with a sharp, acutely brilliant focus.

Moving with liquid grace, he crossed the vast training room with a complex pattern of leaps, kicks, and lightning-fast punches. Fire danced over his skin, leaving scorch marks on the granite floor. He might be a half-breed, but his dragon was particularly strong, allowing him to create enough heat to melt through stone if he wasn't careful.

He was also capable of creating small portals, masking his presence, and killing most creatures with his bare hands. And he had a unique gift of being able to conjure tiny sparks that he could send anywhere in the world. Not a particularly valuable talent, but he'd more than once used them to distract his enemies long enough to gain the upper hand.

Turning to finish his daily routine, Torque found his concentration wavering as a flicker of movement appeared near the door.

"Not now," he growled, leaping high enough to grab the ring hanging from the ceiling.

With a fierce surge of power he was swinging forward, releasing the ring to arc through the air, landing lightly on his feet before he was spinning to kick at the punching bag attached to a steel bar.

"You're wanted," a familiar male voice drawled.

Char.

Like Torque, the male was a half-breed dragon who was in the service of Baine, but that's where the similarities ended.

Torque was a trained solider with short dark hair and brilliant blue eyes. Char was a personal companion to Baine, which meant he had the ability to partially shift into his dragon-form. He had silver hair and gray eyes that turned from smoke to charcoal depending on his mood.

The older male also preferred elegant suits, while Torque wore the plain black uniform of a guard, or casual jeans and sweaters when he wasn't on duty.

Even their personalities were different. Char was sly, sardonic and charming. The sort of male who took pleasure in laughing at the world. Torque, on the other hand, was far more serious. He devoted himself to duty, and keeping his fighting skills at peak condition.

"Wanted by whom?" Torque demanded, whirling to give the bag another kick. "You?"

Char gave a short laugh. "You should be so lucky."

"Yeah, right." Another kick. "According to the harem, there's no luck needed to capture your desire. You spread your interest far and wide."

"True." Char deliberately paused. "But I draw the line at an irritable soldier who thinks a romantic night is kicking bags and lifting weights. Give me a warm woman spread across satin sheets and a cold glass of champagne."

Torque hissed in frustration, slowly turning to face the male who was leaning nonchalantly against the doorjamb. Clearly he wasn't going to get any peace until he could get rid of the unwelcomed intruder.

"Are you going to tell me why you interrupted my training?" he snapped.

Char watched as Torque grabbed a towel to wipe the sweat from his body, tendrils of smoke still clinging to his damp skin.

"Baine had a visit from his father's emissary," he said.

Torque scowled. Baine had walked away from his father, Synge, centuries ago. Dragon family dynamics were explosive to say the least. Many were downright homicidal. But since Baine had found his mate, the two had started a cautious relationship.

Which meant it wasn't entirely unheard of for Synge to send a messenger.

"And?"

"And now he's asking for you to come to the throne room."

"A Council meeting?"

"No. Just you." The gray eyes darkened with something that might have been regret. "I think it's that time."

A chill raced down Torque's spine. He knew the end was drawing near. His betrothed had been born a hundred years ago on this precise date. Which meant she was considered a mature female. Ready for mating.

But he'd done his best to block out the thought of his looming fate.

"Now?" he breathed.

Char grimaced. "Sorry, dude."

Torque turned away. He felt trapped. Had someone put a noose around his neck when he wasn't looking and started to squeeze?

"Tell the master I'll join him after I bathe," he muttered, making a straight line for the side door that led to the locker rooms.

Stripping off his gi, he tossed it on the floor and stepped into a pool overlaid with black and gold tiles. This room was like much of the lair.

Opulent. Lush. Brimming with priceless artifacts.

Dragons were jealous hoarders of beautiful objects, and their homes were a reflection of their status. The more treasure, the greater their power.

There was no doubt that Baine was at the top of the food chain.

He was also a remarkably fair master to his small army of servants. Not that he was weak. Hell, he could be as arrogant and temperamental as the next dragon. But he wasn't unnecessarily cruel.

Something that'd earned Torque's unwavering loyalty over the past century.

Which made this day all the more difficult to endure.

Walking into the center of the bath, Torque sank into the hot water and scrubbed himself clean before leaving the pool. Standing on the tiles, he released a small burst of heat, drying his skin before a robed servant managed to scurry forward to hand him the neatly pressed uniform.

Torque silently pulled on the clothing, his dark thoughts clouding his mind.

He wasn't entirely sure why he was feeling as if he'd been hit by a freight train. Actually, he'd been hit by a freight train not long after they'd returned to this world and it hadn't been nearly so stunning.

Sore. Yes. And aggravated with Char for daring him to stand on the tracks. But not shocked to the point it was difficult to think.

Now he muttered a low curse.

He was being a fool. His destiny had been decided decades ago. No. It'd been longer than that. After all, he'd known he wouldn't have control of his future after his dragon father, Pyre, had bartered him into service to pay a debt to Synge.

At the time he'd assumed he would live out his life as a guard for the ancient dragon. Not an uncommon fate for a half-breed. And one that he'd spent his younger years preparing to excel at. If he had to be a glorified servant, then by god, he was going to be a *great* glorified servant.

Then Synge's favorite concubine had a vision of the future and his entire life had been turned upside down.

Squaring his shoulders, he forced himself to leave the locker room. No point in putting off the inevitable.

Baine was less inclined to death and bloody mayhem than other dragons, but his patience wasn't his greatest asset.

A wise servant didn't keep him waiting.

Pressing open the door, he stepped into the hallway only to come to a sharp halt at the sight of Char leaning against the wall.

"What are you doing here?"

The male straightened with a shrug. "I thought I would walk with you."

Torque scowled. "Was the master afraid I might bolt?"

Char cocked a brow several shades darker than his silvery-blond hair. "Baine assumes that his servants are eager to obey his every command."

Yeah, that was true enough. Probably because every servant was eager to obey his every command.

Heading down the hall, Torque slid a sideways glance at the male who fell into step beside him.

"Then why are you escorting me?"

Char offered one of his most charming smiles. The one that could make an entire harem giggle like a pack of hyenas.

"I assume you'll be leaving us today," he said. "Since we've been together for over a century, I thought we should have a moment together."

Torque rolled his eyes, turning onto a main corridor lined with priceless tapestries, as well as several guards who stood at rigid attention.

"Could this day get any worse?"

Char chuckled, his gaze watching him with a keen intensity.

"You know, most males are eager to be united with their mates," he murmured.

Torque's spine stiffened. It was a subject he never discussed. Not with anyone.

But as Char pointed out, he'd soon be leaving.

There didn't seem any point in keeping it a secret.

"Rya isn't my mate," he denied. "At least not my true mate."

Char looked more curious than surprised. Unlike many immortals, dragons often chose their consorts to consolidate their power base or to increase their hoard. They could mate on an emotional and primal level. Baine was proof of that. But the solitary nature of their beasts, not to mention their violent tendencies, made it less likely they would find true love.

"Then why are you betrothed to her?"

"Her mother is a Shinto," he said.

Char released a low whistle. "Very rare."

They were. The Shinto were a reclusive clan of fey who resided in the deepest forests throughout Asia. They were elusive creatures who avoided contact with the more predatory species. Especially dragons, who prized them for their ability to catch glimpses of the future.

"Yes."

"No wonder Synge was willing to offer her a home." Char's gaze narrowed. "In fact…"

Torque cocked a brow as his companion's words trailed away.

"What?"

"Not to be a prick, but Synge could have negotiated a fortune for her," Char said. "Why choose a half-breed who doesn't want her?"

"She's not a full Shinto," Torque pointed out. Synge was an old-school dragon. He pillaged, he rampaged, and he used his half-breed children as bargaining chips. "Besides, her mother had a vision during her pregnancy that Rya would mate the son of Pyre with the eyes of sapphire, and that together we would discover Synge's lost treasure."

"You were in a vision?" Char gave a slow blink. "Nice."

Torque snorted. "Not really."

"So what's the treasure?"

"Synge refuses to say. But clearly he's convinced it's worth binding us together."

There were a few minutes of silence as they neared the towering double doors made of ebony and inlaid with gold.

"At least she's beautiful," Char at last murmured.

An odd flare of annoyance sizzled through Torque. His betrothed wasn't beautiful, she was hauntingly exquisite. Long, satin black hair that she wore in a complicated braid down her back. A perfect oval face. Skin the color of dark honey. Almond-shaped eyes that glowed with the same amber power as Baine. And a tall, slender body that moved with a mesmerizing grace.

But while he'd naturally had a brief meeting during

their formal betrothal ceremony fifty years ago, and even placed his personal mark on her back, no other male was supposed to be appreciating her attractions.

Wasn't that the whole point of a harem?

"You've met her?"

Char's lips twitched as if aware of Torque's bizarre reaction.

"I've seen her from afar. She's—"

Mine.

The word whispered through the back of Torque's mind even as he interrupted his friend.

"She's suitably attractive," he muttered, deliberately adding an edge of reluctance in his voice.

"But?" Char prompted.

"But I'm a trained soldier, not a treasure hunter," Torque answered, back on familiar ground. He didn't want to think about the nights the image of Rya had crept into his dreams. No, he far preferred to dwell on his brooding sense of injustice. "Not to mention the fact that I prefer to choose my own women."

"Have faith, my friend," Char murmured. "The universe brings us happiness when we least expect it."

Torque glanced toward his companion. "When did you become a philosopher?"

Char flashed his smile. "I'm a dragon of many talents."

"And an ego to match."

"Hey, if I don't appreciate my many fine qualities, who will?" Char reached out to lightly grab Torque's shoulder. "Torque, take care. And if you have need of me, you only have to reach out."

Torque dipped his head in acknowledgement of the genuine offer. The two males might be complete opposites, but they'd formed an unbreakable bond over the past hundred years.

Waiting for Char to turn away, Torque pushed open

one of the doors and stepped into the throne room.

It was just as opulent as might be expected for the formal reception area of a dragon. Nearly three hundred feet long, it had ivory walls inset with mirrors. Overhead the ceiling was painted with a whimsical mural of Aladdin, and in the center, a priceless Venetian chandelier spread a pool of light over the glossy wooden floor.

At the far end a pair of gilded thrones were set on a raised dais where Baine and his mate, Tayla, were waiting for him.

The full-blooded dragon had straight black hair that framed a narrow face, and almond-shaped eyes that smoldered with an amber fire. As usual Baine was wearing a loose pair of dojo pants that revealed the tattoos that crawled over his skin with a metallic shimmer. The markings were more than just decorative. They represented the enormous amount of knowledge the dragon had managed to accumulate over the long centuries.

He was as much a scholar as a warrior.

The female imp next to him had dark gold hair with hints of fire in the silken strands. Her face was pale and dominated by a pair of light green eyes with fissures of jade.

Her beauty was obvious, but everyone in the lair knew it was her gentle soul and boundless capacity to love that had captured Baine's wary heart.

Waiting for Baine to give a small flick of his fingers, Torque walked up the narrow crimson carpet. With every step forward the pulse of the male's power grew more pronounced. The dragon might be sprawled on his throne like an indolent pasha, but only a fool would miss his magic that thundered in the air.

Falling to his knees at the edge of the dais, Torque bent his head in respect.

"Master."

There was a sigh from the tiny woman at Baine's side. "You really have to do something about that."

Baine glanced toward his lovely mate. "What?"

"Master." Tayla rolled her eyes.

"It's my title." Baine shrugged. "At least I don't make my servants crawl on their knees."

"Do other dragons do that?" the imp demanded.

Baine shrugged. "Of course."

Tayla gave a click of her tongue. "Really, we need to have a training seminar to educate your people on how to treat servants. It's not nice to go around terrifying your loyal staff. And don't even get me started on the breathing fire thing."

Baine's lips twitched. "You didn't mind me breathing fire last night."

The imp flushed, even as her eyes twinkled with remembered pleasure. "That was different."

"Did you call for me?" Torque intruded into the teasing banter.

He deeply respected his master, and the entire lair adored the sweet imp he'd taken as his mate, but Torque's nerves were at the point of snapping.

Now that his destiny had arrived, he just wanted to get it over with.

"I did," Baine said, his rare smile vanishing.

The noose tightened around Torque's throat.

"I'm prepared for my fate," he managed to say.

"Actually, there's been a small detour in your fate."

Torque lifted his head, studying Baine in confusion. "What does that mean?"

"My father contacted me this morning to inform me that your future consort is missing."

Torque slowly rose to his feet. He'd been expecting to be led directly to the portal that would transport him to Synge's lair.

Now he frowned, trying to figure out what the hell was going on.

"Missing? I don't understand," he muttered.

"She can't be found."

"But…" Torque gave a shake of his head. "I thought she was in the harem?"

Baine shrugged. "That's what everyone thought."

"Has she been taken by force?"

"No."

Torque's frown deepened, his stab of fear fading as a hint of anger sparked in the pit of his stomach.

"Then what happened?" he demanded.

"From what has been discovered, she slipped away unnoticed."

Slipped away? Meaning she snuck away from the harem like a thief in the night?

"How is that possible?"

"She has fey blood," Baine said. "Like you."

Torque frowned. He never talked about his mother. Primarily because there was nothing to say. He knew nothing about her beyond the fact she was fey. And that she'd abandoned him only minutes after giving birth.

Not exactly the sort of mother anyone would want to brag about.

"And?" he prompted.

"And she was capable of creating a portal to leave her home without alerting anyone to her disappearance."

Torque's hands clenched at his side as his anger spread.

Which meant his female had not only walked away, but she'd deliberately tried to fool her father into believing she was still there.

His chin tilted, his pride rubbed raw by the betrayal.

Wasn't it enough that he'd been commanded to place his mark upon her? Now she had to publicly humiliate him by walking away when they were due to formalize their union?

"Does anyone know how long she's been gone?"

Baine shook his head. "Unfortunately, no. She was residing in the family harem, which meant the guards were only there for her protection. She was free to come and go as she pleased, so they didn't monitor her daily activities," he said. "She could have been gone for hours, or weeks before Synge noticed she was missing."

Torque turned to the side, unwilling to allow his master to see the fierce emotions that scoured through him.

Somewhere in the back of his mind a voice was whispering that he should be relieved. If the female had disappeared then there was no fear he would have to take her as a consort.

But it wasn't relief that was scouring through his body. Instead it was a toxic combination of anger and betrayal.

"Why would she leave?"

Baine cleared his throat. "That's what my father wants you to find out."

Torque turned back to meet Baine's smoldering amber gaze.

"He knows where she is?"

"That's your task."

Torque tilted his chin, trying to pretend an indifference he was far from feeling.

"If she left before completing our mating then our contract is at an end."

Baine tapped his slender fingers on the arm of his massive throne. "I did mention that to Synge."

"And?"

"And he's fully convinced that it's your duty to track her down and return her to the harem," Baine answered.

Torque pressed his lips together. Of course the older dragon would put the responsibility on him.

"What if I refuse?"

Baine grimaced. "You can spend your service as an ambassador to the trolls."

It was the shit-job of the dragon world. No one, not even the most hardened warrior, wanted to be stuck dealing with the smelly, thick-skulled trolls who lived like barbarians in the most remote mountains.

"I don't even know where to begin searching for her," he muttered, still pretending he was reluctant to perform his duty. Inside, however, his beast was stirring with a sharp-edged urgency to be on the hunt. "Her dragon blood will ensure she can cloak her presence."

"Ah." There was the sound of claws scrapping against the wooden floor.

Glancing over his shoulder, Torque shuddered at the sight of the three-foot gargoyle sashaying his way up the red carpet. Levet was a friend of Tayla's, and was a frequent visitor to the lair.

"If you are in need of a tracker, then you are very fortunate that I have chosen to visit my BFF, Baine."

Baine scowled. It was a testament to his love for his mate that the miniature gargoyle hadn't been turned into a charred pile of rubble.

"BFF?" the dragon demanded.

Levet spread his wings that were not only as delicate as a dew fairy, but shimmered in shades of blue and crimson and gold.

"Best friends forever," he told the mind-bogglingly powerful dragon.

Baine looked momentarily horrified. "We are not friends."

"Of course we are." Levet reached up to scratch one of his stunted horns, his ugly snout curled in confusion. "Why else would you give me private rooms in your lair?"

Tendrils of smoke curled from Baine's flared

nostrils. “Private rooms?”

“We’ll discuss it later,” Tayla murmured, reaching out to stroke her hand lightly down Baine’s bare arm. He instantly relaxed, as if she had some magical ability to soothe his inner beast. Once assured the male wasn’t going to bathe the room in fire, she turned her attention to the gargoyle. “Can you track down Rya?”

“But of course.” Levet’s tail curled around his feet, his chest puffing out. “I am the pistachio of locating beautiful females.”

“Pistachio?” Baine snapped.

Tayla made a choked sound, clearly trying not to laugh. “I think he means Picasso.”

Baine hissed with annoyance. “That still doesn’t make any sense.”

Levet gave a flap of his fairy wings. “I am a master of my craft.”

Torque took a step to the side, assuming Baine was about to rid them of the aggravating pest. Instead, the cunning creature allowed a slow smile to curve his cruel lips.

“It couldn’t hurt to take him with you,” he told Torque.

“No. Absolutely not.” The refusal burst past Torque’s lips before he could call it back.

The mere thought of being stuck with the miniature pain in the ass was enough to make his blood run cold.

A hell of a feat, considering he was half dragon.

Baine lifted his brows. “Do you want to spend the next few centuries with the trolls?”

This time Torque managed to bite back his words. He was well aware the dragon was simply trying to rid himself of the annoying gargoyle, but unless he wanted to be stuck with dozens of smelly trolls in a dark hole…

“Fine,” he ground out.

Like he could say anything else.

Levet held out a clawed hand, his gray eyes sparkling with smug satisfaction.

"I will need an object that has a connection to the female," he commanded.

Acutely aware of Baine's warning gaze, Torque reluctantly pulled the pewter ring from his finger. It'd been handcrafted by Rya and held a portion of her magic.

"This was her betrothal gift," he said, dropping it into Levet's outstretched hand.

There was a tiny burst of magic and the ring disappeared.

Torque felt an odd flare of panic. Not that he was attached to the ring, he hastily assured himself. It was just... Hell, he didn't know what it was. All he understood was that he was going to rip off the gargoyle's wings if he lost the betrothal gift.

"Come." Levet abruptly turned to waddle toward the door. "We need to find a witch."

Torque forced himself to follow. "What do you need with a witch?"

Levet continued to waddle toward the door. "Like any great artist I must make use of tools. Do you ask why Renoir needs a brush?"

Torque glanced over his shoulder, meeting his master's amused gaze.

"How long would I have to stay with the trolls?"

Baine pointed a finger toward the door. "Go."

Torque stomped forward, wondering if he'd even make it out of the lair before he torched the tiny demon.

They'd almost reached the door leading out of the throne room when the sound of Tayla's voice floated softly through the air.

"Torque."

Once again he glanced back. "Yes?"

"Be gentle when you find her."

He scowled. The female had publicly humiliated him.

"Gentle?"

Tayla offered a sympathetic smile. "You don't know why she left."

Torque snorted, heading out of the throne room.

He didn't give a shit why she'd left. He only knew that when he found her…

Well, he didn't actually have a plan. But once he got his hands on her, he intended to make damned sure she didn't escape again.

CHAPTER TWO

March was definitely coming in like a lion on the Vatnajökull glacier in Iceland. The temperature hovered below freezing with a fierce wind that cut through the air with a brutal chill.

The terrain was inhospitable to humans, with narrow ridges of snow separated by deep gullies that occasionally dropped the unwary onto shards of razor-sharp ice below. And then there was Grimsvotn, the active volcano that was belching out toxic gases and ash.

The perfect place for a small colony of frost sprites to hide.

The creatures were nearly as rare as the Shinto fey, and just as wary of the predatory species.

Not that they were helpless. They had warriors who were trained to fight with swords as well as their magical ability to form ice around their enemies.

They should have been safe in their frozen part of the world, but of course, no one could ever truly isolate themselves enough to avoid danger.

Four weeks ago the first frost sprite disappeared. They assumed in the beginning that the young male had been struck with the urge to travel to one of the distant villages to enjoy a few nights with the human women. It was something the more adventurous males enjoyed. But when he didn't return they started to become concerned. Then another frost sprite disappeared. And another.

By the time five had gone missing they knew they had a problem they couldn't solve on their own. Desperate, they reached out to Rya's mother, Kai. Her skill at creating a shadow included being able to use her projected image to find missing people.

Unfortunately, she'd been deep in the caves, touching the spot where the last sprite had gone missing, when she'd vanished.

Rya had received the garbled message from the frost sprites several days later and had rushed to organize her journey to Iceland.

First up had been creating a portal that would prevent her father's guards from realizing she was leaving. She was allowed the freedom to come and go from the harem, but only with an armed guard to supposedly provide her protection. On this occasion she wanted to travel unnoticed. Something that would be impossible with a dragon creating chaos around her.

Then, packing a small bag, she'd slipped out of the lair and traveled to the glacier.

By the time she'd arrived the sprite colony had been removed to a hidden location far from their homeland, and only Finn remained behind to continue the search for the missing fey.

The male frost sprite was not only a prince, but he was their most powerful warrior.

Now she watched as the prince pulled himself out of the frigid sea and strolled in her direction. The male had been searching beneath the ice floes for any hint of portals, while Rya had been searching the lava tunnels.

Her dragon blood was violently opposed to the brutally cold water that Finn tried to assure her was invigorating.

"Any luck?" she demanded as Finn wrapped a blue robe around his tall, leanly muscular form.

He reached up to push back his hair that was a pale silver and long enough to brush his wide shoulders. His features were delicately carved, but there was no mistaking he was all male. His eyes shimmered like faceted diamonds in the fading sunlight, and his skin had the luster of a pearl.

The male moved forward, holding out his hand. "This."

Rya frowned as she studied the small golden object that was scored with hex marks.

"A charm," she murmured, capable of sensing the small tingle of magic that surrounded the round disc. "Do you recognize it?"

"It belongs to a fey, but not one of our tribe," he said.

Rya bit her lower lip. "Is it possible that sprites from other colonies are being taken?"

"Possible." The diamond eyes flashed with fury, his fingers closing over the charm. "Or this belongs to our unknown enemy."

Rya wrinkled her nose. "True. Unfortunately, it doesn't get us any closer to discovering who's responsible, or how they're doing it."

"No." The air crackled with the male's power before he was giving a shake of his head and tucking the charm into the pocket of his robe. "Have you eaten?"

Rya blinked at the abrupt change in conversation.

"I'm not hungry."

"Too bad." He narrowed his diamond eyes. "You need food and rest. You can come nicely or I can toss you over my shoulder."

Rya pretended to scowl. "Bully."

He smiled. "You're not the first to call me that."

"No surprise," Rya muttered, even as she allowed the male to guide her over the snow and into the tunnel that led beneath the ice.

"It smells wonderful," she murmured as they entered the surprisingly beautiful cavern lit with thousands of tiny fairy lights that danced, with a dizzying beauty, off the ice.

"I caught the salmon this morning and wrapped them in leaves with spices before placing them in the hot springs." He led her around a stalagmite—or was it stalactite? One of those pointy things that grew from the bottom of the cavern. Her eyes widened at the sight of the small table set with candles and a crystal decanter filled with a golden liquid. "I also have a small serving of nectar that I bought from a fairy when I visited Flúðir."

Her stomach growled as she moved forward to take a seat. She'd expended an enormous amount of energy trying to discover the magic being used to kidnap the sprites.

No one simply disappeared without a trace. There had to be some residual proof of who was responsible for taking them.

Finn moved to a shallow pool in the center of the cavern that bubbled with the heat from the lava flowing beneath them. With surprising efficiency, considering he was a prince who no doubt had dozens of servants who had left the colony to go into hiding with the rest of the tribe, he unwrapped the salmon and placed them on plates along with slices of fresh fruit that he'd gone through a portal to collect the day before.

Heading to the table, he set a plate in front of her before taking his own seat.

"A true feast," she said with genuine appreciation.

Finn gave a lift of his shoulders. "We've worked hard. We deserve a break."

Rya tried to force the gnawing fear for her mother to the back of her mind. Finn was right. She wasn't going to help if she collapsed from weariness.

"I suppose so," she admitted.

"Allow me." Finn reached for the decanter, pouring them each a glass of the nectar.

Rya took a sip, shivering as the delicious warmth spread through her body.

She was only half fey, but the nectar flowed through her like the finest champagne.

"Very potent."

She glanced toward the male who sprawled back in his chair with arrogant ease. He was truly beautiful. A shame he didn't make her heart miss a beat. Or fill her dreams with heated fantasies. Only one male had ever managed to do that.

Torque.

Her back abruptly tingled, as if to remind her that she carried the male's marking. Not that she could forget. His light touch during the ceremony fifty years ago was supposed to have left a small symbol that would seal their betrothal. Instead the image of a dragon had appeared, the vibrant gold and jade colors spreading across her skin.

The tattoo started at the nape of her neck, its long, sinewy body curving down her spine to end at the upper curve of her right buttock. Most startling, it had two sapphire eyes that were a perfect match to her betrothed's.

Only the fact that Torque had seemed as startled as

she'd been by the size and intricate detail of the marking had allowed her to bite back her words of outrage.

"Is something wrong?" Finn's low, musical voice broke through her distracted thoughts. "The air is suddenly several degrees warmer."

Rya pasted a smile to her lips, feeling a blush steal beneath her cheeks.

Dammit. She devoted a large amount of energy trying to forget she possessed a betrothed, let alone the fact that he'd set her blood on fire when she'd seen him. After all, Torque didn't bother to hide his grim regret that he was compelled to take her as his consort.

Jackass.

"As I said, the nectar is very potent," she babbled, focusing her attention on the male seated next to her. "You're not trying to get me tipsy, are you?"

A wickedly masculine smile touched his lips. "Would it work?"

Her brief tension eased. This male might not make her heart race, but he was handsome and charming and the perfect distraction until she returned to the search for her mother.

"Sprites are so predictable," she teased.

Finn reached for his nectar, the delicate crystal glass frosting beneath his fingers.

"I think it has more to do with me being male, not just a sprite," he informed her.

"True," she agreed with a roll of her eyes. "Males are so predictable."

Finn chuckled. "I'll drink to that."

With a rueful shake of her head, Rya grabbed her fork and dug into her dinner.

They ate in silence, both of them in need of the calories to replace their strength. At last full, Rya settled back in her chair and sipped her nectar.

"Thank you," she murmured. "It was delicious."

"It's just a small way of showing my appreciation for helping to look for my people." Without warning he leaned forward, brushing his fingers down her cheek. "I have a more…personal way to share my gratitude planned for later."

Rya chuckled. She'd spent most of her life in a harem. Not one of the harems reserved for courtesans who serviced the dragons, but private rooms in her father's lair that were carefully protected. Which meant she had little experience with males. But she was smart enough to know that Finn wasn't dazzled by her charms. He would happily bed any female who was willing.

Her lips parted to inform him that she had no need of his gratitude when a sudden heat sizzled through the air.

What the heck?

"Remove your hand from her face before I rip it off and stuff it down your throat," a dark male voice commanded without warning.

Jumping to her feet, Rya whirled around to watch as the intruder stalked forward.

Torque.

Her heart slammed against her ribs as her gaze skimmed over his austere features that looked as if they'd been sculpted by the hand of a master. His eyes were a brilliant blue that smoldered with the heat of his inner dragon. Sapphire fire. His mouth was perfectly chiseled, with the bottom lip surprisingly lush, as if hinting at tightly leashed passions. His forehead was broad with dark, arched brows.

He was compelling, rather than beautiful, she silently acknowledged as her gaze lowered to the leanly muscled body covered by a thin black tee and a pair of faded jeans despite the frigid cold.

She unconsciously licked her lips. His power was sternly restrained, but it prickled over her skin. It made her feel as if she was standing in the center of a thunderstorm, waiting for the tempest to be unleashed and batter against her.

Lifting her eyes to meet his smoldering gaze, she tilted her chin in an unconsciously defensive motion at the renegade tingle of excitement that prickled through her.

He'd followed her.

She hadn't expected that.

"What are you doing here?"

Torque sent a glare toward Finn, who'd moved to stand at her side, before returning his attention to her.

"Clearly I'm here to collect my betrothed," he growled, steam swirling around his feet as his irritation threatened to melt the nearby stalagmites. Or were they stalactites? She really needed to figure that out. "Something that wouldn't have been necessary if you were in the harem where you belong."

Rya narrowed her gaze, squashing her stupid excitement.

She'd almost forgotten the male was a jackass. Thankfully, the first words out of his mouth had reminded her.

"How did you find me?" she demanded.

"Ah." A flash of color drew her attention to the tiny demon who was suddenly waddling forward. "You may thank me, *ma belle*. I am a great pistachio at—"

"Not now, gargoyle," Torque interrupted with a snap.

"Hey." The gray creature with large fairy wings and the knobby features of a gargoyle sent his companion an impatient glare. "The world is eager to appreciate my formidable skills, *n'est-ce pas*?" Continuing forward, the demon moved to stand directly in front of Rya, giving a small bow. "Levet, KISA at your service."

Rya studied him in confusion. "KISA?"

"Don't ask," Torque muttered.

Levet sent the dragon a raspberry before turning back to Rya.

"Knight In Shining Armor," he explained, puffing out his chest with obvious pride.

"Oh." Rya tilted her head to the side. Had the dragon lost a bet? That was the only reason she could imagine the arrogant, always-aloof male traveling with such an…interesting companion. "Are you a gargoyle?"

Levet spread his wings. "Not just a gargoyle, but the most famous of all my people."

"You're very…" She allowed her words to trail away.

"Compact?" Levet helpfully supplied.

"Yes."

"Enough talking," Torque growled, abruptly stepping forward. "We're going back to your father's lair."

It was a direct command. As if he had every right to toss out orders.

Her own dragon stirred to angry life.

She stretched her lips into a tight smile. "Feel free to go anywhere you want, in fact, I can give you a few suggestions. All of them are hot and filled with flames. But I'm staying."

Torque blinked, as if baffled by her refusal. "What did you say?"

"I'm. Staying."

The sapphire gaze flicked toward Finn who had moved to stand at her side.

"Are you being held against your will?"

Without warning, the fey prince wrapped his arm around her shoulders, pulling her against him.

"Does it look like she's here against her will?" he taunted.

Torque hissed, fire dancing over his skin as he stalked forward.

"I told you what would happen if you touched her again," he said, his dark voice laced with murder.

Rya instinctively moved forward, planting her hand in the center of his chest.

"Torque, no." She faced him squarely, indifferent to the flames that would have scorched a mere fey. She had no idea what had the male's panties in a twist, but she knew that she didn't want to drag poor Finn into the brewing fight. "Can you give us some privacy?" she asked the prince, her gaze never leaving Torque.

A sharp chill sliced through the air, sizzling as it slammed into Torque's heat.

"I don't think you should be alone with him," Finn protested. "He's clearly violent."

Raw power roared through air, stirring Rya's hair and making Finn grunt in pain.

"You're about to discover how violent I can truly be," Torque promised in awful tones.

"Finn, it will be fine," Rya assured the sprite, keeping herself between the two males. Not only was she capable of enduring the fire that danced around him, but she had enough dragon blood to know she could kick some serious ass when necessary. "I can take care of myself."

Finn hesitated. No doubt because Torque's eyes were blazing with the promise of death.

"Are you sure?"

She shouldn't have been sure. She'd met Torque one time when they'd formalized the betrothal and he'd barely glanced at her. Even when he'd brushed his fingers over her back he'd acted as if he was miles away mentally.

But somehow she knew beyond a shadow of a doubt he would never, ever hurt her.

"I would suggest that you come with me," Levet broke into the tense silence, gesturing for Finn to follow him as he waddled toward the tunnel at the far end of the cavern. "Over the past days I've discovered that it's best not to bother a dragon when they are in a mood." The gargoyle's wings shimmered in the fairy light. "They can be as temperamental as a vampire."

Finn muttered a low curse. "I'll be outside if you need me," he said, sending a warning frown toward Torque.

"Thank you, Finn," she murmured, waiting for both the gargoyle and sprite to disappear through the tunnel before she was slapping her hands on her hips and glaring at the male who had a unique ability to grate against her nerves. "Now. Do you want to tell me just what the hell you think you're doing?"

CHAPTER THREE

Torque felt as if he was perched on top of thin ice.

Quite literally.

No doubt the strange sensation came from the fact that he'd suffered one shock after another.

The first shock had come when he'd stepped out of the portal to realize that he was standing on a frozen wasteland that stretched with empty desolation as far as the eye could see. Why would any female leave the luxurious comfort of a dragon lair to freeze her pretty ass off in the middle of nowhere?

The next shock had been his outrageous fury when he'd entered the cavern and witnessed a strange male touching his betrothed.

Okay. Any dragon would be annoyed to catch his betrothed eating an intimate meal alone with another male. Especially when the bastard dared to touch his female. But the boiling cauldron of rage in the pit of his stomach that urged him to incinerate the male until he was nothing more than smudge on the ice was…over the top.

Only the knowledge that he was acting completely out of character halted his attack.

But had Rya been grateful for his restraint?

No.

In fact, she'd acted as if he was an unwelcomed intruder. And now she was glaring at him without the least hint of remorse.

What happened to the meek, biddable female he'd met during their betrothal ceremony?

It was…what did the humans call it? Bait and switch?

Almost as if to prove his point that this wasn't the same, quiet female who'd accepted his marking, Rya slammed her hands on her hips.

"I asked you a question," she snapped.

Torque stepped forward, ignoring the fact that his heat was melting the ice beneath his feet. For once, he was incapable of commanding his usual composure.

"One I answered." He allowed his gaze to slowly move down her slender form, taking in the soft, blue sweater and the jeans that molded to her slender curves with aggravating perfection. Had the sprite touched the fuzzy material of her sweater? Or studied her fine ass when she'd walked across the cavern? Or sucked in the exotic scent of lotus blossoms that clung to her golden skin? The mere thought was enough to make flames dance over his body. "I'm here to retrieve my betrothed."

The amber eyes smoldered with anger. "You make me sound like a missing piece of property. Of course, I shouldn't be surprised. That's exactly what you think of me, isn't it?"

Torque frowned. Somewhere in the back of his

clever brain, he realized this meeting wasn't going well. But at the moment his male pride was in charge.

Never a good thing.

"Is that supposed to make sense?" he demanded.

"I've never been more than an unwanted duty you're forced to endure to please my father."

The accusing words made Torque falter. How did she know how he much he resented the mating? It wasn't like they spent time together…

He abruptly grimaced. Of course she would know. The fact that he'd gone to such an effort to avoid any contact after the betrothal ceremony would warn the most oblivious female he wasn't eager to take her as his consort. And Rya was far from oblivious.

Now he felt an unexpected pang of regret, swiftly followed by an odd urge to defend himself.

"It's no secret that Synge arranged our mating," he reminded her.

"And no secret how much you resent it."

He glanced around the icy cavern, his dragon blood protesting at their frozen surroundings.

"This is no place for this discussion." He abruptly decided. It wasn't that he was trying to avoid her accusations. Of course not. It was just that he preferred to conduct their conversation in a place that didn't have ceilings with icicles that threatened to impale him. "We'll return to your father's lair."

"You don't listen very well." She leaned forward, her eyes flashing amber fire. "I'm not going back. At least not yet."

His hands clenched. His every instinct urged him to reach out and toss her over his shoulder. No surprise. He was a warrior. Why chat when he could use brute strength to get his way?

But Torque thankfully wasn't a complete idiot. He realized that he'd only piss her off if he tried to force her back to the harem.

Besides, if he was being completely honest with himself, he didn't want to strong-arm her into leaving. He wanted her to be eager to return to Synge's lair.

No, wait. Not Synge's lair.

Once this female became his formal consort he could petition for a private home.

Just the two of them.

The thought of being completely alone sent a sudden thrill of anticipation through Torque.

Over the years he'd been so intent on the knowledge he was being forced into the mating, he'd never truly considered the benefits. Now his body was reacting with an astonishing eagerness to explore the more tangible rewards.

"Is it the sprite?" he abruptly asked.

She blinked, as if caught off guard by the question. "Finn?"

"Is he your lover?"

A flush stained her cheeks. "Of course not."

"He wants you," Torque said, the edge of aggression in his voice startling them both.

"So what? He's like any male." She waved a dismissive hand. "He'll sleep with any female in the vicinity."

The genuine indifference in her voice helped to soothe his restless beast. And ensured the frost sprite would live. At least for now.

"Untrue," he muttered.

"Excuse me?"

"Some men are far more choosy than others," he growled.

She arched a brow. "I suppose you intend to claim you're one of those choosy males?"

He stilled, belatedly realizing why he'd been so uninterested in females since he'd officially put his mark on Rya.

His dragon had accepted that he had his mate. No other woman would do.

Astonishing.

Not that he was about to admit as much to the female currently glaring at him. Instead he folded his arms over his chest. One way or another he intended to get her back to the comfort of the harem.

This cold couldn't be good for her.

"If Finn isn't your lover then why are you here?"

She hesitated, as if she was trying to decide whether to tell him the truth. At last she blew out a resigned sigh.

"Because I'm looking for my mother."

Her mother? His brows tugged together in confusion.

"I thought she had a home in Hong Kong?" Torque said, vaguely recalling Synge sharing his annoyance that the mysterious Shinto fey preferred her own home to the luxurious rooms in his harem. "Why would she be here?"

"Finn contacted her when his people started disappearing."

Torque snorted. He wasn't surprised the sprites would be fleeing from the overly-pretty prince. He was no doubt a terrible leader.

"If his people were leaving he should have devoted more attention to his tribe and less time trying to seduce females."

"Not leaving, vanishing," she corrected with a frown. "As in, they were there one minute and gone the next."

Torque studied her in confusion. Okay, that was strange.

"Magic?"

She shrugged. "That's the assumption."

"Why contact your mother?"

"She has the ability to reach out with her shadow and locate people."

Ah. A powerful gift. Is that why Synge had taken the Shinto as a lover? Did he think she could use her shadow to track down whoever had stolen his treasure?

Or was it simply the hope for a glimpse of the future?

"Did she find them?" he demanded.

"I don't know." Her eyes darkened, her fear for her mother scenting the air with a sharp tang. "She disappeared over a week ago."

Torque sucked in a sharp breath at her confession, instantly furious.

"And you came here knowing that fey were being mysteriously kidnapped?"

Easily sensing his fierce reaction, she tilted her chin to an aggressive angle.

"I have to find out what happened."

"By deliberately putting yourself in danger?"

She met his gaze squarely, refusing to be intimidated.

"What would you do if it was your mother?"

"Nothing," he admitted with blunt honesty. "I have no contact with my mother."

Her eyes widened. "None?"

"None." He shrugged. "I'm not even sure what sort of demon she was, although I have some magic, so she must have been fey."

"Your father never talked about her?"

Torque shook his head. "All I know is that she bartered some sort of deal with my father. I assume she wanted money. Or maybe Pyre took care of one of her enemies." He kept his tone indifferent, as if he hadn't spent endless nights wondering about the female who'd given birth to him. "Once she produced a male child, she'd paid her debt. She left only hours after I was born."

Her delicate features softened, emphasizing her exotic beauty.

"I'm sorry."

Torque took a step forward. He'd seen Rya demure and compliant in the presence of her father. He'd seen her gloriously infuriated when he'd entered the cavern. And now he was offered a fascinating glimpse of her as a tenderhearted consort.

"Why?" he asked.

"Every child should have a mother."

"My father's servants made sure I was adequately cared for."

She shook her head. "Adequate care is not the same as love."

Love.

Torque flinched. Her soft words touched a vulnerable place deep inside him. A place he'd buried when he was just a young hatchling.

Only fools allowed themselves to be blinded by their emotions.

He believed in honor. In loyalty. And strength.

And lust.

He was a big believer in lust. At least when it came to this female.

"We were discussing your reckless disregard for your own safety, not my mother," he said, a grim edge in his voice.

She hesitated, as if considering whether or not to press him. Then she gave a shake of her head, as if annoyed by his refusal to mourn what he'd never had.

"What does my safety matter to you?"

Torque scowled. "That's a ridiculous question."

"It's not ridiculous," she countered. Abruptly turning, she paced across the icy floor, the fairy light gleaming off the ebony darkness of her hair. "If I disappear, you no longer have to worry about our mating."

Torque was instantly outraged. What the hell was she talking about?

"Don't say that."

"Why not? It's true."

"Don't presume to know what I want," he ground out, not bothering to add that *he* didn't know what the hell he wanted.

Instead he moved forward so he could grab her shoulders and turn her back to face him. Only that wasn't enough. He needed…more.

With a muttered curse, he yanked her tight against him.

Her eyes widened as their bodies melded together, a gasp wrenched from her throat.

"Torque."

He glared down at her perfectly formed face. "Why didn't you contact me?"

She blinked. "Contact you?"

"I'm your betrothed," he growled. "If your mother was in danger you should have asked for my help."

***

Rya tilted back her head to stare into the stunning eyes that smoldered with sapphire fire.

This male had pretended that she didn't exist from the day she was born. Even after their formal betrothal. Now he was glaring at her as if he was genuinely irritated that she hadn't rushed to him for help.

And even more disturbing, he had her intimately pressed against his rock-hard body.

How was she supposed to think when his heat was searing through her clothing and his intoxicating scent was clouding her poor brain?

Giving a shake of her head, she tried to remember all the reasons this male was a jackass.

Starting with the fact that he was pretending to be interested in her life fifty years too late.

"Is that a joke?" she demanded.

His lips flattened. "I don't joke."

She rolled her eyes. *Yeah. No crap.* This male was a stoic warrior. All duty and loyalty and blah, blah, blah.

So why did she find him so sexy?

Sucking in a sharp breath, she hastily squashed the renegade thought. Along with the treacherous image of his slender fingers sliding over her body with desire instead of annoyance.

"Obviously I didn't think you would be interested in helping to rescue my mother," she said.

A tendril of smoke curled from his flared nostrils. "If it's important to you, then it's important to me."

She made a sound of disbelief. "Since when?"

"We're soon to be mated."

"And?"

The question seemed to stump him. "And it's my duty to ensure that my consort is content," he at last muttered.

"Content?" she repeated as a stab of disappointment sliced through her. Stupid, of course. Did she expect him to say that he actually cared about her?

"Yes."

"Then let me make this easy for you." Taking an abrupt step backward, she broke free of his grasp, sending him a warning glare. "It would make me *content* if you would return to Baine and let me concentrate on locating my mother."

His hands clenched at his sides. She suspected it was the only way he kept himself from grabbing her and physically hauling her out of the cavern.

"I'm not leaving without you," he said between

clenched teeth.

"Well, I'm not going."

They were glaring at each other, neither willing to back down, when a shrill scream echoed through the air.

Rya sucked in a startled gasp. "What was that?"

Torque scowled. "That stupid gargoyle."

"They must be in trouble," she muttered, a surge of fear clenching her heart as she ran out of the cavern.

"Rya, wait. Dammit."

Rya ignored the angry male voice. Instead she hurried through the narrow tunnel that angled upward.

She'd been so distracted by the arrival of Torque she'd forgotten the danger that stalked this isolated location. Now she skidded onto the icy glacier and searched for some sign of Finn and the tiny gargoyle.

Darkness had fully claimed the bleak landscape, but she could see as easily at night as she could during the day. Which meant that she had no trouble realizing that there was no one around for miles.

"They're gone," she breathed as Torque stopped next to her, his face tight with frustration.

"Don't move," he commanded. "I'll do a sweep of the area."

She clicked her tongue in annoyance. "I'm not helpless."

A dark brow flicked upward. "Have you trained to be a warrior?"

"Has anyone ever told you you're an annoying ass?"

"Yes." He pointed a finger toward her feet. "Don't. Move."

She remained in place as he melted into the darkness. Not because he'd ordered her stay. Nope. Since leaving the harem she'd decided she enjoyed making her own decisions.

But on this occasion, Torque was right.

His training meant he could do a far better job of

ensuring there were no enemies hiding in the area. And since it was obvious that his dragon lurked closer to the surface than most half-breeds, he possessed a physical strength she couldn't hope to match.

Within a few minutes he returned. There weren't many places to hide on the frozen wasteland.

"Well?" she demanded.

He grimaced. "Nothing."

Rya's fear intensified. "Exactly like all the others," she muttered, moving forward, hoping to catch some lingering sense of Finn.

Torque walked at her side, his brow furrowed. "Explain to me exactly how the people have been disappearing."

"I truly don't know, but I suspect it's through portals."

Together they leaped across a sharp crevasse in the ice.

Torque pointed out the obvious. "We should be able to detect where a portal was opened."

"I've tried, but they must have the magical ability to hide their spell."

Rya moved toward the flat area in the center of the glacier. It's where Finn often stood to enjoy the panoramic sweep of the night sky. He said the stars looked close enough to reach up and pluck them from the heavens. Rya thought they looked cold. Like everything else in this goddess-forsaken land.

Unable to pick up any trace of the frost sprite, she was about to turn and head toward the distant shoreline when she caught the unmistakable tingle of magic crawling over her skin.

"Here," she said, abruptly dropping to her knees as she lightly touched the ice.

With a liquid speed Torque was at her side, studying the small scorch mark that marred the ice. "What is it?"

"The gargoyle."

Leaning forward, he touched the blackened ice. "Yes, I can sense that he released a spell." He frowned in confusion. "Can you tell what he was trying to do?"

Rya closed her eyes, concentrating on the unfamiliar threads of magic. It felt like a sticky web. Briefly confused, she tried to imagine what sort of spell would leave that precise residue.

Then she snapped her eyes open. "He blocked the portal," she said, genuinely impressed with the tiny demon's quick thinking.

Without warning Torque reached out to grasp her arm, urging her away from the point where Levet had presumably disappeared along with Finn.

"Stand back," he growled.

"What are you doing?"

"I traveled with the creature for the past three days." Torque shuddered, continuing to pull her away.

She dug in her heels, studying him with a startled glance. The thought of Torque being forced to travel with the gargoyle for more than a few minutes was…inconceivable.

"Why three days?" she demanded.

Torque wrinkled his nose. "The stupid creature had to find a witch who could use your betrothal ring to cast a spell that would allow me to open a portal."

Ah. She'd assumed that Levet must have some special magic. Instead, it'd been a witch's spell. Her gaze briefly darted down, covertly ensuring the ring she'd made for Torque had been returned to his hand.

She felt an odd pang of relief at the sight of the delicate band circling his finger. As if she would have been disturbed if it was missing.

Idiotic.

"So that's how you found me," she forced herself to mutter.

"None of it would have been necessary if you'd just contacted me."

Rya rolled her eyes. "Or you could have remained with Baine and allowed me to look for my mother without interference."

Fire flared in his eyes. "No way in hell."

She blinked at his fierce response. It didn't make sense. She'd been born a century ago, and carried his betrothal mark for nearly fifty years. In all that time, he couldn't be bothered to remember she was alive, and now he suddenly acted like he was a dog and she was the bone.

Unnerved by his possessive gaze, she gave a shake of her head and returned her attention to more important matters.

"So why did you pull me away from the portal?"

"The one thing I learned when I traveled with Levet is that you don't want to be around when he releases a spell."

"Why?"

"Because he blows things up."

Rya pulled her arm free of his tight grip and returned to the edge of the portal.

"This one is no longer active," she assured him, reaching out her hand to lightly trace the edge of the portal.

"Then what's the spell?"

"It's some sort of web," she explained. "It's there to act as a wedge."

"A magical wedge?"

She shrugged. "The only way to explain it is that he stuck his foot in the door before it could slam shut," she said in an absent tone as she concentrated on the mesh of power.

Torque took a step closer, his heat wrapping around her to protect her from the chill. "You can open the portal?"

Could she? Rya sucked in a deep breath. "We're about to find out," she said, using her magic to grasp the edges of the narrow opening.

It was more difficult than she expected. The gargoyle's spell was unfamiliar and the strands kept twisting into complex patterns that made it almost impossible to work her way past. Her limbs were shaking and a thin layer of sweat was coating her skin when she at last managed to shove open the doorway far enough to slip through.

Before she could move, however, Torque reached out to lay a restraining hand on her shoulder.

"Rya, stop," he growled. "We have no idea where this might take us. Or who might be waiting."

She turned her head to send him a frown. "You can stay here if you want. I'm going to find my mother."

The sapphire eyes flared with a burning frustration. "Aggravating female."

His jaw clenched, then without warning, he was bending his head to claim her lips in a kiss that seared through her with a shocking pleasure.

Rya gasped, feeling her inner dragon stir with a sudden burst of flames and fury. It was the first time her beast had ever responded to a male and she trembled at the sheer force of its hunger.

He tasted of heat. And raw male power.

And she wanted more.

Lots more.

Instinctively she opened her mouth, encouraging the thrust of his tongue as he wrapped his arms around her waist and hauled her tight against his torso.

Her hands grabbed his upper arms, savoring the feel of him beneath her palms. His muscles were as hard as granite and perfectly chiseled. Fascinated by his male form, she allowed her fingers to glide up and over his shoulders before exploring the wide expanse of his back.

He made a sound deep in his throat and without warning a glorious fire was dancing over his skin.

She shivered as the flames began to surround her, the sensual warmth as intoxicating as the finest nectar.

"Torque," she breathed, drowning in the erotic sensations.

Time lost all meaning for Rya as he took fierce command of her mouth, kissing her over and over as his hands swept down her body with a possessive confidence.

He touched her as if he owned her.

Something that should have pissed her off, right? She might wear his marking, but he'd barely acknowledged her existence before she'd disappeared from the harem.

Unfortunately—or maybe fortunately—she was too busy melting in pleasure to protest.

Finally, it was a blast of wind that whipped across the glacier that made her push away from his heady touch, her heart thundering with a mixture of excitement and disbelief.

"My mother," she forced herself to mutter, unable to form a full sentence.

The sapphire eyes glowed with a hectic fire. Lust? Need? Sheer annoyance?

Impossible to say.

Sucking in a deep breath he doused the flames that were swirling around him and turned to face the portal.

"I go in first."

Rya bit her lower lip, knowing better than to argue.

Torque was on the edge. She knew beyond a doubt that if she pushed him too far he'd toss her over his shoulder and haul her back to her father's harem.

And there wouldn't be a damned thing she could do to stop him.

Right now she fully understood the proverb that claimed that silence was golden.

CHAPTER FOUR

Finn was floating in a peaceful darkness. At least it was peaceful until he was rudely slapped across the face.

"Wake up," an unfamiliar voice commanded. It had an accent. Was it…French? Weird. "Can you hear me, you overgrown fairy?"

Finn kept his eyes tightly shut, hoping this was nothing more than a nightmare that would pass.

"I'm a sprite, not a fairy," he muttered.

"I do not care if you are an ogre." There was another sharp slap to his face. "You must wake up."

Releasing his breath with a furious hiss, Finn lifted his heavy lids, realizing he truly was in a nightmare. What else could explain the ugly gray face hovering just inches from his nose?

Then a faint memory teased at the edges of his foggy brain.

What was it?

Oh yeah. Missing sprites. The beautiful Rya. And an ugly-ass gargoyle in the company of the half-dragon, Torque.

He'd reluctantly given Rya privacy, which meant he'd been stuck with the gargoyle as he'd moved toward his favorite spot on the glacier. He'd actually been searching for a way to get rid of the tiny demon when a portal had opened in front of him and he'd been sucked inside.

After that everything had gone black.

Trying to determine where he was, he caught a movement out of the corner of his eye. Reaching out, he snapped his hands around his companion's small wrist and squeezed until the creature gave a loud squawk.

"Hit me one more time, gargoyle and I will turn you into a popsicle."

The indignant expression softened to wide-eyed curiosity as the creature gazed down at him.

"Can you truly do that?"

Finn muttered a curse, forcing himself to a seated position. He grimaced, and not just because of the lingering pain that throbbed behind his eyes. Nope. It was mainly in response to the fact that he was in a cramped space surrounded by walls of slick ice that towered toward a thick ceiling made up of the same ice.

It had to be some sort of prison.

"Christ, I must be in the netherworld," he groused, cautiously rising to his feet.

The gargoyle tilted his head to the side, as if he was actually considering Finn's words. "*Non*," he at last concluded with a twitch of his tail. "It is far too cold to be Hades' domain. The god is old, but he can still put out some heat." The gargoyle clicked his tongue. "The last time I visited, he singed my pretty wings."

Finn shoved his fingers through his hair, glaring at his tiny companion. Was the creature deranged? "What did you do?"

Levet blinked. "Do?"

Finn made a sound of impatience. "Where have you brought us?"

"*Moi*?" Levet stiffened, his wings fluttering in outrage. "This is entirely your fault. I was standing next to you when a portal opened and—" He gave a wild wave of his arms. "*Voilà*, we were sucked inside. Since no foe is foolish enough to dare my wrath I must presume they wished to capture you."

Finn scowled. Okay. It'd been a stupid question. Gargoyles, even miniature ones, didn't have the skill to make portals. And they most certainly didn't have the talent of forming ice prisons.

It had to be the work of the mysterious stalker who'd been kidnapping his people. Ironic, really. He'd been doing everything in his power to find his tribe.

Now it turned out he'd managed to fall into the same trap.

Grimly he moved to place his hand against the slick wall that reflected his image. He had the power to endure the most brutal cold. He could also manipulate ice. But even as he released a tentative flare of magic, he knew it would have no effect on the wall.

The ice was…odd. Almost fluid. And heavily spelled by a magic-user that Finn had never sensed before.

"Damn," he rasped, lowering his hand.

Levet gave a small sniff. "Precisely."

Accepting he wasn't going to be able to easily force his way out, Finn turned back to the gargoyle. "Did you see who created the portal?"

"*Non*." Levet hesitated, as if struck by a sudden thought. "But I smelled rosemary as the portal opened."

"Rosemary?" Finn clenched his hands. So this was the gargoyle's fault. "Is she a gargoyle?"

Levet blinked. Then blinked again. "Rosemary is not a person. It is a plant."

Ah. Finn shuffled through his considerable knowledge of demons. He'd never heard of any of them smelling like rosemary.

"A witch's spell?" he at last guessed.

Levet gave a shake of his head. "A Sylvermyst."

Sylvermyst? Finn knew about the dark fey, although he'd never encountered one. They were distant cousins who had been banished centuries ago.

"I thought they left this world?" he said.

Levet wrinkled his short snout. "A few remained in hiding, and it is possible that there were some who snuck through during the battle with the Dark Lord."

Finn scowled. Was the tiny demon making shit up to sound important? Or could the outrageous claim be true?

Finn shrugged. He knew the vampires had recently battled the ancient evil. Maybe a few nasty surprises had managed to return to the world during the fight.

It wasn't like he had a better suggestion.

He folded his arms over his chest. "Why would they capture frost sprites?"

Levet gave a lift of his hands. "That is your duty to discover. Along with the means of getting us out of here."

"My duty?"

The gargoyle shrugged. "I have done my part."

"What part?" Finn growled. "Slapping me in the face?"

"Hey." Levet puffed out his chest. "I used my magic to ensure that the dragon can follow us. Not to mention standing guard while you napped." He gave a full-body shudder. "I cannot, however, endure such cold. I have to shift before I freeze."

Realizing the creature was about to turn into his stone form, Finn held out his hand. "Wait."

Levet clicked his tongue. “What is it now?”

“What do you mean, you used your magic so the dragon could follow us?”

The wings fluttered as Levet smiled with smug satisfaction.

“I used my considerable talents to make sure the portal could not be completely closed,” he said. “Let us hope that Torque has the intelligence to follow.”

Finn grimaced. He didn’t know anything about the half-breed Torque. Well, nothing beyond the fact that he’d felt an instinctive antagonism. A typical response between two alpha males. But he did know Rya. She would most certainly search for him. And once she found the open portal, she would follow.

And no doubt become trapped.

“You have to close it,” he commanded in urgent tones, his words falling on deaf ears as a flurry of sparkles surrounded the small demon.

Finn squeezed shut his eyes, nearly blinded as the light bounced off the ice. When he at last dared to open them again he discovered that Levet was already turned to stone.

“Shit,” he breathed.

Feeling oddly abandoned by his companion, Finn turned to walk back to the wall, placing his hand against the ice. If there was a way into the frozen prison, there had to be a way out.

Right?

Especially if the gargoyle truly had managed to keep the portal open with his magic.

Calling on his powers, he released a series of pulses that made the ice hum at a low frequency. The vibrations would reveal any hidden openings. If nothing else, the pulses might eventually weaken the ice and cause cracks that he could use to bust his way out.

Refusing to consider the knowledge it might take

days, if not weeks, to do any true damage to his prison, Finn concentrated on his task.

Over and over he released his magic, moving from one wall to another until he was distracted by the sound of crackling. Like water being poured on water.

Was a portal opening?

Hurrying to stare at the place where the murky density of the wall was beginning to clear, Finn instinctively held out his hand. A cloud of mist swirled around his fingers, the ice droplets hardening until they formed a perfect dagger.

It looked harmless, but his enemies swiftly learned that it was sharper than any metal blade.

Usually when it was slicing through their flesh.

The murkiness continued to dissipate, until it was as clear as glass despite the fact it was several feet thick. Finn frowned. A shadowed form was approaching from the other side of the wall.

A female form.

Fury exploded through him, along with something else. Something that made him gawk at his captor with a fascination that was entirely unacceptable.

She was fey. He could tell that much by the provocative beauty of her heart-shaped face and the delicate lines of her slender body. But he'd never before seen eyes that looked as if they were made from pure platinum, or hair that was threaded with the colors of autumn. The long tresses tumbled over her shoulders in a cascade of gold and red with copper highlights.

She was wearing a white robe that blended into the tunnel of ice behind her, but that did nothing to diminish her stunning beauty.

Trying to banish his odd response to her, he placed his hand against the ice. Her exquisite eyes widened as he unconsciously allowed his magic to continue to pulse, sending vibrations through the air.

"You must stop," she said, her voice throaty. She glanced over her shoulder before returning her attention to him. "If you keep trying to escape they'll hurt you."

Finn lowered his hand, startled by the fact that he could hear her as clearly as if she was standing next to him. It had to be magic. Perhaps a miniscule portal that she could speak through?

The thought sent a jolt of hope through him.

If she could create a small portal to talk through, there was no reason she couldn't create a bigger one that would allow him to escape.

Hiding the dagger behind his back, he offered her a charming smile. At least he hoped it was charming. It felt remarkably close to a grimace.

"Who are you?" he asked.

"Adair," she murmured, her husky voice sending zings of pleasure through Finn.

"Adair." His smile widened. "A fascinating name for a fascinating female."

She blinked, as if caught off guard by his blatant flirtation.

"It's very common among my people."

"You're a Sylvermyst," he breathed, his gaze skimming over the pure ivory of her skin before lingering on the lush curve of her lips.

The sort of lips that could send a male to paradise.

Hastily he squashed the renegade thoughts.

She nodded. "Yes."

"I've never met one in person." He stepped forward, his nose nearly pressed against the ice wall. "Are they all so lovely?"

Her long lashes fluttered, the scent of rosemary filling the air.

"I…I must go."

"Wait." He tried to look entreating. It felt weird on his face. He was a male who demanded, not pleaded.

"Can you tell me where I am?"

She shook her head. "Don't ask."

"Why not?" he pressed. "Is it your secret lair?"

She hesitated, the scent of rosemary deepening. At last her hand fluttered toward her throat, as if she was afraid.

"Dragon dreams," she whispered.

"Dragon dreams?" Finn stilled, his brows drawing together in confusion. "What does that mean?"

She shook her head. "I'm not sure."

He bit back his curse. For now it didn't matter where he was. Or what the hell 'dragon dreams' might mean.

"Tell me why I'm here," he instead demanded.

"My family has need of you," she said.

"What do they need me for?" he asked.

"I can't tell you. Just do as they ask. Otherwise…" She allowed her words to trail away, a shudder shaking through her body.

"Otherwise?" he prompted.

"They'll kill you." She shuddered. "They'll kill both of us."

Finn fought his primal response to the fear that flared through the platinum eyes. This female didn't need his protection, he fiercely reminded himself. She was the enemy. Which meant she was quite likely trying to earn his trust so she could…

Well, he didn't know what she wanted, but he wasn't going to be bewitched into forgetting she was the bad guy. Or bad female.

Bad, sexy, delectable female.

Abruptly as furious with himself as the Sylvermyst who'd taken him captive, he allowed his smile to fade.

"Where are my people?" he snapped.

She flinched. "They're safe."

Finn slammed his hand against the ice. "Where?"

"Shh." She glanced over her shoulder, pretending

she was terrified of some unseen enemy lurking behind her. "I told you—"

"Don't screw with me," he interrupted, his anger sending plumes of frost through the air. "I want to be taken to them."

She jerked her head around to send him a horrified glance. "No. That's impossible."

Finn narrowed his eyes even as he tried to reassure himself with the knowledge that his people must be near.

"Why?"

She reached out to lightly touch the wall that stood between them.

"The labyrinth is preparing to change. It won't be safe to try and open a portal until after it settles."

Finn made a sound of impatience. What labyrinth? And why would it change?

Giving a shake of his head, he glared at the female who regarded him with a tragic expression. As if he was stupid enough to believe she was actually disturbed by his fury. "I'm willing to take the risk."

She shook her head, taking a step backward. "They're calling for me." She sent him a warning frown. "You must be quiet. The next time, it will be one of my siblings who will come." She bit her bottom lip. "Trust me. You don't want them angry."

Panic flared through him as she continued to back away. "Will you return?" he demanded.

She shook her head. "I don't dare."

"Please."

"I have to go." The ice began to cloud, turning her slender form into a shadowed silhouette.

"Adair." He pounded his hand against the wall. "Don't go."

She disappeared as the scent of rosemary began to fade. Finn clenched his jaw, refusing to give in to defeat.

His position as prince wasn't an honorary title. He

had actual royal blood running through his veins. Which gave him gifts few other fey could claim.

The only problem was that using them meant he would be dangerously weakened.

At the moment, however, it didn't seem he had much choice. He couldn't wait in the cell. Not when his people needed him.

Laying his hands flat on the wall, Finn emptied his mind of everything but the ice beneath his palms.

His magic shimmered around him. It didn't try to bang against the barrier. He'd already discovered that was a losing battle. Instead, he called his most ancient powers to alter his body, allowing him to change his very cellular structure.

Slowly and surely, he sank into the wall, becoming one with the ice.

***

Torque ignored the painful cold as he sat on the floor of their frozen prison.

Any other time he would be furious.

Not only had they walked directly into a trap, but his most powerful weapons were ineffective in breaking through the thick ice walls that surrounded him.

But at the moment nothing mattered but the slender woman he had cradled in his lap.

Gently his fingers slid over her cheek, testing the warmth of her golden skin.

She'd been struck unconscious only seconds after entering the portal behind him. He'd assumed it was caused by the sudden wrench as they'd stepped between dimensions. With a low hiss, he'd managed to turn and scoop her in his arms before she could fall and hurt herself.

As a guard for Baine, he'd trained to endure the

backlash of magic that could happen when forced through a portal. Finn and Levet had clearly been sucked inside by an unknown enemy and the potent vacuum had remained when they'd entered.

Thankfully he'd recognized the familiar dizziness as they were jerked through the void and he'd managed to brace himself. Rya, however, hadn't been expecting the recoil. Which meant she was susceptible to the disorienting sensations.

But even knowing why she was lying unconscious in his lap didn't ease the fear that was twisting his stomach into a tight knot.

He didn't understand his intense reaction.

He'd never worried about Rya before she'd left the harem. Of course, there was no safer place in the world than a dragon's lair, a voice whispered in the back of his mind.

But now…

Shit. He was suddenly terrified that something might happen to her.

Instinctively his arms tightened around her delicate form, his gaze locked on the steady pulse that beat at the base of her throat.

Her warm, exotic scent teased at his nose, stirring something deep inside him.

Not lust. Or at least not entirely. It was raw and profound and unnamed.

Keeping them both wrapped in a bubble of heat, he grimly waited.

And waited.

And waited.

Just when he feared his dragon might go apeshit crazy and do something desperate to try and get them out of the prison, Rya softly stirred against him.

"Torque?" she breathed.

"I have you." His hand gently cupped her cheek.

"Are you hurt?"

Her lashes fluttered upward, her amber eyes still dazed as she tried to make sense of where she was.

"No, I'm fine." Her brows tugged together. "There must have been something in the portal that made me pass out." She studied his concerned expression. "It didn't affect you?"

Torque shook his head. "I've traveled through a void before."

"Void?" She blinked in confusion. "What does that mean?"

"It's a portal used during battle," he explained. "When it opens it sucks in any creature who happens to be in its path."

"Oh." Her gaze flicked toward the towering ice walls that surrounded them. "Where are we?"

He grimaced. That was a question he'd been trying to answer since he stepped out of the portal.

Even without being able to see anything beyond their frozen prison, he could sense the flux beneath his feet. It was like standing on quicksand that was threatening to suck them under at any moment.

"I would guess that we're somewhere between worlds," he admitted. "Our surroundings feel fluid. As if it's moving around us."

"Yeah, I can feel it." She wrinkled her nose. "It's weird."

"More than weird," he muttered.

"What do you mean?"

He grimaced. "We're trapped."

Without warning she was wiggling out of his grip so she could scramble to her feet. Instantly his arms felt empty. As if he missed the sensation of her slender curves snuggled against him.

The knowledge had him slowly rising, his hands clenching to keep from reaching out and jerking her back into his embrace.

What the hell was wrong with him?

She was standing fewer than three feet away. How could he possibly be convinced that she was in danger if he wasn't physically holding her?

It was ridiculous.

Still, he couldn't halt his need to follow her as she moved to place her palm flat against the frozen wall.

"This is ice." She turned her head to send him a puzzled frown. "Can't you use your dragon-fire?"

Standing at her side, he reached to place his hand next to hers on the wall.

"I tried, but the walls must be spelled," he told her. "As soon as it starts to melt, it refreezes."

He released a burst of fire, allowing her to watch as the heat seared through the first layers of ice before it was rapidly re-forming.

Her eyes widened. Dragon-fire could melt through pure steel. The fact that it couldn't dissolve the ice meant it had to be protected by a powerful magic.

"Amazing," she breathed.

"That's not the word I'd use."

Lowering her arm, she turned to inspect their cramped cell.

"I don't understand." She shivered at the brutal chill in the air. "The portal should have taken us to Finn and your gargoyle."

"Levet is not my gargoyle." Torque protested any connection to the aggravating pest, releasing enough heat to keep her warm.

Despite having Synge as her father, it was growingly obvious she'd inherited far more of her mother's fey blood. Which meant she was more fragile than most dragon half-breeds.

He would have to take great care to ensure that the unnatural cold didn't cause her harm.

She moved around the cramped space before turning back to face him. "Did you try to contact him?"

"I haven't been able to contact anyone," he said, not about to admit he'd made no effort to locate the missing gargoyle. Instead he'd reached out to try and link his mind with Baine.

When that had failed, he'd tried to contact his father. Their shared blood and magic meant that nothing should be able to block their connection.

But he'd been unable to reach out telepathically.

He didn't know if there was some sort of buffering spell around their cell. Or if the instability of the space around them was interfering.

She bit her lower lip, slowly beginning to realize they were truly stuck.

"What about another portal?" she demanded.

He shrugged. "Whoever constructed the cell made sure one couldn't be formed to get out of here."

Of course she couldn't simply accept his word. She lifted her hand, her magic prickling through the air. The rich scent of lotus blossoms teased at his nose, making his inner beast rumble in pleasure.

A few minutes later she muttered a curse and allowed her hand to drop.

Torque wisely resisted the urge to point out that he'd told her it couldn't be done. He even managed to watch her pace the icy floor without giving in to the impulse to scoop her off her feet to make certain she wouldn't fall.

See. Old dragons could learn new tricks.

"There has to be some way out," she muttered.

He stood near the wall as she moved from one end of the cell to the other, fascinated by the soft glow of light that shimmered over the glossy ebony of her hair and added a hint of honey to her skin.

She was exquisite.

Desire coursed through his body, the pulses of heat

filling the cell with enough warmth to create a mist in the air.

"None that I could discover," he managed to mutter.

Time passed, but Torque was too distracted by his companion's graceful movements and the lingering scent of lotus blossoms to realize the looming danger.

Not until Rya abruptly lowered herself to sit cross-legged on the icy floor, her expression determined. "Perhaps I can find something."

With a sharp motion, Torque was at her side, glaring down at her with concern.

"Wait," he commanded. "What do you intend to do?"

She laid her hands on her upper thighs, her palms turned up.

"I can use my shadow to search for someone to help us."

He scowled. "What does that mean?"

"I've inherited a few Shinto talents," she said, her voice edged with impatience. "I can create a shadow."

"Like the one your mother used before she went missing?" he demanded.

She shrugged. "No one is sure what happened. The sprite who was with her disappeared at the same time."

He made a sound of disbelief. "And now you want to repeat her mistake?"

"We don't know if it was a mistake—" She bit off her words, giving a shake of her head. "We have to try something."

Torque narrowed his gaze. "Explain what happens when you create a shadow."

"It's actually a part of my essence that I release to travel through space and—"

"No," Torque snapped.

He'd heard enough.

There was no part of her…essence that was going

anywhere.

Not without him.

She scowled. “Is no your favorite word?”

Squatting down, he leaned forward until their noses were nearly touching.

“I spent the past hour holding you in my arms, unable to wake you,” he growled. “At least give me a few minutes to recover before you try to get yourself killed again.”

Her eyes widened, as if shocked by his accusation. “I’m not trying to get myself killed.”

His gut twisted with…

He didn’t know exactly what it was.

Anger. Betrayal. A terrible dread that he’d nearly lost something infinitely precious.

“Are you sure?” he muttered.

“Why would you think I’d want to die?”

He spoke his darkest fear before he could halt the words. “I assume death is preferable to the horrible fate of becoming my mate.”

She pulled back, genuine confusion darkening her amber eyes.

“That’s insane.”

“Is it?” He reached to cup her chin in his hand, careful to keep his touch light. The last thing he would ever want to do was bruise her smooth, delicate skin. He might be a dragon-shifter, but he wasn’t an animal. Okay, that wasn’t true. He *was* an animal. But he could usually control his beast. “You accused me of not being properly excited about our betrothal, but I didn’t disappear from my home on a reckless mission that put my life in danger.”

She stuck out her chin. Stubborn female.

“I had to find my mother.”

Her explanation only fueled his sense of injustice.

“And you trusted a frost sprite to help you instead of

reaching out to me," he scolded.

"I told you, I didn't think you would care."

His fingers drifted down the curve of her throat, lingering on the rapid beat of her pulse.

"But you knew I cared when you insisted on opening a portal and entering it despite my protests," he muttered.

A part of his brain recognized he wasn't being entirely fair. But that didn't stop him. This female stirred the primitive side of him that didn't care about logic or justice.

With a frown, Rya reached up to smack his hand away. "Are you blaming me for us being trapped here?"

He heaved a rough sigh, grasping her shoulders as she tried to scoot away.

"No, I'm blaming you for scaring the shit out of me," he rasped.

She blinked, as if startled by his revelation. "Torque."

"And if you dare claim that I would be happy if you were dead, I'll…"

"You'll what?" she demanded.

"This."

Torque didn't know what demon prompted him to swoop his head down to claim her lips in a stark kiss. At least not until he felt her mouth soften beneath his fierce demand.

Only then did he acknowledge that he'd been aching for any excuse, no matter how flimsy, to kiss her again.

He'd harbored a precise memory of her sweet taste. And the way her lips parted when he swept his tongue over their lush temptation.

Now he wrapped an arm around her shoulders and tugged her tight against his body.

She had heat, but not the scorching heat of his own dragon. Hers was a smoldering, exotic warmth that enticed his beast even as his fey blood bubbled with the intoxicating magic that sizzled between them.

Allowing his fingertips to touch the satiny smoothness of her cheek, he plundered her mouth. He wanted to drown in the sensations that thundered through him.

Why the hell had he been so reluctant to claim this delectable female?

Reluctantly lifting his head, he watched as her fingers fluttered toward her reddened lips, her eyes still dazed.

"Why did you kiss me?"

"Because I can't stop myself," he admitted in a gruff voice.

She blinked, her expression oddly wary. "You're just saying that to try and manipulate me."

He flinched, guilt blistering over his raw nerves. Of course she didn't trust him. He'd never given her any reason to believe he cared about her.

"I'm sorry," he whispered, his hands smoothing over her fragile shoulders.

He felt her tense, her tongue peeking out to lick her lips.

"For kissing me?"

He scowled. Was that supposed to be a joke? He rarely understood humor.

"Hell, no," he snapped. "That's the one thing in my life that I'll never regret."

"Then why are you apologizing?"

His skimmed his hands down her arms, grasping her hands in a tight grip.

"I allowed my reluctance to relinquish my life as a warrior to tarnish our betrothal," he admitted. "I never considered how my lack of attention was affecting you. It was selfish and unnecessarily cruel."

Something vulnerable flared through the amber eyes.

"And now?"

He tilted his head to the side. "Now?"

"How do you feel about our mating?"

He didn't hesitate. "I'm fully prepared to do my duty."

The air cooled, her expression suddenly impossible to read.

"Duty?" she demanded.

"Yes."

"Awesome."

She tugged her hands free, closing her eyes as she sucked in a deep breath.

"Rya." Torque frowned, baffled by the scent of singed blossoms that filled the air. Rya was pissed, but he didn't have a clue why. "What's wrong?"

"The fact that you even have to ask proves you know nothing about me," she muttered. "Or any other female."

Her eyes remained closed, as if she was trying to block him out. The sight made tiny flames dance over his skin.

Dammit. He'd just told her that he regretted not treating her with proper respect as his soon-to-be consort. And even told her that he was ready to complete their mating.

What more did she want?

"I have no talent for reading minds," he groused.

Her lips twisted. "What is your talent?"

"Killing things," he informed her in bleak tones, belatedly wondering if she'd hoped for a mate who was artistic or poetic or philosophical. He'd never had time for anything but training to protect his master. "It's all I've ever known."

She bit her lip, but she still refused to look at him. Instead she squared her shoulders as the feel of her magic swirled around him. "I'll be back."

Fear exploded through Torque.

Shit. Shit. Shit.

He grabbed her arms, roughly hauling her into his lap, but he instantly knew he was too late. She lay limp in his arms, her essence already leaving her body to travel beyond the walls of their prison.

CHAPTER FIVE

Char felt…unsettled.

At first he assumed it was a result of his long sexual drought. Despite his teasing with Torque, it'd actually been weeks since he'd visited the harem to enjoy the various females who were always eager to invite him to their beds.

Not since he'd seen his master with his beautiful mate, Tayla.

The sight had been a revelation.

Suddenly he was witnessing the relationship between a mated couple.

Not just lust, although Baine could barely keep his hands off his lovely consort. But teasing and laughter and a soul-deep affection.

It made the thought of a fleeting night of passion…

Hmm.

He wasn't sure.

He only knew that he wasn't as content with sex as he had been before he'd seen what was possible.

But as the hours passed, he accepted that his restlessness wasn't just sexual frustration. Instead, it was directly connected to Torque.

His fellow guard had been gone for a few days, but it wasn't until that morning that Char had felt a jarring sense of loss as his mental connection to the younger male had been abruptly severed.

All of Baine's warriors shared a telepathic bond that allowed them to fight as a seamless unit during battle.

It should only have been broken if Torque…

The thought didn't have time to form as a massive fist smashed into the center of his face, sending him flying across the gym to land flat on his back.

Pain exploded through Char.

Shit. He knew better than to try and train when he was distracted. Especially when his sparring partner was a six foot six half-breed dragon with massive muscles and a burning desire to earn a place among Baine's warriors.

A shadow fell across him before a lean face with smoldering black eyes and a gleeful smile was hovering directly above his head.

"Do you give?" Vynom demanded.

"Fuck that," Char growled, surging upright to lunge toward his companion with a wicked speed.

His hands were a blur of movement as he hammered the young male with a series of blows that quickly had him retreating across the practice mat.

Fire spilled around them as Char spun through the air and landed a kick that cracked at least two ribs.

"Stop." Vynom dropped to his knees, holding up a hand of surrender.

Clenching his aching jaw, Char leashed his beast, his body trembling with the effort not to shift. He was one of the very few half-breeds who could actually become a dragon. He had to take care he didn't accidentally lose control of his inner animal.

Warily straightening, the younger male lifted a hand to touch the blood welling from a cut on his lower lip.

"Damn, dude. What crawled up your ass?"

Char grimaced. "I need to go see our master."

Vynom shook his head, his long, dark hair that was pulled into a braid brushing against his back.

"While you're at it, why don't you get laid?" the warrior-in-training suggested. "You seem a little on edge."

Char shrugged, moving to grab a towel to wipe the sweat from his bare chest and arms.

"Or I could come back here and kick your ass again," he suggested, drying his face before he tossed aside the towel.

Vynom headed toward the nearby baths. "I vote for the getting-laid option."

Char rolled his eyes, leaving the gym.

He ignored the startled gazes that followed his slender form as he marched down the wide corridor that was lined with priceless tapestries. It was rare that he ever left his private rooms without being elegantly attired in black slacks and a silk shirt.

He took great pride in his grooming.

At the moment, however, he was wearing a loose pair of yoga pants and his hair was mussed from his sparring. It was no wonder the natives were gawking.

Moving from the communal area of the lair into Baine's private rooms, he followed the pulse of energy to the vast library.

He stepped into the room that had towering shelves filled with books as well as glass cases that protected the more fragile manuscripts. A quick glance revealed Baine sitting behind a large desk with a map spread across the polished top.

Coming to a halt in the center of the room, Char offered a deep bow. "Master."

"Char." Baine arched a dark brow, his amber gaze skimming over his servant's rumpled appearance. "Are you coming from the gym or the harem?"

"The gym."

"That's a relief." Baine's lips twitched as he deliberately studied Char's battered face. "I'd hate to think one of the females gave you that black eye."

With a small burst of power, Char rapidly healed his injuries.

He really was rattled not to have done it before he left the gym.

"I was distracted and Vynom got in a lucky punch," he muttered.

Baine slowly stood. Like Char he was wearing nothing more than a pair of loose pants, but his pale skin was covered in a dizzying array of tattoos that possessed a metallic sheen in the candlelight.

"I assume the distraction is the reason you sought me out?"

Char gave a jerky nod. "I can't sense Torque. I think there might be something wrong."

Baine's brows snapped together, his heat blasting through the room as he closed his eyes. Char knew the dragon was concentrating on his own connection to his servant.

Since it was far greater than Char's bond with Torque, he hoped the older male could make contact and reassure him that there was nothing wrong with his friend.

Abruptly Baine's eyes snapped open. "When did you last sense him?"

Char clenched his hands. He didn't need Baine to tell him that he couldn't reach Torque. The worry was etched on his narrow face.

"Our bond was broken when I woke up," he said in grim tones. "I don't know exactly when it occurred."

Baine gave a slow nod. "There's something blocking him from me."

Relief exploded through Char. "So he's not—" He couldn't bring himself to say the words.

Torque might have annoyed the hell out of him on occasion. And there was no denying that he could be a stick-in-the-mud when it came to his rigid sense of duty. But there was no one that Char would rather have at his side.

And the thought that he might have died had hurt more than Char wanted to admit.

"No." Baine gave a sharp shake of his head. "Torque is still alive. But he's no longer in this world."

No longer in this world? Char blinked in surprise. "What the hell is going on?"

***

Finn re-formed his body as he stepped out of the wall.

Instantly he swayed, nearly falling to his knees as weariness slammed through him. It'd taken even more energy than he'd expected to move through the ice. No doubt because it kept fluctuating.

More than once he'd feared he was stuck. In fact, if he hadn't possessed the ability to manipulate the ice around him, he might have become permanently lodged in the strange barrier.

Now he sucked in deep breaths, a fine layer of frost covering his skin.

Realizing that he was dangerously close to collapse, Finn tensed as he caught a familiar scent of rosemary.

Adair.

She'd passed this way.

Recently.

With an effort, Finn forced his heavy feet to carry him forward. The shifting ice had seemingly given him a shortcut through the Sylvermyst lair.

The first stroke of good luck he'd had since his people started to disappear.

Keeping a hand on the icy wall, he moved along the narrow tunnel. It felt like he was walking through a maze that might change or even disappear at any second.

It was unnerving as hell.

Refusing to dwell on the creepy sensations that prickled over his skin, he moved silently through the eerie light that glowed from the surface of the ice.

He was rounding a large curve in the tunnel when he caught the sound of voices. Slowing his pace, he pressed his back against the wall and inched his way forward.

At last he could see Adair standing near an opening in the tunnel. His heart stuttered, his gaze lingering on the striking beauty of her finely sculpted profile and the copper highlights in her hair.

It wasn't until he noticed the way her hands were balled into tight fists of tension, and her slender body trembling beneath her white robe, that he turned his attention to her companion.

The female bore a striking resemblance to Adair. She had the same delicate features and odd metallic eyes, although the stranger's were bronze in color. Her hair was also darker, without the stunning copper highlights. Finn also suspected that the other female was older by several years.

No doubt most males would find her attractive, but Finn was instinctively repelled by her cold disdain as she reached out to grab Adair's upper arm.

"Lila," Adair murmured, her tone wary. "What are you doing here?"

"Obviously I was looking for you."

"Me?" Adair cleared her throat. "Why?"

"You left your rooms." The female gave Adair a sharp shake. "Where have you been?"

Finn stiffened, infuriated as he watched Adair cower in obvious fear.

"Nowhere," she breathed.

"Don't act coy," Lila snapped. "Tell me where you went."

"I…I was bored and I took a walk."

"Liar." Lila gave the smaller woman another rough shake. "You went to see the prisoner."

Finn watched as Adair lowered her lashes over her eyes. She didn't want to tell this female that Finn had been trying to escape.

She was…protecting him.

An odd tightness wrapped around his chest, making it hard to breathe.

"I needed to ensure that pulling him through the portal hadn't injured him."

Lila gave a sharp laugh. "Right. And it has nothing to do with the fact that you've been gawking at the male since we opened the gateway?"

Even from a distance, Finn could detect the blush that touched her cheeks. It only emphasized her rare, astonishing beauty.

"I was told to monitor the entire tribe," Adair muttered.

The older female sneered at Adair's flustered expression. "Maybe, but no one told you to spend hours staring at the lovely prince, did they?"

She'd been staring at him? For hours?

He should have been creeped out by the thought. Who wanted to be watched by unseen eyes? Instead it warmed something deep inside him.

"Is there a reason you're here?" Adair asked.

"Micah is anxious to get the prince working," Lila said, glancing over her shoulder. Was she afraid of the mysterious Micah? And what the hell did she mean by work? "Do you know when he can be brought to the treasure room?"

Adair made a sound of frustration. "I've told Micah that it's impossible to keep a portal open during the flux," she said. "To even attempt to release the prince from his prison might kill him." She held her companion's gaze. "Or me."

Lila shrugged, her lack of concern for Adair's welfare blatantly obvious.

Bitch.

"Our brother is impatient to complete our task," she insisted.

Finn's brows snapped together.

A violent urge to rush forward and shove the female away from Adair surged through him. He could grab her by the front of her white robe and send her skating down the tunnel. Like a penguin skimming across an ice floe.

Only instead of plunging into the ocean, she would smack her smug face into the wall.

Adair hunched her shoulders. "He'll have to wait. Even when the fluctuations cease, it might be hours before the prince wakens," she said.

Finn bit back his curse. Why was she trying to protect him? It couldn't be a trick to earn his trust. There was no way either female knew he was eavesdropping.

So why?

Lila grimaced, as if she had a bad taste in her mouth. "The fey in this world are weak," she groused. "They should have spent some time with the Dark Lord. He would have given them a spine. Or they would have been destroyed."

Finn ignored his weariness as he released a concentrated burst of power to create an ice dagger that he clutched tightly in his hand.

He didn't know much about the Dark Lord, but there were rumors that his followers were cruel, ruthless bastards who sold their souls to gain the power the evil deity offered them.

Which meant that they could be doing anything to his people.

He had to find them.

Now.

Adair hunched her shoulder. "You speak as if being tortured was a good thing."

"It made us tough," Lila argued, her tone sharp. "We're survivors."

Adair shook her head. "No, we're thieves who hide in the shadows."

Without warning, Lila lifted her hand and slapped Adair across her face. Finn hissed, barely resisting the primal urge to lunge forward and give Lila a taste of her own medicine.

He didn't approve of violence toward females, but the sight of Adair lifting a hand to touch the mark on her cheek made him tremble with a vicious need to punish Lila.

Only the knowledge that he didn't have any idea how many Sylvermyst might be lurking in the ice tunnels kept him hidden in the shadows.

Acting impulsively might put Adair in even more danger.

"Don't ever say that again," Lila said in shrill tones. "We're the forerunners who will return the Sylvermyst to their former glory."

Adair ducked her head, an air of defeat slumping her shoulders. "I don't want glory," she muttered.

"Really?" Lila sneered. "What do you want?"

"Peace."

"Talk like that in front of our brothers and you'll

discover the true meaning of torture," Lila warned.

"Don't you hope for more?" Adair's words were so low Finn nearly missed them.

Lila stiffened, a strange expression tightening her features. "All I hope for is to live through the day," she said in harsh tones. "Tomorrow, I'll hope for the same thing."

Adair sucked in an audible breath, her hand tentatively reaching toward her sister. "Lila, listen to me. We could—"

Crack. The female once again slapped Adair, halting her soft words.

Finn growled low in his throat, lifting his hand. One flick of his wrist and the ice dagger would be flying through the air to sink in Lila's throat.

The thought had barely formed when Lila was taking an abrupt step backward. Almost as if she sensed she was about to become a shish kebab. Unfortunately, her new position meant that it was impossible to have a clear shot at her.

"No. Stay here until you're called for," Lila commanded, pointing her finger toward the opening behind Adair. "Next time I discover you've left your rooms without permission I'll turn you over to Micah."

With her warning delivered, the female swiftly headed down the tunnel, disappearing around the curve. At the same time, Adair turned to head down a separate passageway that presumably led to her private lair.

Finn moved forward, his jaw clenched as he battled against the instinctive urge to follow Adair.

His duty demanded that he locate his people and find a way to free them from the icy prison. After that, he needed to concentrate on how to destroy the Sylvermyst so they could never again use their powers to enslave his tribe.

The last thing on his mind should be Adair and the

certainty that she was as much a victim of her family as his own people. No matter how distractingly lovely she might be.

Keeping his back against the icy wall, he cautiously continued past the side tunnel, following the faint scent of nettles.

It was impossible to determine how far he traveled, or even how much time had passed, but at long last the tunnel began to widen. He slowed until he was barely inching his way forward, catching the scent of more Sylvermyst along with something…dark.

And dangerous.

Very, very dangerous.

Stepping out of the tunnel, he discovered he was standing on a ledge that overlooked a deep, massive cavern. Ensuring there was no one near, he glanced over the edge, discovering there was a large bulge of ice in the center of the chasm. It was impossible to determine what caused the odd lump, and at the moment Finn didn't care.

Not when he caught sight of the slender, pale-haired fey that were chained around the edges of the cavern.

Frost sprites.

A grim joy raced through him.

They were alive. He could sense their spirits, although they were oddly muted. As if there was an unseen barrier around them.

Glancing from side to side, Finn was focused on finding a path to reach his people when there was a stir of air behind him.

He cursed his distraction even as a hand was placed over his mouth and he was yanked back into the tunnel.

Tightening his grip on the dagger, he prepared to turn and slice through his attacker. It was only the sudden scent of rosemary that halted his killing thrust.

Adair?

Glancing over his shoulder in shock, he met her furious glare.

"Have you completely lost your mind?" she rasped, her eyes flashing with genuine fury.

***

Rya allowed her shadow to drift through the ice, heading for the nearest opening. There had to be one. It was just a matter of getting through the barrier to search from the outside.

While she drifted, however, her mind wasn't on her task.

Instead she was still seething.

Torque was a jackass.

No. Calling the aggravating male a jackass was an insult to the ass.

How dare he imply she should be pleased because he condescended to accept his duty? Did he think she wanted to become a burden he was forced to endure?

Then, to make matters worse, he'd kissed her.

Just like that.

And she'd *responded.*

It was nuts. Full-blown crazy.

For so long she'd told herself that she would have to force herself to accept Torque into her bed. No matter how gorgeous or sexy or enticingly male he might be, she had her pride. What sort of female could become aroused by a mate who barely acknowledged she was alive?

But she had been aroused.

Achingly, savagely aroused.

And the hunger continued to burn deep inside her.

She had no idea how much time passed as she allowed herself to dwell on her dark thoughts, but it was too long.

She should have already been through the wall, even if the ice was a mile thick. Instead she continued to move through the frozen barrier, belatedly sensing that it was constantly moving to ensure she didn't escape.

Crap.

It had to be magic, but she didn't recognize it. Worse, she didn't have any idea how to get back to the cell.

She was well and truly trapped.

Refusing to panic, Rya concentrated on releasing a small burst of fire. She didn't think she could melt her way out of the ice, but she hoped to leave a scorch mark so she at least would know if she were traveling in circles.

She moved what she assumed was forward, leaving small marks as she traveled through the ice. At one point she paused, catching the unmistakable scent of rosemary, but it disappeared before she could use it to find her way out of the ever-shifting ice.

Cursing, she tried moving to the side. She didn't know if it would help, but she was determined to keep trying until she found an exit, or managed to return to Torque.

Almost as if the thought of him was some sort of trigger, Rya discovered her scenes filled by his male scent. She stilled. Had Torque managed to follow her?

No. That wasn't possible. He might be a skilled warrior, but he couldn't walk through solid ice.

Trying to pinpoint the source of the smell, Rya was distracted by a tiny spark that was visible in the ice directly in front of her face.

What the heck?

She frowned. She hadn't created the tiny flame. Which meant…

Torque?

Yes. It had to be.

She didn't know how, or why, but she wasn't going to ignore the vague hope that the small flame might help her escape.

Sliding her shadow toward the glowing spark, Rya watched as it darted to the left. With grim determination she followed, turning when the flame turned and slowing when it slowed.

It would be easy to wonder if she'd gone crazy and was destined to spend the rest of her immortal life chasing after an elusive flame.

There were worse ways to spend eternity.

But not many.

Oddly, however, Rya had full faith that Torque had found a way to reach out and save her.

Nearing the point of complete exhaustion, Rya grimly pushed forward, unprepared when the ice abruptly disappeared and she slid back into her body with an unexpected jolt.

She made a sound of alarm even as strong arms tightened around her, silently reassuring her that she was safe.

"Torque?" Rya opened her eyes to discover she was cradled in Torque's lap as he leaned against the wall, his legs stretched across the icy floor.

His face was oddly pale as he glared down at her, his eyes shimmering with sapphire fire.

"Shit. No more," he snapped. "Do you hear me?"

She blinked in shock. She didn't know what she'd expected, but it wasn't his outraged anger.

"I think everyone can hear you," she muttered, trying to push herself out of his arms.

She might be grateful that he'd rescued her, but he was still a jackass.

Without warning he tightened his arms around her. At the same time he lowered his head to bury his face in her hair that had escaped from her braid.

"Gods," he whispered, tiny flames dancing over his skin. "I nearly didn't find you."

Oh. He'd been worried about her. Her anger melted away. She didn't even protest when he squeezed her so tight she could barely breathe.

Instead she absently rubbed her hand over his chest in a soothing motion until the flames disappeared.

"How did you create the spark?" she eventually asked.

Slowly he lifted his head, studying her with a brooding gaze.

"It's childhood trick I discovered when I was still in the nursery," he admitted, his fingers brushing through her hair as if savoring the softness of the strands. "I never thought it would have any value beyond distracting my enemies. Not until this moment."

Rya frowned. Something teased at the edge of her mind. Something that had to do with creatures who could use sparks…

"Fire imp," she breathed as she suddenly recalled a story her mother had told her.

His brows drew together in a confused frown. "What?"

"Your mother must have been a fire imp."

His frown deepened. "I've never heard of them."

"Not surprising," she assured him, no longer trying to wriggle out of his arms. She was still too weak to stand, right? It had nothing at all to do with the delicious heat cloaked around her. Or the comforting sensation of his fingers combing through her hair. Nothing at all. "My mother has devoted her life to studying rare fey species," she continued. "She's spoken about the fire imps and their ability to create sparks that can travel great distances. They use them to communicate, to spy on other tribes, and even as weapons."

He hesitated, his expression unreadable. "I suppose

it's possible," he at last conceded, his tone offhand.

She frowned. Torque was stoic by nature, but she expected him to be a tiny bit excited by the thought he might discover something about his mother.

It wasn't until she noticed the clenched muscles of his jaw that she realized she'd touched a nerve.

Idiot, she silently chastised herself. Torque was convinced his mother had walked away without a second thought for her child. Over the years he'd no doubt managed to convince himself he didn't care who she was or why she'd left.

Biting her lower lip, she was searching for some way to change the conversation to a less painful subject when she was struck by an astonishing suspicion.

"Dear goddess, that's it," she impulsively muttered.

He looked predictably puzzled. "What's it?"

"Why she disappeared."

"Why who disappeared?"

"Your mother, of course."

His eyes narrowed. "Are you delirious?"

"No." She released a rough sigh. She was making a mess of this. "I just remembered something my mother told me."

"Rya—"

"Please just listen."

"Fine," he muttered, his tone flat.

Rya ignored his less than encouraging attitude. She was beginning to suspect that beneath all his grim control was a male who harbored intense emotions.

"Fire imps live deep in volcanoes. Many spend their entire life never traveling away from their home," she said, trying to recall as many details as she could about the elusive fey. "That's why so few people know about them."

Torque snorted. "Obviously my father did."

"Yes." She gave a lift of her shoulder. There was

one obvious reason a fey would have attracted the attention of a dragon. "They must have petitioned for a favor."

"And I was the payment." The sapphire eyes darkened. "I'd already figured out that much."

She slid her hand up to lightly touch his throat. "But you assumed that your mother abandoned you."

Smoke curled from his nose. "She did."

"She didn't have any choice," she told him. "A fire imp has to be near lava to survive."

He scowled. "What?"

"From what my mother managed to discover, the creatures have a magical dependency on the lava."

Torque looked far from impressed by her revelation. "If that was true she would have died in the harem," he scoffed. "The last time I checked there was no lava there."

"Any fey can survive for a short length of time even if they are separated from the source of their magic."

"Just as they can easily be separated from their child."

She resisted the urge to roll her eyes. She couldn't blame Torque for being reluctant to consider the idea that his mother might have a legitimate reason for leaving. Hope could be a dangerous thing.

Still, she wasn't going to let him turn his back on a potential explanation. It was important to her. Why? Hmm. Not because she was coming to care about him. Of course not. But…she simply couldn't bear the thought of anyone living with the belief his mother had never loved him.

Yeah. That was it.

"Don't you see? That would explain why your mother had to leave so quickly after your birth," she insisted. "She must have been desperate to get home."

His expression remained hard. "Even if that is true,

she could have returned to visit me."

"Are you sure?"

"Sure about what?"

She clicked her tongue. He was being deliberately obtuse.

There were times when he was so…male.

"Are you sure she didn't try to see you?" she said in slow, concise tones. "You would have been the property of your father, which meant he would decide who could or couldn't visit the nursery. She might have returned only to be denied entrance into Pyre's lair."

Something flared through his sapphire eyes before he was giving a sharp shake of his head.

"I don't want to discuss my mother."

"But—"

He rudely overrode her protest. "I want to discuss your suicidal tendencies."

"Stop saying that," she snapped, wondering if he was deliberately trying to piss her off. What better way to distract her? "I'm not trying to kill myself. I was just trying to find a way out of here. I didn't expect to be caught in a maze."

"That's why you don't rush into unknown places without making sure you won't be trapped."

He had a point. She'd impulsively used her shadow without a full understanding of the prison surrounding them.

That didn't mean, however, she was going to admit she had been reckless. Not when he was doing his best to annoy her.

"Since when did you become my father?" she instead muttered.

"Father?" he snarled, horrified shock rippling over his lean face.

She sent him a chiding frown. "You scold like one."

There was an explosive silence as Torque glared at

her with eyes that smoldered with sapphire fire.

"You scared the hell out of me," he at last burst out. "Again." Another glare. "My nerves can't take any more."

Once again he managed to steal her righteous outrage. Aggravating creature.

Rya heaved a resigned sigh. Maybe they should discuss more important things. Like how to find her mother and the others so they could get the hell out of there.

"Could you recognize the magic of the maze?" she demanded.

He continued to glare at her, no doubt anxious to continue with his sermon. She was reckless, she was foolish, she was…yadda, yadda, yadda. Then, no doubt sensing he was wasting his breath, he leashed his desire to lash out and forced himself to concentrate on her question.

"It smells of dragon-magic," he said grimly.

She blinked in surprise. "Dragon?"

"Yes, but it's strange."

"Everything about this place is strange," she said in dry tones.

"True."

She glanced toward thick ice walls, a shudder racing through her. It would be a long time before she forgot the terrifying sensation of being trapped in the frozen barrier. "How are we going to get out of here?"

He shrugged. "For now, we remain patient."

She grimaced. "I'm not very good at that."

His humorless laugh echoed through the small space. "Yeah, I've noticed."

"Hey," she protested. "Anything is better than just waiting around."

He studied her flushed face for a long, unnerving moment.

"I could offer a distraction," he finally murmured, the heat in the air notching up several degrees.

A strange, electric jolt of anticipation arrowed down her spine.

"What sort of distraction?" she demanded.

He lowered his head without warning, stealing her protest with a kiss that sent pleasure searing through her body. She made a sound deep in her throat, her toes curling.

Intoxicating excitement bubbled through her blood, making her lightheaded.

That was the only reason her fingers were curling into the fabric of his T-shirt to pull him closer to her trembling body. Right?

Of course, that didn't explain why her lips were parting as his tongue stroked into her mouth. Or why she was arching upward in a silent invitation.

But at the moment, she couldn't make herself care.

Not when he was tugging on her hair to tilt back her head. And his roaming lips were taking advantage of her exposed neck to plant dozens of kisses down to the pulse that thundered at the base of her throat.

Oh…lord.

She shivered as his heat danced over her skin. She could smell his dragon in the air. Taste him lingering on her tongue.

Such raw, ruthless power.

It was enough to make any female melt into a puddle of gooey need.

As she wrapped her arms around his neck, Rya's lashes were fluttering downward when she caught sight of a gathering darkness out of the corner of her mind.

She stiffened, turning her head as the darkness spread, heading toward them at a frightening speed.

"Torque," she cried in warning.

His arms tightened around her. "I've got you," he

muttered, cloaking them both in the power of his dragon.

Rya released her own inner dragon. It wasn't as strong as Torque's, but the two easily melded together, creating a blaze of magic as the darkness washed over them.

CHAPTER SIX

Torque held Rya in his arms, protecting her with his larger body as the blackness swept over them. There was the sensation of being whisked through dimensions. Not a portal.

Just pure magic.

Heat prickled over his skin. It didn't feel like a threat. It was more a brush of curiosity. Then slowly the darkness receded and a soft glow of light revealed a large room that looked like it'd been carved out of stone.

With a muttered curse, he set Rya on her feet and stepped back. He didn't want to let go of her, but he needed space to fight.

Spinning in a circle, he searched for a hidden enemy, flames dancing over his skin.

When nothing leaped out of the shadows, he returned his attention to his companion even as his senses remained on high alert. Nothing would be allowed to sneak up on them.

"Are you okay?"

"I'm fine." She pushed her hair from her face, her own power thick in the air. As fragile as she might look, she was still a dragon-shifter. She was far from helpless. "What happened?"

"I..." His words faltered as he allowed himself to truly take in their surroundings. "Shit," he breathed.

"Torque?" Rya murmured in confusion.

He shook his head, studying the familiar black leather couch and matching chair that was set near a large, stone fireplace.

"It's not possible," he muttered, crossing the barren floor to touch the leather-bound books that filled the wooden shelves on one wall.

"What's not possible?"

He pivoted back to meet Rya's worried gaze.

"These are my private quarters," he told her. "Or at least the illusion of my lair."

Widening her eyes, she glanced around with blatant curiosity.

"It feels real," she said, studying the large space before lifting toward the vaulted ceiling. "Did you create it?"

"I don't have the power. As far as I know, only a full dragon can produce an imprint," he admitted, referring to a dragon's ability to tap into a person's mind to create a space that echoed their personal lair.

They could also call on a creature's deepest fantasy or their worst nightmare, depending on the dragon's mood.

Thankfully, he'd never been subjected to that particular torture.

Rya's brows pulled together. "You did say the maze felt like dragon-magic."

He moved toward the deep hearth with a rough wooden mantel built over it. Char had often teased him for enjoying a roaring fire while he read a book in peaceful solitude. He was half dragon, after all. He could create his own flames.

Was it possible that his love for the roaring heat came from his mother? He gave a sharp shake of his head. Dammit. He hadn't thought about his mother in decades. Now wasn't the time to start.

Instead, he concentrated on his companion's words, recalling the distinct power that'd sizzled around him as he'd searched for Rya's essence that was lost in the ice.

"Yes," he said. "I don't know why, but there was a definite dragon vibe."

She nodded, accepting his vague explanation without question.

Nothing short of a miracle.

"Your father?"

Torque shook his head, glancing toward the small gift from Baine's mate that was set on a low table. The delicate pewter figure had sapphire chips as the eyes and a scroll in one hand. Tayla had adamantly ignored his assurance that he had no desire for a dragon's hoard, revealing that she'd had the gift personally made for him.

That knowledge had made him treasure the little figurine.

"Doubtful. The details are far too perfect," he said, his lips twisting at the mere thought of his father wasting his energy creating anything that didn't gain him an obvious advantage. "Like Synge, my father has always concentrated on honing his battle skills. He's a big believer in the 'might makes right' philosophy."

Rya nodded in understanding. She might have lived in a separate harem, but she would be well aware that her father ruled with brute strength.

"What about your master? I've heard that he is far more…civilized than most dragons."

Torque gave a short laugh. Baine and civilized should never be spoken in the same sentence. Still, she was right that the younger dragon had a reputation for subtle cunning.

"Baine has the skill, but I would recognize his power," he assured her.

She gave a slow nod. "So it has to be another

dragon."

"Or an enemy who wants us to let down our guard," he pointed out, not willing to take anything for granted.

She wrinkled her nose. "Neither thought is very comforting."

Without hesitation he was moving the short distance to wrap her in his arms. Instantly something eased deep inside him.

As if he wasn't quite…settled without the feel of her warmth pressed against him.

Which was ridiculous, of course. But for now he didn't question the odd sensation.

"Nothing's going to happen to you, Rya," he swore in low tones. "I've pledged my life to protect you."

For a moment she leaned against his chest, seeming to take comfort in his embrace. Then, without warning, she became rigid in his arms, her scent changing as she tilted back her head to glare at him.

"More duty?" she demanded.

He studied her tight expression with a puzzled frown. He'd been trying to offer her comfort, but clearly he'd done something wrong.

"Why does that word bother you?"

"Who said it does?"

He made a sound of impatience. "I'm not very good at reading minds, but you smell like scorched lotus blossoms when you're angry."

She jutted her chin, her eyes a rich amber in the muted light. "I don't like the knowledge that you see me as a constant burden."

"A burden?" What the hell was she talking about?

She hunched her shoulders. "What else would you call a duty?"

He reached up to lightly touch her cheek. Inwardly he cursed his past mistakes. He'd made her feel unwanted. Now she doubted every word he said to her.

"My duty toward you isn't a burden, Rya. It's a sacred promise," he murmured in a soft voice, considering his words with care. "One that is etched upon my soul. What could be more important?"

She didn't look entirely convinced. "That still doesn't change the fact you were forced into the betrothal."

"Just as you were," he gently reminded her. "But while our meeting was fated by your mother's vision, how we choose to build our relationship from here is entirely in our hands. I think we could create something very, very special."

"Oh." Something vulnerable flared through her eyes as a warm flushed touched her cheeks. "Torque—"

"Shh." He pressed a finger against her lips as he felt the approach of an intruder. "Someone's coming."

Pulling back, he started to pivot toward the entryway, when Rya suddenly reached out to grasp his arm.

"Wait." She frowned as he turned his head to meet her narrowed gaze. "You get to put yourself in danger, but I can't?"

"Exactly," he agreed, wondering why she'd asked such a foolish question. Gently he tugged his arm free of her grip. "Stay here."

She growled low in her throat. "This conversation isn't done, mister," she warned.

"Mister?"

She shrugged. "It's better than jackass."

Torque headed out of the main living chamber with a shake of his head. Rya was without a doubt the most complex, aggravating creature he'd ever met.

Or maybe it was just the emotions she inspired that were aggravating.

After all, he'd spent his entire existence pretending that he didn't have feelings. That was what was expected of a warrior in his father's lair. It made life much easier.

Now he didn't know what to do with the tangled mess of emotions.

"Females," he muttered, moving through the small entryway and into the corridor that was a perfect match for the one in Baine's lair.

"Yes." A lightly accented voice murmured before there was a shimmer of magic and a small creature appeared before him. The stranger had a pretty oval face with long, brilliant red hair and odd, pale eyes dotted with flecks of color like opals. "I believe I am a female."

"Shit." Torque spread his feet and squared his shoulders, prepared to be attacked.

The power pulsing in the air was heavy. Thunderous.

Ancient.

The intruder, however, did nothing more than smooth her hands down the linen robe that covered her slender body.

"Language," she chided, the air filled with pinpricks of heat.

Torque gave a cautious nod of his head. The female was a delicate wisp, and her pale features made her look as if she was still barely more than a foundling. But he wasn't stupid.

A dragon could take any form they wanted. And this one had the sort of presence that only came from a very old creature who wielded an unimaginable magic.

It seemed best to treat her with a wary respect.

"Forgive me," he murmured.

The threatening power eased as her eyes suddenly twinkled with starbursts of color.

"Of course." She seemed to float forward, patting him on the cheek. "I do adore a handsome male. There was one…" Her words trailed away, her voice becoming distant. "So long ago."

Torque remained wary. Dragons were fickle

creatures who could go from charming to lethal in the blink of an eye.

“I’m Torque, son of Pyre,” he said, waving his hand toward the doorway behind him. “My companion is Rya, daughter of—”

The female interrupted his introduction. “Synge.”

Torque instinctively stepped to the side, blocking the doorway with his body. Not that he could hope to stop the female if she wanted to get to Rya. He wasn’t sure even his powerful father could match this dragon in a fair fight. “Do you know her?” he demanded.

The woman blinked in confusion, the colors dimming in her eyes to leave them oddly opaque.

“Of course not.”

Okay. Torque cleared his throat. He was sensing there was something not entirely…stable about the female.

“Can you tell me where we are?” he asked, keeping his voice light.

He feared if he pressed her too hard, she might disappear.

Or worse, turn him into a crispy critter.

“No.” She glanced around, as if confused by the sight of the wide corridor and high ceiling. “You shouldn’t be here.”

“It wasn’t our intention to intrude,” he rushed to assure her. “We were searching for Rya’s missing mother when we were trapped in the ice.”

She frowned, perhaps silently testing his words to search for any hint of deception. Finally, she tilted back her head and sucked in a deep breath.

“A portal,” she abruptly said.

He nodded. “Yes. It was a portal that brought us here.”

“How?” Her frown deepened. “It doesn’t smell of you.”

"No." He shrugged. "It was formed by an unknown enemy who has been kidnapping frost sprites along with a Shinto female." She continued to frown and he was struck by a sudden thought. "Oh, and it was kept open by a miniature gargoyle."

The dragon looked at him as if he was some sort of whackadoodle,

"A miniature gargoyle?"

Torque grimaced. "Yeah."

"Have you taken a blow to the head?" she demanded.

"It does sound…" Torque struggled for the right word. "Unlikely."

The dragon tilted her head to the side, and Torque was hit by a sudden suspicion. Was she listening to voices he couldn't hear?

Time passed, but Torque wisely bit his tongue. She'd speak when she was ready.

At last she focused her full attention on him.

"You said frost sprites have been brought to this place."

"We believe so," he said. "We were searching for them when we were sucked through the portal. Of course, we haven't actually seen them."

She gave a click of her tongue, her luminous beauty marred by an expression of irritation.

"Such an annoyance," she announced.

It was a hell of a lot more than annoying. Still, Torque was careful to keep his expression bland. Until he knew more about this female he was going to treat her with excessive courtesy.

Dragons were oddly OCD about good manners.

"Excuse me, but are you trapped here as well?" he asked.

She considered for a long moment. "In a manner of speaking."

He was assuming that meant 'yes.'

"Then perhaps we can work together to find a way out," he suggested.

The scent of warm cinnamon filled the air, the female's brilliant hair floating on an unseen breeze.

It was eerie as hell. Torque felt his skin prickle with unease.

"I can't leave," she told him.

"Why not?"

"I don't remember," she said, her tone puzzled rather than angered.

Torque paused. His first instinct was right. This dragon was clearly unstable. The question was if it was a natural phenomenon or if someone had caused her muddled confusion.

"Can you tell me who trapped you here?"

"I..." Her words trailed away as she gave a shake of her head.

He swallowed a sigh, trying a new approach. Maybe he could lead her slowly to how she'd become a prisoner in the ice.

"You haven't told me your name," he reminded her with a small sigh.

"Oh." She wrinkled her nose. "Did I have one?"

"I assume you did."

"It disappeared."

Torque grudgingly accepted defeat.

Whoever or whatever had managed to capture a dragon had also destroyed her ability to remember what had happened.

All he could hope for was her cooperation in getting them out of there.

"Please let me help you," he murmured, taking a step toward her.

She instantly moved away, the scent of cinnamon almost choking him.

"You can't," she rasped. "No one can."

"Together it's possible," he said. "If the three of us combine our fire we could surely melt through our prison and—"

She abruptly interrupted his words, a shimmer of magic surrounding her. "I must go."

"Wait." He held out a pleading hand. To hell with pride. "Please."

The shimmers thickened, but she didn't disappear as he'd feared.

"You mustn't leave this lair," she commanded.

"Why not?"

The pale eyes narrowed. "Madness waits for you out there."

"Madness? From what?"

There was a silence, and Torque suddenly wondered if he'd gone too far. Offending a dragon was remarkably easy. Especially one who wasn't thinking clearly.

At last she heaved a rueful sigh. "I had forgotten how very persistent males can be."

He realized a silent sigh of relief. At least she hadn't turned him into a charred pile of ash.

"I don't mean to be persistent, but we can't stay here forever," he said, his voice gentle.

"Why not? You have to be someplace." A sly expression touched her beautiful features. "And with someone. This is as good a place as any."

Torque felt a jolt of shock. Had she sensed his increasingly tangled bond with Rya? Or had she read his secret fantasy of having his lovely betrothed locked in his bedroom for the next few centuries?

"Our families will be searching for us," he forced himself to say.

"They will eventually forget you." A sad, melancholy smile touched her lips. "They always do."

The corridor seemed to darken, as if her mood had

dimmed the soft glow.

Torque resisted the urge to reach out and touch the ruby-red hair. Trying to comfort a dragon was a risky proposition.

"I won't deny it's a temptation," he reluctantly admitted. "But we can't stay."

When he had Rya in his bed it would be because she wanted to be there. Not because they were trapped.

"It's too dangerous to leave now," she said in unexpectedly firm tones. "I will return when it's safe."

"But—"

She lifted a silencing hand. "Patience."

The shimmers whirled around her before she disappeared, leaving behind a small puff of smoke.

Patience.

Torque rolled his eyes. He'd just used the same word with Rya. No wonder she'd looked like she wanted to kick him in the nuts.

"Just perfect."

CHAPTER SEVEN

Finn was furious as he felt himself being yanked through the portal to land in a small, icy cave. Glaring at the tiny female in front of him, he allowed his powers to fill the air with a white mist.

"What the hell did you do?" he hissed between clenched teeth.

With a brief glance toward the dagger he still held in his hand, she met him glare for glare.

"Are you trying to get yourself killed?" Adair snapped.

He leaned down until they were nose to nose. "I'm trying to rescue my people."

The platinum eyes darkened, but she refused to back down. "By getting caught?" she challenged. "Do you think the sprites aren't being constantly guarded? The moment you stepped on the ledge you would have set off the magical alarms."

Slowly Finn straightened. He wanted to continue yelling at her. How else could he release his bubbling frustration?

Well, he could always press the exquisite little Sylvermyst against the frozen wall and claim her mouth with a kiss that would melt…

No, no, no.

There might be a temptation to believe that she was an innocent victim of her family, but he didn't allow himself to think with that particular body part.

For now she was the enemy.

End of story.

"Is this a devious plan to distract me so your family can slip away with my people?"

Her eyes widened. "No, I'm trying to help."

"Right." His lips twisted in a humorless smile. "The fey of this world aren't all weak, useless fools. And we're not stupid."

"Oh." Her face heated with a delightful color as he repeated Lila's claim.

Finn ground his teeth together. The urge to reach out and discover if her skin was as soft as it looked was nearly overwhelming.

With an effort he forced himself to concentrate on the brief glimpse he'd had of his tribe. He couldn't be sure, but he'd thought he had caught sight of chains around their ankles.

"Tell me the truth," he snarled.

She took a small step backward as his angry mist swirled around her.

"The truth about what?"

"Did you deliberately keep me from my people?"

"No." She lifted her hand, almost as if she intended to touch him, only to abruptly let it drop.

Finn grimaced, telling himself that he wasn't

disappointed. Nope. Not at all.

"I was saving you," she insisted. "If you'd tried to get down to your tribe you would have been captured. Or worse."

He scowled. He actually didn't doubt her claim. His people would have escaped if they weren't being magically guarded. That didn't, however, ease his seething fury at being whisked away from them.

"Why would you try to save me?"

"I…" She paused, licking her lusciously full lips. "I don't know."

Finn's cock went on full alert. Dammit. He was supposed to be rescuing his people, not being distracted by his uncomfortable, unquenchable hunger for this female.

"Adair," he said on a low growl. "Talk to me."

She wrapped her arms around her waist, her expression troubled.

"You must return to your cell."

"Not until you tell me what's going on."

She shivered, her eyes darkening. "If my family find you…"

She allowed her words to trail away. Finn didn't need her to be more specific.

He didn't doubt for a second that they would kill him.

At the moment, however, he wasn't concerned with himself. He needed to figure out a way to rescue his people.

"Adair." He stepped toward her, the scent of rosemary settling somewhere deep inside him. "Tell me."

She shook her head. "Stubborn."

He held her wary gaze. "More stubborn than you could ever imagine."

For a painful second he feared she might shut him

out. Or worse, turn him over to her family.

Then, heaving a deep sigh, she turned away. "Come with me," she muttered.

Finn's lips parted to protest. He wanted answers. And he wanted them now. But before he could speak, there was crack of ice as a narrow crevice appeared.

Adair darted through the opening, ignoring Finn's command to stop.

Left alone, Finn briefly considered using his powers to try and return to the cavern. After all, Adair had just warned him that he would never be able to reach his people without tripping the alarms.

If he took the proper precautions, there was no saying he couldn't rescue them.

Then, with a muttered curse, he was moving through the crevice.

He might not fully trust the pretty Sylvermyst, but he did accept that he was going to need more information if he intended get his tribe out of this icy prison alive.

Stepping out of the opening, Finn came to a sharp halt. His eyes widened, his senses on full alert.

He glanced around, trying to adjust to the abrupt change of scenery. Gone was the endless ice and muted glow that was the only light. And in its place was a rolling meadow dappled with wildflowers. Daffodils, daisies and tulips were clustered in splashes of color. Nearby, a narrow stream danced over flat rocks, the gurgles of swirling water mixing with the cry of sparrows as the only sounds to break the silence.

Overhead was a bright blue sky with tiny puffs of clouds that moved on a lazy breeze.

It had to be an illusion. Right? Still, it felt remarkably real.

"What is this place?" he breathed, cautiously crossing the grass that was spongy beneath his feet.

"I'm not entirely sure."

Adair tilted her head back, allowing the sunshine to bathe her delicate face in golden warmth. She was still wearing her white robe, and her glorious copper hair was left free to spill down her back.

His heart seized in his chest.

She was as rare and mysterious as a frost flower.

Seeming to sense his intense scrutiny, she lowered her head to meet his fierce gaze.

"It appeared after I claimed the cave as my private lair," she explained. "As far as I know it's the only place like it in the labyrinth."

"Labyrinth?" he demanded.

She waved a hand. "That's what I call it. If it has a real name, I don't know what it is."

Hmm. Labyrinth seemed to fit.

"Is it magic?"

She shivered. "Dreams."

He frowned. "You said that before. Dragon dreams," he reminded her. "What does it mean?"

"I'm not sure." Genuine fear darkened her eyes. "The words whisper in my head when I sleep."

Finn gave a slow shake of his head. This was a place that could give anyone nightmares. Even a frost sprite who lived in dark, icy tunnels. At least in his homeland he knew that the walls wouldn't be appearing and disappearing. And that his magic could free him from any potential danger.

He gave a shake of his head. Now was not the time to worry about the hows and whys of their surroundings. Instead he needed to focus on the larger picture.

"Start at the beginning," he demanded.

She absently moved to perch on a rock that overlooked the narrow stream. At the same time Finn stepped into the shade of a towering oak tree. The pocket of summer was a pleasant relief from the crushing sense of menace in the ice prison, but he would never be a sun-lover.

"You know that we're Sylvermyst," she murmured softly, her gaze locked on the sparkling water.

"Yes." He pretended he didn't feel a childish resentment because she wasn't looking at him. *Yeesh.* "And that you worshipped the Dark Lord."

She released a short, humorless laugh. "It's not like we had much choice."

"Everyone has a choice in who they worship," he corrected.

"Not us," she insisted. "My family were slaves who did whatever was necessary to survive."

He bit back the urge to argue. He didn't really care if they'd been disciples of the Dark Lord or slaves.

Why should he?

The past didn't matter.

"You came through during the war?" he asked, referring to the recent attempt by the evil deity to return to this world.

She nodded. "There was enough chaos for us to slip through unnoticed. Once we were here we disappeared in the wilderness of Alaska."

"Why didn't you seek out the Sylvermyst who'd fought against the Dark Lord?"

"It's what I'd hoped for," she said softly. "Shortly after we arrived, I sought out information on our people. I discovered Ariyal and his tribe were already established in an isolated area in the Midwest."

Finn frowned. "I think I heard about him."

"He was forced to stay hidden at Avalon and serve Morgana le Fay," she said.

"Ah. Yes." Finn had heard stories about the reclusive fey who'd been used as sex slaves by Morgana le Fay. And the fact that they'd been instrumental in the defeat of the Dark Lord.

"I tried to convince my family that Ariyal and his people already understood this world and would have a number of allies among the other demons. Who better to help us adjust to our new home?"

Finn lifted a brow. "So why didn't you join them?"

She grimaced. "My brothers claimed Ariyal and his people were without honor for not following the Dark Lord when he was banished. They're determined to create a separate colony that will include only those Sylvermyst who returned at the same time we did."

He didn't miss her word *claimed.*

"You think there's more to their refusal to join with an established tribe?"

"After an eternity of being mere slaves they want to be the ones to give the orders," she admitted. "Something that would have been impossible unless they founded their own colony."

He folded his arms over his chest, his attention locked on the delicate lines of her profile. "And you?"

Puzzled by his question, she at last turned to meet his searching gaze. "What?"

"Did you want to give orders?"

She shuddered as she shook her head. "God, no. I just want a home." Her voice lowered to a mere whisper. "And peace."

Her words held a compelling sincerity that eroded Finn's attempt to convince himself that she was a ruthless adversary.

"What happened after you arrived in Alaska?"

Her gaze returned to the stream that swirled and eddied as it cut through the meadow.

"My brothers sent out word for others to join us. I think they assumed the dark fey would flock to Alaska." She didn't bother to hide her own opinion of her brothers' plan. "But no one responded."

"Shocking," he drawled.

A gentle breeze rushed past them, tugging at her coppery curls. Finn froze. In that moment, he made the irreversible decision to see that satin hair spread across his pillows.

There.

He'd accepted it.

Good or bad. Evil or innocent.

This woman was going to be his lover.

A weight he didn't even know he was carrying abruptly fell from Finn's shoulders.

Thankfully unaware that her fate had just been sealed, she gave a small shrug.

"Micah, my oldest brother, decided that we needed wealth to lure our people to such a remote location."

Finn made a sound of disgust. As a prince he understood that being a leader meant loyalty and commitment, and self-sacrifice. His people and their needs always came before his own.

A philosophy that petty dictators were never willing to accept.

"He wanted to buy a tribe?"

Her lips twisted at his flagrant disdain. "I'm not sure he thought of it in those terms."

"I'm not sure what other terms there are," he muttered. "How did he get his money?"

"They tried panning for gold," she said. "And then searching the abandoned mines."

"I assume you didn't strike it rich?"

"No." She glanced toward the crevice. "Unfortunately."

This time he didn't try to resist the need to step forward so he could cup her chin and tug her face toward him.

Instantly he felt small tingles of excitement as he savored the warmth of her skin. Her heat would be an intoxicating thrill when it was pressed against his chilled flesh.

"Why was it unfortunate?" he forced himself to ask.

She stilled, but she didn't pull away from his light touch.

"My brothers were becoming increasingly frustrated by our isolation, and the lack of interest in joining their colony. They insisted that I use my gift to search for the riches they were convinced would solve all our problems."

His thumb absently brushed the lush temptation of her lower lip. "Your gift is creating portals?"

She hesitated. Almost as if she feared revealing her secret talent.

Understandable. Clearly her family had exploited her for years. Maybe centuries. She would naturally assume he intended to do the same.

"More than that," she grudgingly admitted. "I can concentrate on a particular object and open a portal that will lead me to it."

The scent of rosemary deepened. Fear, or a response to his touch? The fact he couldn't be sure made him snap out in frustration.

"An object like a frost sprite?" he sneered.

She lowered her lashes, flinching as if he'd physically struck her.

"Yes," she breathed. "I can connect with people as well as objects."

Finn heaved a rough sigh. Her rare talent was clearly responsible for the disappearance of his people, but his anger was directed at his vulnerability to her feminine allure.

A waste of energy that wasn't getting him any closer to saving his people.

He turned the conversation to more important matters. "What did your brother make you do?"

A sadness rippled over her pale face. "They

demanded I focus on finding a treasure."

"What sort of treasure?"

"They weren't specific so I just imagined a chest filled with jewels and gold coins." She lifted her lashes, her platinum eyes blazing with a silver shimmer in the sunlight. "I thought it might lead us to a buried pirate booty."

He blinked. There were thousands of bank vaults spread around the world. Not to mention museums with priceless works of art. And she chose a pirate chest?

"Are you serious?"

"I like to watch old human movies," she muttered in defensive tones.

Finn flattened his lips. Dammit. He wasn't going to smile.

"What happened?"

She waved a hand toward the crevice. "The portal opened into this labyrinth." She pulled away from his light grip, wrapping her arms around her waist. "I tried to warn them that it was unstable, but as soon as they entered the lower cavern they caught sight of the piles of gems buried beneath the ice. After that they wouldn't listen to anything I had to say." Her lips twisted into a humorless smile. "Of course, they never listen to me."

"Gems?" Finn muttered, trying to make sense of her words.

He'd assumed the labyrinth was a strange jumble of magic that had no purpose or meaning. But if it held gems, it changed the entire purpose of the place.

She abruptly scowled, looking oddly disappointed. "Not you, too. Is there anyone not obsessed with treasure?"

Finn jerked, instantly offended by her accusation. "I have no interest in gems."

"But you just said—"

"I was trying to figure out who created this place,"

he interrupted in stern tones. “I don’t need sparkly stones to rule my people.”

She flushed. “I’m sorry. I watched you with your tribe. You’re a very good leader.”

Her confession that she’d spied on him should have been infuriating. Instead, Finn found his anger instantly fading. Hell, he was preening at her soft words of praise.

Clearly the labyrinth was turning his brains to mush.

“My only interest in the gems is whether they’re a part of the cavern or if someone brought them here to keep them safe.”

“Oh.” Her brow furrowed. “I don’t think they’re an actual part of this place. They looked liked someone had deliberately piled them along the edges of the cavern and then iced them over.”

His brain raced. What sort of demon could create such an elaborate maze to hide his expensive baubles?

At last he gave a shake of his head.

The truth was that he didn’t have a clue.

“I know why your family is here, but you haven’t explained why my people are being held hostage,” he said, the words clipped.

She sent him a confused glance. As if the reason should be obvious.

“Because of the ice that covers the gems,” she told him. “We tried everything to get them loose. Fire. Explosions. Magic. Nothing would free the treasure.”

He clenched his hands at his side, a fine film of frost coating his skin. His people had been kidnapped because an idiotic family of dark fey needed money?

“Whose bright idea was it to use frost sprites to act as your personal miners?”

She nervously licked her lips. “It was my younger brother, Jarvis, who suggested your tribe might be the answer to our problem.”

“I’ll be sure and give him my personal thanks,” he

growled.

She was wise enough not to try and plead for mercy for her brothers. They would have to pay for their sins.

“He assumed it would only take one sprite to destroy the ice surrounding the gems,” she instead admitted.

Like that was supposed to make it better?

“But?” he pressed.

“The sprite couldn’t penetrate more than a few layers.”

“So you kidnapped more of my people.” It was an accusation, not a question.

She gave an embarrassed nod. “Yes. Their combined magic has allowed a few of the jewels to be taken from the ice.”

“So why kidnap me?”

“There’s a large object in the floor,” she said, reminding Finn of the bulge he’d noticed in the center of the cavern. “My brothers are convinced it must be even more valuable than the treasure at the fringes.” She gave a small shake of her head.

Disbelief that the mystery item was valuable? Or that her brothers could be so stupid as to risk everything by kidnapping a prince? Finn couldn’t say.

“The sprites, however, haven’t been able to penetrate the magic that protects it.”

He flicked his brow upward. “And you assume I can?”

“We’ve seen that you’re more powerful than any of your people.”

He shrugged. There was no denying what she already knew. “What if I refuse?”

Her face paled. “They’ll kill your people one by one until you agree,” she rasped.

It was exactly what he’d expected, but his power still lashed out, icing over the stream.

The bastards.

"And if I agree?" he ground out.

"I…don't know." The platinum eyes darkened with distress. "I truly don't."

CHAPTER EIGHT

Char returned to Baine's lair and headed straight to his private rooms. His visit to the pack of trolls who were hidden in the mountains of Siberia had been…satisfying.

Usually he allowed his master's younger guards to collect on overdue debts. It not only gave them a sense of purpose, but it offered the opportunity to release their aggressive nature. After all, the creature who was stupid enough to try and renege on a deal with a dragon needed to be taught a lesson.

On this occasion, however, Char insisted on taking care of the problem himself. His smoldering frustration at Torque's continued absence was making him twitchy. Beating a handful of trolls into a bloody pulp was just what he needed to release some steam.

Now he was in dire need of a hot bath.

Something that was going to have to wait, he wryly accepted as soon as he felt the ground tremble beneath his feet.

Seconds later, Baine appeared from a portal.

For once, the dragon was wearing a formal robe in a dark jade color. Which meant he was just returning to the lair.

"Char," the male said, stepping into the corridor next to him.

Char offered a bow of his head. "Master." His nose flared as he caught the scent of Synge clinging to Baine's robe. "Were you allowed to speak with your father?"

Baine's eyes flared with amber heat. "For all the good it did."

Sharp disappointment sliced through Char. "He doesn't know where Torque is?"

"He claims he doesn't."

Char clenched his hands. "Do you trust him?"

Baine released a humorless laugh. "Not as far as I can throw him."

Yeah. That was pretty much how Char felt. Synge was a cunning, greedy bastard who would happily sacrifice Torque if it would somehow be to his advantage.

"What about Rya?" he demanded. Synge might not give a shit about Torque, but from all reports he did have a soft spot in whatever passed as his heart for his half-breed daughter.

Baine's expression hardened. "She's missing as well."

"Damn." Smoke curled around Char's feet as he struggled to contain his worry.

Baine reached out to lay a hand on his shoulder. "I've sent servants to try and locate Rya's mother," he assured Char. "As a Shinto she'll have the skill to locate her daughter no matter where she might be."

"Her mother doesn't stay in the harem?" Char asked

in confusion. Most concubines preferred to remain within the luxury of a dragon's lair.

"No. She has a home in Hong Kong," Baine explained.

"What if she's not there?"

"Then I'll send the servants to search for Rya's grandparents." He grimaced. "Unfortunately, that could take some time."

Char's brief flare of hope dimmed. Baine's expression wasn't encouraging.

"Why?"

"The Shinto tribe travels through the deepest forests of Asia, and they're very good at hiding from others. Even dragons."

Char scowled. "What do we do in the meantime?"

Baine gave his shoulder a squeeze. It was as much a warning as an offer of comfort. The older male knew Char wanted to be out there hunting for his missing friend.

"We wait," he said in tones that told Char there was no use in arguing.

Char heaved a resigned sigh. "Great."

***

Rya wasn't happy.

Not an unusual occurrence when it came to her aggravating betrothed. Usually, however, it was because he was intent on ignoring her. What female wouldn't be offended by the knowledge her potential consort couldn't be bothered to spend five minutes in her company?

This time it was because he was deliberately putting himself in harm's way.

Suddenly she understood why he'd been so frustrated when she'd impulsively leaped into danger. Of course, the realization did nothing to ease her temper.

Pacing the barren floor, she whirled toward the doorway when she at last heard approaching footsteps.

Seconds later, Torque returned to the main chamber, his expression impossible to read.

"Well?" she demanded, moving to stand at his side.

His lips twisted into a humorless smile. "I was right about the dragon."

Torque wasn't a male who easily revealed his inner emotions, but she was fairly certain he wouldn't look quite so grim if they were about to escape.

Still, she had to ask. "Is he willing to help us?"

"It's a she." He gave a small lift of his hands. "And not exactly."

Her brows drew together. He'd been out there with another female while she'd been worrying herself to death?

"This isn't the time for puzzles," she snapped.

He blinked, clearly startled by her sharp response. "I agree. Unfortunately, I don't have any answers," he admitted, his gaze sweeping over her face.

She sucked in a deep breath, telling herself that she was being ridiculous.

Of course he was talking to the female. *Yeesh.* How else was he supposed to communicate?

"Did you ask the dragon if she knows who is holding us captive?"

"I did." He hesitated. Which couldn't be good. "Unfortunately she's clearly suffering from some sort of mental distress," he at last said.

Rya studied him in confusion. "What does that mean?"

"She didn't make much sense," he said in rueful tones. "If I had to guess I'd say she's trapped in the ice the same as we are. Perhaps for a very long time."

Her eyes widened. "What sort of demon has the

power to hold a dragon captive?"

"I don't know," he admitted, glancing back toward the doorway. He clearly wasn't any happier than she was about the thought of being in the hands of a demon who could imprison a full-blooded dragon. "And she couldn't tell me," he continued. "She doesn't remember how she got here. Or who was responsible. She couldn't even remember her own name."

A shiver inched down her spine. Until this moment, she'd been more frustrated than frightened. She'd just assumed they would find a way out of the ice. Or that someone would come in search of them.

Now…

Now it felt as if the walls were closing in on her.

"Why did she create this place for us?" she abruptly demanded.

She wouldn't give in to panic.

Or at least she was going to pretend she wasn't panicking.

"I think she's trying to protect us," Torque said, stepping closer. Had he detected the sudden leap of her pulse? "She wants us to stay here."

"For how long?"

He shrugged. "I don't think she knows."

The walls inched in closer.

"So we're supposed to sit here and wait for an unhinged dragon to tell us we can leave?"

His brows drew together at the shrill edge in her voice. "It's certainly preferable to our previous cell."

She wrapped her arms around her waist. "That's not the point."

His gaze studied her tight expression. "What is the point?"

She licked her lips. She had a point. Of course she did.

"I came here to search for my mother," she at last

muttered. "It's more important than ever that I find her."

"And how do you intend to do that?" he pressed. "We can't force our way through the ice, and your powers don't work here."

She turned on her heel, pacing toward the large fireplace. "I have to do something."

He moved so silently she didn't hear him. It wasn't until she felt his fingers skim lightly up her arms that she realized he was standing directly behind her.

Astonishingly, the feel of his gentle touch sent a soothing warmth through her. As if his mere presence was enough to banish her looming freak-out.

On cue, the tension melted from her muscles and the claustrophobic fear that was gripping her began to ease.

Dear goddess. He was better than a shot of Prozac.

"Listen, we're both exhausted. We'll take enough time to regain our strength." Tightening his grip on her shoulders, he firmly turned her to meet his steady gaze. "If the dragon hasn't returned then we'll consider how we can continue your search."

"I…" She grimaced. Now that Torque had eased her panic attack, she could think clearly again. Which meant accepting that he was right. She was still weak from her attempt to use her shadow to find a way out of the ice. It would take time to regain command of her magic. "Fine."

His lips twitched. "Was that so hard?"

She heaved a deep sigh. "We've already established that I'm not very fond of waiting."

His hands slid beneath her hair before exploring down the curve of her spine. The dragon tattoo that spread across her back tingled. As if the mating mark recognized Torque's touch.

"How did you spend your time in the harem?" he demanded.

The temperature in the room amped up by several

degrees, evaporating any lingering anxiety. Was it her dragon or his causing the heat?

Did it matter?

Suddenly her racing heart had nothing to do with fear.

She cleared her throat, trying to ignore the fire that smoldered to life in his sapphire eyes at her ready response to his touch.

"When my mother was there she trained me to use my magic," he told him. "I was also her scribe. She would bring me texts from endangered fey she'd studied and I would translate them so they could be preserved in the Shinto library."

An unmistakable pleasure raced over his face at her words. "A scholar?"

"I find it fascinating to learn about other species," she admitted. "Although I'm not sure I would qualify as a scholar."

He gave a slow nod, his gaze resting with a brooding intensity on her lips.

"I would enjoy reading your mother's stories," he murmured. "I've been fortunate enough to have Baine as my master. He encourages all of us to make use of his extensive library. He believes knowledge is the greatest of weapons."

"I've heard he's dangerously intelligent."

"Without a doubt."

Rya had encountered Baine once. She'd been very young, but she'd never forgotten the male's choking power when he'd entered the room. She'd been frankly terrified of him.

"What about his mate?" she abruptly asked.

"Tayla?" He looked confused. "What about her?"

"How does she deal with being mated to such a ruthless predator?" she clarified. "She's a purebred fey. He could crush her without even trying."

Torque's gaze widened before he released a low chuckle. "Trust me, Baine would destroy himself before ever harming one golden hair on Tayla's head." He shrugged. "If anyone's terrified, it's poor Baine. I've never seen a male so anxious to ensure his mate's happiness."

Something perilously close to jealousy speared through Rya.

What would it feel like to know her mate was desperate to please her? That his very existence was meant to bring her joy?

"She's a lucky female," she muttered.

"Yes," he agreed without hesitation. "Baine is a mate who will keep her well protected."

She rolled her eyes. "I meant that she's lucky to have a mate who clearly feels an affection for her. It's what most females hope for."

He stilled, a sudden suspicion darkening his eyes. "Did you ever leave the harem?"

"What do you mean?"

"Did you travel from your father's lair?"

"I wasn't a prisoner," she told him, caught off guard by the sharp edge in his question. "I often visited my mother's tribe in Hong Kong."

"Were there males?"

"Male Shinto?" She sent him a confused frown. "Of course."

"Did they give you the affection you say you believe is so important?" he said in dark tones.

She jerked at the unexpected attack. Was he mocking her? Just because he was a dutiful warrior who had no interest in tender feelings didn't mean she hadn't hoped she would be cherished by her mate.

"That's none of your business," she snapped.

"It is now." His hands gripped her hips as he pressed her against his hard body. "No more."

Stunned by his unexpected flare of anger, she watched in fascination as a curl of smoke escape his nostril.

"Excuse me?" she at last demanded.

Tiny flames danced in his sapphire eyes. "I don't like the thought of you with other males."

"Why not?" she demanded. "It's not as if you've ever actually cared about me or my feelings."

Without warning his hand slipped beneath her sweater, touching the tattoo on her back.

"You carry my mark," he husked.

The air was jerked from her lungs at the feel of his fingers pressed against her bare flesh. The mating tattoo tingled, the searing heat of his touch sending tiny jolts of excitement crackling over her skin.

Oh, yes.

This was it.

This sizzling desire was why she hadn't been able to banish him from her thoughts since their betrothal. And why she trembled whenever he was near.

"Because you were forced to give it to me," she said in husky tones.

She sensed his anger easing as he stroked his hand up her spine, inching her sweater upward.

"Ah, Rya." He bent his head downward, wrapping her in the power of his dragon.

Inside, her own beast stirred. Her fey blood might sparkle through her veins, but deep in her soul, she was still a dragon.

His lips brushed her forehead. "I've been a fool."

"True," she agreed, although she wasn't sure what exactly he was referring to.

He'd been a fool about so many things.

He nuzzled a path to her temple. "It's going to be different from now on."

Rya shivered, shocked by the need blasting through

her.

Dear goddess, she wanted him.

She wanted to arch against his hard muscles. To feel his lips exploring her bare skin from head to toe. She wanted to drown in the flames of his desire as she pleaded for him to ease the ache that was becoming unbearable.

It was the sheer intensity of her craving that had her jerking away from his roaming hands.

Nervously tucking her hair behind her ear, she turned to pace toward the well-worn leather chair set near the fireplace.

Torque might tell her that he regretted treating her like an unwanted burden, but she'd been an idiot to forget that she was still nothing more than a duty as far as he was concerned.

The thought of exposing her most raw, vulnerable emotions was…unnerving.

"So, this is your lair," she inanely muttered.

She could feel his heat beating against her back before he was leashing his dragon and moving to stand at her side.

"An illusion of it," he said, his voice deliberately light.

She breathed a sigh of relief. He had to sense that her withdrawal from him was nothing more than a fragile pretense. He could easily vanquish her resistance. But instead of pressing his advantage, he allowed her a graceful retreat.

The knowledge chipped away a little more of her lingering resentment.

"It's very…" She faltered as she struggled to come up with the proper word.

"Yes?"

"Stark."

He arched a brow, casting a glance around the barren

room.

"It's functional," he corrected. "I have my books and a small gym where I can work out in private if I want." He waved a hand toward the door at the back of the room. "I also have a sleeping chamber. What more do I need?"

She studied his lean, compelling features. He was serious. Unlike most dragons, he wasn't motivated by avarice, or the lust for power.

Instead he honored things like loyalty and integrity.

"There's nothing on the walls." Her gaze skimmed around the room before lowering to her feet. "Or the floors. It's just plain stone."

He shrugged. "I don't spend a lot of time here."

"Why not?"

"I'm usually on guard duty," he paused, as if having to consider what he did with his time. "Or I'm training."

"Or visiting the harem?" The words left her lips before she could halt them.

"Ah." A slow, satisfied smile curved his lips. "I'm not the only one troubled by the thought of sharing."

She tilted her chin. She'd have her tongue cut out before she would admit she was jealous. "As you said, we're betrothed."

"Hmm. So we are." His gaze swept downward, taking a slow, disturbingly thorough survey of her body. "And soon to be mated."

A treacherous thrill of awareness curled through the pit of her stomach. *Yeesh.* He wasn't even touching her and she was aroused.

Time for another distraction.

"What then?" she asked.

His gaze snapped back to her face. "I don't understand."

"After we're mated do you intend to stay with Baine?" she asked. "Or will you join my father's guard?"

"I assumed that Synge would send us in search of his lost treasure." He shrugged, as if he hadn't given the question much thought. And in truth, he probably hadn't.

It was obvious that he had done his best to block out their future together.

The fluttery awareness remained. He was a gorgeous, impossibly sexy male. That didn't mean, however, she wasn't tempted to give his dangly male bits a good, hard kick.

"If my father knew where to send us, we'd already be there," she pointed out between clenched teeth.

"Your mother hasn't had any other visions?"

"Not that she's shared."

"Good." Seemingly indifferent to the edge in her voice, he smiled with satisfaction. "Then we'll stay with Baine. Or if you prefer, we can find a lair of our own and wait for Synge to decide where he wants us to search."

Rya had assumed Torque would choose to continue their current arrangement until Synge or her mother discovered some clue that would send them on their mysterious quest.

She hadn't even considered the possibility that they would…play house. "A lair? Together?"

He arched a brow at the squeak in her voice. "Mated pairs usually share a living space, don't they?"

She nervously cleared her throat. "I suppose."

He stepped toward her. "Does the thought trouble you?"

Did it? Yeah. But not for the reason he was imagining.

It wasn't that she was repulsed. Just the opposite. Without even trying, she was capable of picturing a small, cozy lair, complete with Torque comfortably settled next to her. As if a part of her had already been fantasizing about the day she would be living with her consort.

Realizing he was waiting for her response, she gave a shrug.

"A little," she admitted.

Something flashed through his eyes. Something that Rya might have thought was pain if it wasn't so ridiculous.

"Why?" he demanded.

"We're still strangers," she said, not willing to share the truth behind her unease.

He moved with a shocking speed, wrapping her in his arms as he studied her with a fierce expression.

"We're not strangers," he growled, something in his voice warning her that she'd touched a nerve. "Not anymore."

"Torque," she breathed, shocked when he buried his face in the curve of her neck.

"You know who I am," he muttered, his lips branding fiery kisses over the pulse that pounded at the base of her throat.

She shivered, her lashes fluttering downward as liquid heat flowed through her body.

She'd been trying so hard to ignore the aching desire that pulsed between them. As if she could make it go away by pretending it didn't exist.

Now she struggled to breathe as his lips branded her skin, his dragon-fire dancing between them.

"I suppose I know that you like to read," she husked, her heart missing a beat as he sank his teeth into the soft flesh of her shoulder. Not deep enough to draw blood, but enough to leave his mark. "And work out," she forced herself to continue, a groan wrenched from her throat as his hands slid beneath her sweater to cup her breasts. "And that you have a thing for duty," she finished with a hiss of pleasure.

"I have a thing for more than just duty." His lips

moved to nuzzle the corner of her mouth, his thumbs strumming over the hardening peaks of her nipples.

Bliss streaked from her breasts to the empty ache between her legs. She instinctively pressed her hips forward, seeking the hard pressure of his thickening cock.

"What's that?" she asked in a breathy whisper.

"This." He kissed her with a blazing urgency. His arms tightened around her, one hand tangling in her hair. Rya leaned against him, a molten desire making her feel boneless. Her lips parted, inviting the thrust of his tongue. "This," he murmured, giving her one last lingering kiss before his lips were sweeping over her flushed cheeks and along the line of her jaw. "And this."

He lifted her sweater to expose her breasts, his eyes smoldering with a fevered need.

"Torque," she said on a soft exhale, her hands grabbing his shoulders as his head lowered.

"Rya." He licked a pebbled nipple, chuckling as she gave a gasp of stunned pleasure.

"And do not forget Levet," a lightly accented voice called from the outer room as the sound of a door being slammed shut echoed through the air. "Did you miss me?"

"Shit." Torque jerked his head up, a furious cloud of smoke swirling around him. "I'm going to kill that stunted gargoyle."

CHAPTER NINE

Torque released his hold to allow Rya to hastily arrange her clothing. At the same time, he silently considered the easiest means to rid the world of the miniature, first-rate, champion of all pains in the ass, Levet.

Unfortunately, he didn't actually know how to kill a gargoyle. Not even a teeny tiny one.

He'd heard they were one of the few creatures impervious to dragon-fire. And that human weapons couldn't hurt them.

There was a chance he might be able to wait for the aggravating pest to turn to stone and chisel him into a pile of rubble, but that wasn't going to ease his immediate frustration.

Not nearly as upset as she should be, Rya moved to stand in the center of the floor as the gargoyle waddled into the room.

"Levet," she murmured.

"Ah, *ma belle*." With a flap of his ridiculous wings the demon hurried forward, reaching up to grasp Rya's fingers. "I knew you would be clever enough to find the opening I left for you."

Rya smiled even as Torque stalked forward to tug her hand away from Levet's grip.

It wasn't that he was jealous of the undersized creature. Of course not. That would be silly. But he didn't want any male touching his female.

Especially not one who'd just rudely intruded at the worst possible moment.

Dammit. Rya had finally been warm and willing in his arms. And his bedchamber had been so close.

Then…*bam*. He'd been cock-blocked by a talking lump of stone.

"I don't know about clever," Rya murmured, not even glancing in his direction. Had he suddenly become invisible? "We'd barely entered the portal when we were trapped in a frozen cell."

"Ah." Levet wrinkled his tiny snout. "We endured the same unfortunate fate."

Torque scowled with sudden suspicion. "If you were trapped then how did you get to this lair?"

The gargoyle flapped his wings. "I am not entirely certain. One moment I was enjoying a peaceful nap, and the next…" He gave a dramatic wave of his hands. "Poof." Another wave. "I was standing outside the door."

Torque wrapped a protective arm around Rya's shoulders. "Convenient."

Levet gave a decisive shake of his head. "*Non*, it is not convenient at all. If I was to be poofed somewhere, I would have preferred a lovely villa on the Seine. Or even my new home. I do have a very successful business that demands my attention, after all."

Rya leaned forward. "You have your own business?"

"*Oui*. A matchmaking business. If you are interested in a love connection I can—"

"Instead you were brought here," Torque sharply interrupted, a startling fury clenching his gut.

How dare the miniature demon offer his woman a love connection?

Rya belonged to him.

End of story.

Levet frowned, easily sensing the danger that prickled in the air.

"Why are you staring at me?" The gargoyle narrowed his gray eyes. "You are not a crawly, are you?"

Torque blinked. "Crawly?"

Rya cleared her throat. "I think he means creeper."

"*Oui*, a creeper." Levet pointed a claw in Torque's direction. "I do not entirely trust you, *mon ami*."

Torque leaned forward, his power sizzling through the air. "If anyone is suspicious in this room, it's you."

"Moi?" The gossamer wings fluttered, shimmering in the muted light. "That is absurd."

"Is it?" Torque countered. "You were the one who left open the portal so we could enter and become trapped in a frozen, impenetrable maze. Then just when we were rescued from the icy cell to be brought to this place, you suddenly appear."

"Fah." Levet's tail curled around his clawed feet. "If I wished to hurt you, I would not need to lure you to this bizarre nightmare. And I would certainly not be here myself." He gave a violent shudder. "I detest the cold."

Okay. There was a small part of Torque that admitted it was unlikely the gargoyle was involved.

For one thing, the creature didn't have the power to create the elaborate trap. For another, he was utterly committed to Tayla. He would never do anything that would cause her distress.

And killing one of Baine's most trusted servants would certainly upset the tenderhearted imp.

Still, he wasn't in the mood to give anyone the benefit of the doubt.

"Just know that I'm keeping my eye on you," he warned.

Levet gave a *tsk, tsk, tsk* sound with his tongue. "Dragons."

"Where is Finn?" Rya abruptly asked, no doubt hoping to ease the tension.

Instead, the reminder of the overly-pretty frost sprite made Torque release a low growl.

He didn't know what was wrong with him.

He'd never been one of those selfish males who was always fretting and fuming that someone might steal something from his hoard. Of course, he'd never really had anything he'd considered of value, he silently conceded.

Not until now.

Thankfully unaware of his rare sense of uncertainty, the gargoyle remained focused on Rya.

"I was forced to shift, but I sensed him leaving the cell," he admitted with a grimace. "I cannot say if he escaped or was taken by our captors."

Indifferent to what had happened to the frosty prince, Torque asked the most obvious question. "I don't suppose you have any clue who our captors might be?"

Levet slowly turned to face him, his arms folding across his narrow chest. "I suspect they are Sylvermyst."

Torque lifted his brows in confusion. Not surprising. The Sylvermyst had disappeared from the world centuries ago. It took a minute to recall that he'd heard a vague rumor about the creatures returning to this world after the defeat of their evil master.

"Why would you suspect the dark fey?" he demanded. "They have no talent for creating or manipulating ice."

Levet gave a small sniff. "I recognized their scent. I assume they must be working for another demon." He curled his tiny snout in disgust. "The dark fey have few morals about selling their services."

Torque gave a frustrated shake of his head. "Dragons, and now Sylvermyst. This makes no sense."

"Dragons?" Levet instantly perked up, his tail twisting in excitement, like a dog offered a special treat. "Where?"

Rya broke the bad news. "She's already disappeared. Thankfully she created this place to keep us safe before she left."

Levet glanced around, his gaze lingering on the barren walls before he turned his attention to Torque. "These are your rooms, are they not?"

"How do you know that?" Torque demanded. As far as he knew the tiny demon had never been near his private quarters.

"Who else would reside in a dragon's lair, where he could have any luxury that he desired, and choose to live like a monk?"

Torque scowled, watching as Rya struggled to hide her smile.

His rooms weren't that bad. Were they?

He allowed his gaze to skim the stone walls and the bare floor before taking in the black couch and chair.

Well, maybe they were a little…stark. But he was a warrior, not a froufrou designer. What did they expect?

"I don't live like a monk," he muttered.

"Perhaps not," Levet murmured. "The Holy Brothers tend to have more fun."

Torque released a hiss of outrage. "You are a—"

Rya hastily stepped between them, speaking to Levet. "Does your magic work?"

The gargoyle shrugged, pretending he didn't notice

the furious dragon half-breed who was glaring at him with murder in his eyes.

"I fear not." His wings drooped. "I attempted to create a portal when we were first captured. There is a dampening spell that is interfering."

"A dampening spell." Rya gave a slow nod. "That would explain why I couldn't use my shadow. Do you think it's Sylvermyst magic?"

"*Non*. I would guess that it is the spell of an ancient dragon." Levet shot a glance toward Torque. "No doubt your female is responsible."

Torque curled his fingers into tight fists. He was going to kill the gargoyle. It was that simple.

"She's not *my* female," he snapped. "I've never seen the dragon before today."

"Hmm." The gargoyle allowed a suggestive smile to touch his lips. "She created your lair."

Rya made a strangled sound of warning. "Levet."

Perhaps realizing the danger of poking at an enraged dragon, the gargoyle heaved a small sigh. "Fine." Levet sent him a challenging frown. "Did you ask the dragon how we can leave this place?"

"Of course I did," he snapped.

"And?"

"And…" Torque considered his words. "She's confused."

Of course the annoying pest couldn't just leave it there.

"What do you mean, confused?"

"I'm not entirely certain. Perhaps she's mentally traumatized," he said between clenched teeth.

The idiotic creature gave a small squeak, his tail twitching. "There is a crazy dragon nearby?"

Torque's gaze jerked toward the doorway, half expecting a blast of dragon-fire.

"Perhaps you could call her crazy a little louder?" he

snarled. "I'm not sure she heard you."

"Enough." Rya sent them a mutual glare of impatience. "I believe the dragon is trying to protect us."

Levet turned toward Rya, deliberately flicking his tail in Torque's direction.

"Protect us from what?" the tiny demon demanded.

Rya grimaced. "That's the question we're still trying to answer."

Levet muttered something beneath his breath, his claws scraping against the stone floor as he paced toward the fireplace. Abruptly he whirled back around, pointing toward Torque. "You must do something."

"Do what?" Torque snapped.

"Discover who has captured us." The gargoyle sent him a smug smile. "You are a warrior, are you not?"

Torque snorted. "I seem to remember your incessant chatter about being some sort knight in shining armor."

The gargoyle grabbed his tail and busily started to polish the tip. "It is true that I am a hero."

"So why don't you do something to rescue us?"

"I told you," he muttered. "I do not like the cold."

Torque stepped forward, his dragon-fire dancing over his skin. Before he could reach the aggravating pest, however, Rya was once again moving to stand between them.

"The female dragon requested we wait," she said in stern tones. "For now, that's what we'll do."

Levet gave a small sniff. "And then?"

"Then we'll toss you out the door and see if the crazed dragon desires gargoyle for dinner," Torque snarled, pivoting on his heel to storm toward the nearest doorway.

He might as well spend his time lifting weights.

It wasn't like he was going to have an opportunity to relieve his frustration by more pleasurable means.

***

Finn folded his arms over his chest.

Absently he was aware of the call of a finch, and closer, the rustle of leaves in a nearby tree, but his focus remained locked on the female Sylvermyst who had lowered her head to hide her expressive features.

The movement allowed the sunlight to pick up the copper highlights in her hair that spilled over her shoulders and down her back.

His fingers suddenly itched to reach out and discover if it was as silky soft as it looked.

Muttering a curse at his treacherous fascination with the female, he clenched his hands into tight fists.

Dammit.

The female had just revealed her brothers intended to kill him. The last thing he should be thinking about was threading his fingers in that glorious mane of hair so he could yank her against his body.

"How many entrances are there into the cavern?" he demanded, his voice sharper than necessary.

Adair abruptly jerked her head up to study him with a horrified gaze.

"You can't go there," she protested. "It's too dangerous."

His lips twisted in a humorless smile. "You've just told me I'm a dead sprite regardless of what I do. I'm not going to wait and be led like a lamb to the slaughter."

She stretched her hand toward him, her expression pleading. "I can try to return you to your homeland."

He stiffened, outraged by the mere suggestion he would allow her to take him home while his tribe remained enslaved.

"And leave behind my people?"

She hunched a shoulder. "You would be alive."

"Not for long."

"I don't understand."

He glanced toward the wildflowers that swayed beneath a soft breeze. The illusion truly was remarkable. The pretty view, however, wasn't the reason he'd turned his head from Adair. No. It was the sincere concern shimmering in the platinum eyes that he was trying to avoid.

"If some frost sprite didn't track me down and destroy me for being a coward, I would kill myself," he muttered. "A prince does not abandon his people."

"So you'll die trying to rescue them?"

His answer came without hesitation. "If necessary."

"That makes no sense."

"It does to me."

There was a tense silence before she heaved an audible sigh. "I won't help you if you're determined to get yourself killed."

"Fine." He didn't bother to glance at her as he swiveled around to head toward the narrow crevice that would lead them back to the icy labyrinth. "I'll do it on my own."

"Finn." She muttered a curse as he continued forward, then without warning she was quickly darting around him to stand directly in his path. "Wait," she pleaded.

He scowled. "Wait for what?"

There was another pause, as if she waged some sort of inner battle.

"I can try to create a portal that will open in the cavern," she at last offered, the words a mere whisper that floated on the breeze. "It might allow us to bypass the magical security system."

A flicker of hope eased the black dread that was lodged in the pit of his stomach. "Now?"

She gave a grudging nod. "Yes, but I can't guarantee

that I can hold it open long enough to allow your people to escape."

He waved aside her warning. There was no way in hell she was going to be around when it came time for him to bust out of the labyrinth.

"Just get me to them. I'll worry about escaping once I have them unchained."

"This is crazy." An indefinable emotion rippled over her lovely face, but squaring her shoulders, she reached out to grab his hand. "Hold on."

Finn felt the surroundings melt away as she tugged him forward. There was a familiar sensation of traveling through a portal along with a disorienting sense of floating in nothingness. It was almost as if they were standing still and the world was moving around them.

He didn't know if it was because Adair was a Sylvermyst, or as a result of the strange magic in the labyrinth. All he did know was that it was making his stomach lurch. And not in a good way.

Battling the urge to puke, Finn wasn't ready for the weird motion to come to an abrupt halt. Stumbling forward, he would have fallen on his face if Adair hadn't grabbed his arm and held him upright until he regained his balance.

"Thanks," he muttered, pulling free of her grasp.

He was a prince. It was downright embarrassing to lurch around like a drunken dew fairy.

Perhaps sensing his discomfort, Adair turned her attention toward the small, icy cave that surrounded them.

"We're at the backside of the cavern," she murmured. "The gems have all been taken from this area, so there shouldn't be anyone around."

Once again in control as the ground stopped shifting and his stomach settled, Finn moved across the slippery floor. Reaching the ice wall, he peered through a narrow crack.

He easily determined that they were indeed at the bottom of the cavern, but the bulk of his view was blocked by the mass of ice that bulged from the center of the floor.

He didn't need to see, however, to know that his people were close.

The crisp scent of frost sprites filled the air.

Barely leashing his impulse to rush toward them, he turned his head to watch as Adair moved to join him at the opening.

"Are there guards down here?" he murmured, his voice pitched low enough it wouldn't carry into the cavern.

"At the top," she said, her voice equally soft. "They only come down here when my brothers have the sprites released so they can work."

He grimaced. One day very, very soon he intended to have a chat with the male Sylvermysts. It was a chat that would no doubt lead to death and dismemberment. And not necessarily in that order. In this moment, however, he was hoping to avoid them.

"Where is your charming family?"

A shamed blush touched her cheek at his sneering tone.

"I don't sense them nearby. They've probably returned to our lair in Alaska to hide the latest gems. That's what they usually do when they're forced to allow the sprites to rest, but they won't be gone long." She took a step forward, clearly intending to head through the fissure. "We have to hurry."

"We?" With lightning speed, Finn was grabbing her upper arm. "Hold on," he growled, tugging her backward.

She sent him a startled frown. "What's wrong?"

"Where do you think you're going?"

She looked confused. "To help you release your people, of course."

He shook his head. "There is no 'of course' about it."

"What do you mean?"

He absently loosened his grip on her arm, allowing his fingers to trail up to her shoulder. Her hair brushed the back of his hand. Yep. It was just as soft as he'd imagined.

"Why are you helping me?" he abruptly demanded.

She flinched, as if his words hurt her.

"It's not a trap, if that's what you're thinking," she muttered.

Was that what he was thinking? In truth, he didn't know.

"Just answer the question," he commanded.

Her lips flattened, as if annoyed by his tone. "I love my family, I truly do. But…"

"But?"

"I'm not like them."

Finn gave a short laugh. "No shit."

She arched a brow. "What does that mean?"

He shrugged. He wasn't about to admit that he refused to believe he could be attracted to a female who was truly evil.

That was just lame.

"Why are you different?" he instead demanded.

She lowered her head. Did she know that her face revealed her every emotion?

"I don't care about power or wealth or being a ruler of a tribe of Sylvermyst," she muttered.

She trembled, and Finn slid his hand down her back before he could halt the soothing gesture. Hell, he didn't want to halt it.

He wanted to feel the heat of her body that seeped through the loose robe. And savor the scent of rosemary that suddenly spiced the air.

"There's more than that," he said in a husky voice.

She gave a slow nod, unconsciously swaying toward him.

"It's wrong to turn the sprites into slaves," she said, slowly lifting her head to meet his searching gaze. "Just as it was wrong for us to be enslaved. I can't stand aside and let that happen."

His hand splayed across her lower back, urging her even closer. "If you felt that way then why did you help them?"

"They're my family. Without them I have nothing."

"You have your honor."

Anger at his soft reprimand darkened her platinum eyes. "And how long would I survive alone in a world surrounded by my enemies with just my honor?"

She was right, of course. A lone Sylvermyst needed the protection of a tribe to survive. Finn, however, didn't want her to think she had to remain at the mercy of her family.

"Perhaps you aren't as alone as you fear," he murmured.

Their gazes locked, a strange sizzle of anticipation zapping through Finn.

Something had just happened. Something big.

But before he could actually define what it was, she was taking a step backward, her heart pounding so loudly he could hear the frantic beat.

"We should go," she rasped.

He wrapped his arm around her waist, holding her captive. "Not you."

She blinked in surprise at his fierce tone before her lips were flattening in frustration. "You don't trust me."

He ignored her accusation.

"What will happen if your family discovers you've helped me?" he demanded.

"I…"

His lips twisted as her words trailed away. She didn't have to tell him. He was well aware that her brothers would treat her as a traitor.

She would be punished. Perhaps even killed.

A stark, mystifying stab of pain sliced through his heart.

"Exactly," he snapped in harsh tones. "Return to your rooms, Adair."

She narrowed her eyes as she glared at him. "You'll never get out of here without my powers."

"I have my own magic."

"I know, but creating a portal in this place is extremely difficult."

He stuck out his jaw. "Dammit, female. I won't be responsible for putting you in danger," he snapped.

She blinked. Then blinked again.

"You're worried about me?"

Unable to resist temptation, he lowered his head and kissed her with all the frustration that bubbled deep inside him.

He sensed her shock before she released a small sigh, her lips parting in silent invitation. Finn dipped his tongue into the warm welcome of her mouth. He groaned. She tasted of sweet herbs and earthy desire.

A combination that made his head swim.

The air misted around them, tiny snowflakes floating on the air as his chilled powers meshed with her dark, evocative magic.

Glorious…

The word drifted through his stunned mind even as he was sharply pulling away. What the hell was wrong with him?

Infuriated by his inability to think clearly when Adair was near, he moved with a blinding speed into the cavern. Then, turning, he gave a wave of his hands, unleashing his magic to fill the fissure with a thick layer of ice.

With her path blocked, the female had to accept that this wasn't her battle. Right?

She could return to the safety of her private rooms. And he could concentrate on the only thing that mattered.

Rescuing his people.

CHAPTER TEN

Rya watched Torque march out of the room, his spine ramrod straight and trails of smoke following in his wake.

He was in a huff.

No doubt about it.

Oddly, Rya found herself pleased by the male's foul mood.

Not because Levet managed to annoy him. Okay, that wasn't entirely true. She might take an itsy bitsy amount of pleasure in the gargoyle's unique ability to piss off Torque. But it was mainly relief that the stoic male could feel *anything*.

After the formal betrothal, Rya had been worried that her future mate was incapable of normal emotions. He'd been so detached during the ceremony while she'd been a quivering mass of nerves.

Now she at least knew he could feel anger.

And desire.

White-hot, all-consuming desire.

A tiny shiver racked her body.

As if sensing her inner turmoil, Levet waddled to stand at her side, reaching up to lightly pat her hand.

"I am so sorry, *ma belle*," he murmured.

She glanced down at him in confusion. "For what?"

"That you're being forced to mate with such a surly brute."

Another shiver raced through her. If she was being honest with herself, she wasn't nearly so sorry about the upcoming mating as she'd been just a day ago.

In fact…

"He's not a brute," she breathed.

"Non?"

Her lips twitched at the patent disbelief in Levet's tone.

"No. Although I thought he was."

"And now?"

She took time to consider what she'd discovered of Torque over the past hours.

"Now I realize that he's serious, but he isn't stern," she slowly admitted. "And he's dedicated. And loyal. And—"

"Handsome?" Levet overrode her words.

Heat raced through her. Handsome was such a mundane word. Certainly it didn't capture Torque's potent male beauty.

"He is…gorgeous," she at last muttered.

The gargoyle heaved a deep sigh. "I thought vampires were trouble."

Vampires? What did bloodsuckers have to do with Torque? "Excuse me?"

"In my experience, females always choose the tall, dark and annoying creatures." The delicate wings fluttered as Levet gave a resigned shake of his head. "It makes no sense to me."

"You don't have a mate?"

The gargoyle paused, before delicately clearing his throat.

"*Non*. I have no mate. In my house, I do have a young fairy that I recently rescued, but I am merely her protector," he revealed, placing his hand against his chest as a soulful expression settled on his lumpy face. "It is my nature to spread my love," he explained. "Not to have my wings clipped."

"I see."

"It is my destiny to be a toy boy."

Rya struggled to hide her amusement. "You mean, be a boy toy?"

"Oui." With an airy wave of his hand, Levet turned his attention to their surroundings. "If you are forced to mate with the dragon-shifter I do hope you intend to improve his taste in lairs," he murmured. "My heart aches at the thought of you living in such a dismal place."

Rya aimlessly wandered toward the shelves that consumed the far wall, her hand lightly touching one of the precious leather-bound books.

"Torque has suggested we build a lair together," she said.

"Is that what you desire?"

A thrill of anticipation inched down her spine. "I'm not sure. Just a few days ago I would have said no. Now…things have changed."

Levet clicked his tongue. "Ah well, do not blame yourself," he assured her. "Being in danger does tend to stir the emotions."

Was that it? Was danger responsible for her sense of bonding with Torque?

It would be an easy explanation. Unfortunately, it didn't ring true.

"Perhaps," she said with a shrug, eager to change the conversation. "Not that it matters until we manage to get out of here."

Levet started toward her. "We will escape. You can trust in me." He came to an abrupt halt, the gray eyes widening as if he'd been struck by inspiration. "In fact…"

Rya frowned as the gargoyle tilted back his head and spread his wings.

"What are you doing?" she demanded.

"My magic cannot work, but I might be able to use my ability to speak mind to mind," he told her.

Rya hesitated, wondering if the small demon was teasing her. She didn't know much about gargoyles or their powers. But as his pretty wings shimmered with a flare of magic, she allowed herself to experience a surge of hope.

"You can truly use telepathy?" she asked.

"*Oui*. I am a demon with many gifts."

Rya crossed the floor to stand at his side. "Can you contact my father?"

He wrinkled his short snout. "It would be simpler to try and reach out to Tayla. We already have a mental connection."

Rya nodded. That made sense. "What can I do?"

He gave a dramatic wave of his hands. "You may watch me in amazement."

Her lips twitched. "Okay."

Levet closed his eyes, presumably reaching out to Baine's mate. Rya stood beside him, waiting for…

Well, she didn't really know what she was waiting for. But as the minutes ticked past, she grew increasingly restless.

Levet, on the other hand, stood so still she started to wonder if he'd shifted into his statue-form.

Then, with a gusty sigh, he abruptly opened his eyes.

"Sacre bleu."

"Is something wrong?" she asked.

He gave a click of his tongue. "The magic is too thick for me to penetrate."

Rya grimaced, her hope fading. "Damn."

Levet's wings drooped. "I even tried to reach Finn, since he is within the maze with us."

A cold dread twisted her stomach. Over the past few days she'd become fond of the prince of frost sprites. She couldn't bear the thought of him being hurt.

Or worse.

"You couldn't find him?"

"He is blocking me," the gargoyle muttered. "The imbecile."

"Can you tell if he's okay?"

"He's alive," Levet muttered, his tail twitching around his feet. "That is all I can say."

Rya nodded. At least she knew he hadn't been killed by their unseen enemy.

On the point of suggesting they spend a few hours resting to regain their strength, Rya abruptly stiffened.

What was wrong with her brain? She had the perfect solution to their troubles.

"What about my mother?" she eagerly demanded. "Could you reach out to her?"

Clearly caught off guard by her request, Levet held up a clawed hand.

"I can make no promises, *ma belle*. I have never met your mother, which makes it much more difficult to touch her mind."

She held his gaze, her hands pressed together. She was desperate to reach her mother.

"Will you try?" she pleaded.

There was a short pause before the gargoyle was performing a deep bow.

"For you, *ma belle*? Anything."

She chuckled at his flamboyant antics. He truly was a charming companion. She couldn't understand why Torque found him so annoying.

Stepping back, she watched as he once again closed his eyes and lifted his hands. His wings shimmered with a pulse of magic, and then…nothing.

Prepared this time for his absolute stillness, Rya forced herself to remain patient. Just a few minutes later, however, Levet gave a strangled cry and tumbled face-first onto the stone floor.

Instantly dropping to her knees, she reached out to roll him onto his back, careful not to bend his fragile wings.

"Levet?" She touched his cheek, uncertain whether his chilled skin was natural or if something was truly wrong with him. "Levet, can you hear me?"

There was the sound of hurried footsteps as Torque rushed back into the room.

"Rya," he rasped, swiftly bending down next to her. "Are you hurt?"

A strange warmth filled her heart at the genuine concern that smoldered in the sapphire eyes.

He was really and truly worried about her.

"No, I'm fine," she assured him, nodding toward the unconscious demon on the floor. "But something's happened to Levet."

Torque made a sound of disgust. "Do you want me to throw him out of the lair?"

She sent him a chiding frown. "Of course not."

He shrugged. "Just a suggestion."

Ignoring his ridiculous words, she grabbed Levet's shoulder and gave him a small shake. The gargoyle groaned softly, but his eyes remained shut.

"He was trying to reach my mother when he collapsed," she muttered.

"Reach your mother?" Torque demanded. "How?"

"Levet claims to be a telepath."

Torque snorted. "He claims to be a lot of things."

She turned her head to study him in confusion. "I thought he was your friend?"

"Friend?" Torque shuddered. "He is a barnacle that is impossible to scrape off."

"Hey," Levet protested, his eyes fluttering open. "I am no banjo."

"See?" Torque growled, straightening as Levet pushed himself to his feet. "Aggravating pest."

Rya concentrated on the tiny gargoyle, still worried that he'd hurt himself. "Are you okay?"

"Non." He absently rubbed one of his stunted horns. "My head is throbbing."

Rya grimaced. "I'm sorry, Levet. I should never have asked you to use your gifts in this place."

"It is not your fault, *ma belle*," the gargoyle assured her. "Your mother is very…*formidable*."

Rya pressed a hand to her chest as her heart missed a painful beat. "You spoke to her?"

Levet's wings gave a violent flutter. "Actually, she spoke to me."

Rya blinked back sudden tears of relief. Until that precise moment she didn't realize just how worried she'd been. "She's alive."

"Very much so," Levet muttered.

Rya reached out to grab his arm. "Could you tell if she was nearby?"

"*Non*, I am sorry. I sensed that she's trapped in the same icy prison as we are, but it is impossible to know her precise location."

Rya slowly rose to her feet, vaguely aware of the heat that scalded down the length of her back as Torque moved to stand directly behind her. Her attention never wavered from the tiny gargoyle. "Did she speak to you?"

"Oui." Levet shivered at the memory. "She was

frighteningly insistent."

Rya smiled with wry amusement, growingly confident that he had indeed contacted her mother.

She was a female who let people know exactly what was on her mind. In very vigorous fashion.

"What did she say?"

Levet grimaced. "She told me that we're all in danger."

Torque's arm abruptly wrapped around her waist as Rya gave a small gasp, tugging her protectively against the hard strength of his chest.

"We already knew that," he growled.

She glanced over her shoulder to send Torque a reprimanding frown before returning her attention to Levet.

"Anything else?"

Levet nodded. "She insisted that we must wake the dragon."

"What dragon?" Torque demanded.

Levet glanced toward him with an overly innocent smile. "I assume that she meant your female."

Torque swore beneath his breath. "For the last time, she isn't mine," he ground out.

Levet shrugged. "So you say."

Feeling Torque stiffen, Rya rolled her eyes.

Men…

Did they all feel the need to bicker and fuss like rabid orcs?

"Is that all she said?" she asked, trying to diffuse the sizzling tension in the air.

"Oui." Levet nodded. "Just that we are in danger and that someone must wake the dragon."

Slowly turning in Torque's arms, she met his narrowed gaze.

"Rya—"

She overrode his protest. "We have to find the

dragon. And we have to do it now."

CHAPTER ELEVEN

Finn turned away from the closed fissure to study the strange mound that consumed the majority of the cavern floor.

Unlike the ice that made up the labyrinth, it was denser. And far too cloudy to determine what was beneath it.

Not that Finn intended to find out.

His magic easily determined that it wasn't just one big chunk of frozen liquid. Instead, there were thousands of thin layers that covered a hidden object.

Clearly someone had gone to a lot of trouble to keep the thing buried. He had no intention of disturbing it.

With a shiver, he made his way along the edge of the cavern, his gaze lifted toward the ridge far above him. He could sense at least one guard, but the weird flux of the labyrinth meant he couldn't be sure there weren't more.

Inching around a thick stalagmite, he discovered a male frost sprite lying on frozen ground, his thin face drained of color and his pale hair tangled.

Finn didn't have to ask his friend to know that he'd been forced to use his magic to the point of complete collapse.

"Tasko," he murmured in low tones, reaching out to grasp the male's shoulder and give him a small shake. "Tasko, you must wake."

Putting a punch of magic behind his command, he watched as Tasko grimly forced his eyes open. For a second the male looked confused, as if Finn was the last person he expected to see.

Then, with a shaky hand, he reached up to lay his fingers against Finn's cheek. "My prince. Is it really you?"

"Shh." Finn quickly glanced around, ensuring nothing was sneaking up on them. "It's really me."

The male grimaced. "You shouldn't have come here."

Finn ignored the soft chiding. Tasko was his strongest warrior, and the one tribesman who felt comfortable speaking his mind.

"How is the cuff locked?" he instead demanded, crouching down so he could study the heavy manacle wrapped around the male's ankle.

"By magic," Tasko said, his voice thick with disgust. "I've tried every trick I know and haven't been able to put a dent in it."

Finn reached out to touch the heavy metal, hissing as pain shot from his fingers up his arm.

"Iron," he breathed, jerking his hand away.

"Yeah, our idiotic captors expect us to use our magic to retrieve gems from the ice, but they keep us so drained we can barely function."

Finn swiftly considered their options. There weren't

many. The iron meant he couldn't physically break open the manacles. And the unknown magic prevented him from turning the metal to frost.

His only hope was his rare talent to move through ice.

"I'll have to share my powers for you to escape," he said. "Be ready to run."

"No, Finn," the younger male protested, well aware that the effort would drain Finn of his magic. "Don't waste your strength on me. Release the others first."

Finn gave a decisive shake of his head. "It might not be official, but we both know you're the obvious heir to take my place if something happens to me," he pointed out. "The tribe needs you."

Grabbing the male's leg just below the knee, he released his magic. It was intoxicating. Like champagne bubbles dancing through his veins. Focusing his will, he allowed the power to flow through his palm and into Tasko's leg.

Immediately his foot began to sink into the floor, as if it was melting through the ice. Tasko bit his lower lip, shuddering as the cold sliced through his body. Finn, however, didn't relent, continuing to pump his magic through his leg until the manacle was fully surrounded by ice. Then, jerking Tasko's leg up, he shut off his magic.

With a flurry of sparkles, Tasko's calf and foot re-formed. This time without the heavy iron cuff that remained trapped beneath the floor.

"I'm free," Tasko rasped, his shaky tone revealing his fear that he was destined to die in the strange labyrinth.

Finn straightened, grasping Tasko's arm so he could tug him to his feet. "Can you create a portal?" he demanded.

A grim determination flared in Tasko's light blue

eyes. "I'll force one open."

Finn nodded. "Good. I'll release the others."

Depending on his warrior to find a way to get them out of the cavern, Finn concentrated on moving forward. His feet felt oddly heavy, but he refused to acknowledge his weariness.

Adair had said her brothers would soon be returning.

The clock was ticking.

He found the next sprite curled in a small cavity dug into the wall.

Ineke was a tiny female with a mass of silver hair and gray eyes. She barely looked big enough to be fully grown, but her magic was off the charts. Which was no doubt why she'd been kidnapped.

Containing his flare of fury at the sight of her ashen complexion and the purple shadows beneath her eyes, Finn bent down to grab her leg, leaving her asleep until he'd managed to use his powers to press her foot into the ice. She at last woke when he was finishing, as if jolted when he removed his magic.

Like Tasko, she blinked in confusion. "Finn?"

He leaned forward, placing his hand over her mouth as he whispered directly in her ear.

"Tasko is waiting at the back of the cavern," he told her. "See if you can join your powers with his to open a portal for the others."

She rose to her feet, briefly swaying. Still, her concern was focused on him.

"You need to rest, my prince," she murmured softly, reaching up to press her fingers to his cheek.

He shook his head. "Later."

"But—"

Finn gave her a small push toward the narrow pathway that led to the back of the cavern. "Go."

She hesitated, tears filling her beautiful eyes. "Thank you."

He gave a short nod, waiting for her to spin on her heel and disappear in the shadows that appeared to be thickening.

Finn swayed, but with grim determination he was once again moving forward.

Nothing was going to stop him from freeing his people.

End. Of. Story.

He found the next two tribesmen chained together. Motioning for them to remain silent as they parted their lips in shock at his sudden appearance, he performed the same ritual. Thankfully, they were close enough that he could free them both at the same time.

Ordering them to join Tasko and Ineke, he went in search of the last of his tribesmen.

It took a few minutes to at last find Daq at the very front of the cavern. The young male had a bloody lip and a dark bruise on his cheek that spoke of a recent beating.

Bastards.

Finn contained his fury, using his rapidly fading magic to get rid of the manacle. Then, gently shaking the young male awake, he helped him to a sitting position.

"Can you stand?" he asked in a low whisper.

"Yes." With a pained grimace, Daq rose to his feet. Then, with a choked cry, he grabbed Finn's hand to squeeze his fingers. "Bless you, my prince."

Finn offered a rueful smile. "Don't thank me yet," he warned. "We still have to get out of here."

As if the words had conjured his worst fear, there was a sudden movement on the ridge just above them. Finn cursed as a tall, thickly muscled male dressed in jeans and a long leather coat headed down the stairs carved into the ice. He had a bow angled across his back, along with a full quiver of arrows.

"Get to the back of the cavern and tell Tasko to get through the portal," Finn commanded. He had to distract the approaching stranger or none of them were making it out of the labyrinth. "Once you're back home I want you to head to Nome and lock yourselves in the safe house."

Daq's lips parted to argue, then, meeting Finn's determined gaze, he gave a reluctant nod and turned to hurry away.

At the same time, Finn moved to block the path.

"There you are," the male drawled from the edge of the ridge, the faint scent of herbs revealing he was a Sylvermyst.

Finn narrowed his gaze, studying the stranger. He had light red hair that was pulled into a braid that hung down his back. His face was narrow, with small eyes and a strange mark branded into the side of his neck. A gift from the Dark Lord? Impossible to say.

Finn was far more interested in the faint resemblance to Adair in the platinum eyes that warned him this wasn't just another Sylvermyst, but one of her brothers.

With a sudden leap, the male was landing directly in front of him.

Finn folded his arms over his chest. The longer he could keep the male preoccupied, the greater the chance his people could escape. "I didn't realize you were looking for me."

An ugly sneer touched the male's cruel mouth. "I should have known you would try to escape. Royalty always has to be a pain in the ass."

Finn arched a brow, not missing the edge in the male's voice.

Clearly he had authority issues.

"You have no idea just how much of a pain I intend to be," Finn assured him with a mocking smile.

Anger flared through the man's eyes before he was deliberately assuming a nonchalant manner. "Tsk. Tsk. You aren't in a position to be issuing threats," he drawled, his gaze flicking to the side as another male abruptly stepped out of the ice.

Finn scowled, belatedly sensing the hidden tunnel. Dammit, this place was like a twisted funhouse.

"I see you found our prisoner, Micah," the newest stranger said, his face almost a carbon copy of the first male, although his eyes were darker and his chin weaker.

Finn also had the sense that he was the younger of the two.

Micah frowned. "Did you see the other prisoners?"

"No, but Lila is searching for them."

"Damn." Micah clenched his hands into tight fists before he was sucking in a deep breath. "No matter. They can't have gone far."

Finn silently prayed the male was wrong. With any luck, Tasko would have already opened a portal and whisked his people far away.

"Do you want me to take this one back to his cell?" the second male demanded.

"No, now that he's here we might as well put him to use," Micah said, strolling forward to study Finn with a dismissive gaze. "So, you're a prince."

"And you aren't," Finn mocked, knowing he was touching a raw nerve.

The male's nose flared, but he grimly held on to his temper. "Smirk if you want, but I shall soon be a king," he informed Finn.

"Really." Finn deliberately glanced toward the male standing off to the side. "And what about you?"

The Sylvermyst blinked in confusion. "Me?"

"Do you get to be king?" he pressed, sensing he was the weaker of the two. "Or does your brother get all the glory?"

"I—"

"That's none of your concern," Micah interrupted.

The second male scowled. "Micah."

"Shit, Jarvis, he's just trying to cause trouble," the

male snapped.

"But I get to be king," Jarvis demanded. "Don't I?"

Micah sliced his hand through the air. "We'll discuss this later."

"Later." Finn chuckled, keeping his gaze on Jarvis. "That's the code word for 'he doesn't intend to share the throne.'"

"Shut up," Micah growled, abruptly slamming his fist into Finn's face. "You will do as I say or you'll pay the consequences."

Finn swallowed the blood from his split lip, his smile never fading. The punch had hurt like a bitch, but there was no way he was revealing any vulnerability in front of the Sylvermyst. "I'm not afraid of you."

"Then you're an idiot," Micah assured him, lifting his hand. "I learned how to inflict pain from a master."

Prepared for another blow, or even an arrow through the heart, Finn was caught off guard when a blinding pain sliced through his head.

Dark magic.

A cry was ripped from his throat. It felt as if someone was carving a knife through his brain. *Slice. Slice. Slice.*

"Stop." The word passed his lips before he could halt it.

Micah chuckled, clearly tickled by his little trick. "I have discovered that there are worse things than death," he taunted.

Finn pressed his palms against his temples and squeezed. As if he could somehow halt the searing agony. "What do you want from me?" he rasped.

The pain continued as the male leaned down to speak directly in his ear.

"Remove the ice from the center of the floor," he told Finn. "Simple."

Finn's breath was released on a hiss. "If it was so

simple, you would do it."

The pain abruptly intensified. "Just do it."

Finn battled back a looming darkness. Holy shit. He'd never endured such torture.

"I can't do anything if I'm unconscious," he snarled.

The pain began to ease, and Finn lifted his head to meet the glittering platinum gaze. It didn't take a mind reader to know that Micah enjoyed seeing him on his knees.

"One wrong move and I'll make sure you regret it," the Sylvermyst promised.

Finn rose to his feet, his knees threatening to collapse. Covertly he placed his hand behind his back, using the wall to keep himself upright.

"What's beneath the ice?" he demanded. Not that he gave a shit, but he needed time to recover his strength.

Once he could conjure his magic, he intended to collapse the entire cavern. He'd see if the bastards could crawl out of several tons of ice.

"Obviously that's what you're going to find out," Micah sneered.

Finn turned his attention toward the swell of ice that towered just a few feet away. Once again he was struck by the sense of…wrongness.

He asked the question that'd been preying on his mind. "Did it occur to you that someone went to a lot of trouble to cover it in so many layers?"

The scent of herbs deepened as Micah glanced toward the looming mound. Naked greed tightened his narrow features.

"Of course it did. Which is precisely why I want it uncovered." Micah stepped toward the mound, his body vibrating with excitement. "It must be priceless."

Finn frowned. The more he concentrated on the strange heap of ice, the more unnerved he was at the thought of messing with it. "Or dangerous," he muttered.

"What are you talking about?" Jarvis demanded, his expression torn between his brother's lust and a wary unease.

Could the younger Sylvermyst sense the menace that throbbed beneath the ice?

"Nothing," Micah snapped, his seething frustration prickling through the air. "He's just playing for time."

That'd been the original intent. Now, however, he was genuinely concerned.

The more he concentrated on the ice, the more certain he was that it was there to keep something trapped.

Something they wanted to *stay* trapped.

"No. We shouldn't mess with it," he muttered in distracted tones.

Jarvis inched a step toward him. As if Finn could offer him protection from whatever was lurking just out of sight.

"Why not?" he asked Finn.

Finn shuddered. "Darkness."

"Micah," Jarvis muttered. "Maybe we should wait until—"

"What is wrong with you?" He whirled to glare at his brother. "The sprite is trying to screw with us."

"Listen to me," Finn insisted. "Whatever is under the ice isn't treasure."

"Liar," Micah rasped, his eyes glowing with a weird frenzy. Almost as if he'd already been touched by madness. "Remove the ice."

Finn took a deliberate step away, his back pressed against the frozen wall.

"No."

Micah's face flushed with fury. "Have you forgotten what I can do to you?"

Finn shook his head. "Then do it. I won't help you."

"You say that now." Micah lifted his hand, the air

heating with his magic. "But eventually you'll do exactly what I want."

"When hell freezes over," Finn said in wry tones. He was still weak, but he was fairly confident he had enough strength to pull down the ceiling.

Or at least that was the hope.

Micah blinked, caught off guard by Finn's response. Clearly he'd assumed Finn would do anything to avoid the pain.

"Do you think I won't kill you?" he growled.

Finn shrugged. "I don't care."

There was a tense battle of glares as Micah prepared to use his magic. Then, perhaps sensing that Finn wasn't going to budge, he released a sharp breath.

"Find the others," he snapped toward his brother.

Jarvis gave a grudging nod, but before he could move, the sound of the female sliced through the air.

"They're gone, but I have something better."

Finn turned his head to watch the tall, slender female Sylvermyst step into sight from the side of the cavern. He easily recognized the female he'd seen with Adair earlier.

What was her name? Lila? Yes, that was it.

"Where have you been?" Micah barked.

The female's bronzed eyes flashed with temper. "Solving your problems, as usual."

Micah curled his lip with disdain. "I don't need a female to solve my problems."

"Is that right?" Indifferent to her brother's scorn, Lila stepped around the curve of the icy mound, revealing that she wasn't alone. "Come along, dear sister."

Adair.

Finn sucked in a shocked breath. Not because she was in the company of Lila, but because it was obvious she'd been severely beaten.

Her copper hair was tangled around her pale face that was bruised and bloody. One eye was nearly swelled shut, and the arm her sister was holding was hanging at an awkward angle. It was either ripped out of joint or broken.

Her robe was torn in several places and she was limping, which meant that it wasn't just her face that had suffered from the tender hand of her sister.

Anger blasted through Finn.

The bitch. Finn had a natural aversion to hurting females, but Lila had just sealed her fate.

She was going to die along with her brothers.

Oblivious to the cloud of frost that filled the air, Micah stepped toward his sisters with a small frown.

"Adair?" His gaze flicked between the two women before landing on Lila. "What's going on?"

Lila glared at her sister. "I found her at the back of the cavern, helping the sprites escape through a portal."

Finn's heart clenched. He was suddenly certain she was the one who'd opened the portal. Dammit. She'd saved his people and now she'd put her own life at risk.

Confirming his worst fear, Micah stormed forward, lifting his hand to smack Adair across the face. Her head rolled backward, blood dripping down her jaw from a wide cut in her cheek.

"Treacherous bitch," Micah thundered, his hand lifting to hit her again.

"Stop," Finn rasped, his hands clenched at his side as he leashed the urge to attack the male.

He had to conserve his strength. Especially now.

He could no longer consider the idea of becoming a noble martyr, willing to die to take out his enemies.

Not when that would also mean the death of Adair.

He would sacrifice himself. But not her.

It didn't matter that she was related to his enemies. Or that he barely knew her.

He wasn't going to let her die.

Period.

Glancing over his shoulder, Micah took in Finn's grim expression, a slow smile curving his lips as he realized he had the perfect weapon in his hands.

"Ah," he drawled, moving to wrap his arm around Adair's shoulders. "Perhaps you're not as worthless as I always feared, sweet sister."

Adair shuddered, her expression pleading. "Micah, please."

"Don't worry, pet," he mocked, tugging her forward until they stood directly in front of Finn. "I don't intend to kill you. Not yet, anyway. First your prince is going to remove the ice for us."

Adair swayed and no doubt would have fallen on her face if her brother hadn't been holding her up. Her gaze, however, remained locked on Finn.

"I'm sorry," she breathed, as if any of this was her fault.

Frost coated Finn's skin as he glared at the smugly smiling Micah. "Hurt her and I'll destroy you."

"Isn't that sweet?" Micah roughly patted Adair's wounded cheek. "The pretty sprite is worried about you. Did you let him have a taste of your body to earn such concern?"

"Let her go," Finn commanded.

Micah's eyes narrowed, his expression already one of anticipation. "Do as I ask and I promise I'll release her."

"Don't listen to him—" Adair's words broke off in a scream as Micah released his magic.

"Shit," Finn muttered, his gut twisting as Micah shoved Adair onto the ground. Still screaming, she writhed in pain, but reaching out a pleading hand she released a low groan.

"Don't, Finn," she managed to gasp. "They'll kill

me either way."

Micah cursed, landing a vicious kick to the side of Adair's head. The female went limp, knocked unconscious by the blow.

Satisfied that Adair couldn't cause any further trouble, Micah glared toward Finn.

"Do it." He pointed at the icy mound. "Now."

Trying to ignore the fear that he was making a terrible mistake, Finn held out his hand. Then, with a sharp blast, he released the last of his magic.

CHAPTER TWELVE

Torque scowled at Rya and the ridiculous gargoyle who were gazing at him with expectant expressions.

Did they think he had some sort of special magic that allowed him to locate missing dragons?

"How am I supposed to find the female?" he asked.

Levet clicked his tongue. "And you call yourself a hero?"

"No." He glared toward the miniature blight on gargoyles everywhere. "I have *never* called myself a hero."

Rya stepped forward, no doubt eager to halt yet another squabble. Torque swallowed a curse. The annoying creature provoked him into acting like a cranky hatchling.

"You're a much better tracker than I am," Rya pointed out in soothing tones. "Can you use your senses to find her?"

He grimaced. Even standing in a place that looked so familiar, he was eerily aware of the strangeness of their surroundings. The truth was that he had no idea how to go about picking up a trail.

"I might be able to if we weren't in the middle of an ice maze," he grudgingly confessed. "Once I leave these rooms there's a very real possibility that I'll become lost." A small shiver raced through his body. "Or worse, stuck in another cell."

Rya nodded, but her expression remained troubled. "We have to do something. My mother can be a bit bossy—"

"Not a bit, *ma belle*," Levet interrupted, his tail twitching around his feet. "She is *très* bossy."

"Okay, very bossy." Rya waved a dismissive hand, while Torque made a mental note to treat the Shinto female with proper respect. He didn't know why, but it was important that Rya's mother approve of him. "Still, if she says we need to waken the dragon, then we can't ignore her warning."

Torque heaved a resigned sigh. Obviously he wasn't going to get any peace until he at least tried to locate the damned dragon.

"Fine," he muttered. "Remain here."

"Non." Without warning, the gargoyle stepped forward. "You will need me."

Torque didn't bother to hide his horror. It was bad enough to be wandering through the weird-ass ice without being burdened with the three-foot demon from hell. "You are the last thing I need."

The gargoyle puffed out his chest. "Can you detect illusions?"

Torque planted his hands on his hips, refusing to budge. "The ice isn't an illusion."

Levet gave a flick of his wings. "True, but I can sense where there are hidden pathways."

Torque stiffened. The gargoyle could find a way through the maze? And he hadn't told them earlier?

What the hell?

"If you had the means to escape, then why didn't you?" he growled, his voice thick with suspicion.

Levet stomped a clawed foot, his expression petulant. "I have told you and told you. It is too cold."

There was a movement next to him as Rya stepped to stand next to the gargoyle. "I'm going as well."

"No." Torque nipped the suggestion in the bud. "Absolutely not."

Her gaze narrowed. "If you're concentrating on finding the dragon you'll need me to watch your back."

"It's too dangerous."

A tense silence filled the room as the gargoyle took a dramatic step backward. As if trying to get out of the direct line of fire.

Clearly the demon was smarter than Torque had given him credit for.

"My dragon might not be as strong as yours, but I'm not completely worthless," Rya at last said in flat tones.

Prickles of heat danced over Torque's skin. Clearly his female wasn't happy.

"I know that," he said in cautious tones.

"Good." She moved forward, pressing her finger into the center of his chest. "Then you won't try to keep me locked away."

He reached to grab her hand, pressing it against the beat of his heart.

"Rya—"

She overrode his protest. "Torque, I appreciate your desire to protect me. But right now we all need to work together if we're going to locate the dragon and hopefully get out of here."

He gazed down at her flushed face and smoldering amber eyes and realized she'd never looked more beautiful. Even more astonishing, he realized that as much as he wanted to keep her safe, the thought of working with her as a partner felt oddly right.

His lips twitched with a rueful smile, accepting that she'd won the argument.

Again.

"How did I ever assume you were a quiet, biddable sort of female?" he muttered.

Something that might have been hurt rippled over her delicate features.

"Is that what you prefer?"

He cupped her face in his hands, gazing down at her with blatant need.

"You know what I prefer," he said in husky tones.

There was the scrape of claws against the stone floor as Levet moved to wiggle between them.

"*Non*. No kissy-face until we have completed our quest," he groused, pushing against Torque's leg. "It is a rule."

Torque stepped back as he formed a ball of dragon-fire in his hand. Rya released a small gasp, reaching to grab his wrist.

"Torque, no," she pleaded.

With an effort he forced himself to extinguish the fire. "When this is done I'm going to crisp him into a tiny briquette," he warned.

"Fah." Levet sniffed. "The joke is on you. I adore brisket."

"I—" Torque bit off his words. Christ, what was wrong with him? This was no time to be distracted. "Never mind. Let's go," he snapped.

He crossed the floor with long strides, stepping through the opening that led to the small foyer. He was pulling open the front door when Levet suddenly darted in front of him.

"Allow me to go first," the gargoyle commanded.

Torque waved a mocking hand. “Knock yourself out.”

Waddling out the door, Levet gave a flick of his tail. “This way.”

Torque rolled his eyes, but he followed the tiny gargoyle into the narrow tunnel of ice. He felt Rya directly behind him, the sizzle of her dragon-magic brushing over his back.

Clearly she was taking her duties as rear guard seriously. A delicious excitement tingled through him, his own beast roaring with satisfaction. As a half-breed he couldn’t fully shift into dragon-form, but that didn’t mute his animal instincts.

He liked feeling her heat.

In silence they moved through the tunnel, an ominous sense of claustrophobia pressing down on Torque. He hated the sensation of being trapped in the endless tunnels. And the knowledge he was at the mercy of the damned gargoyle.

And while Levet never hesitated as he moved forward, Torque couldn’t shake the sensation they were going in circles.

Trying to ignore the knowledge that his nerves were being rubbed raw, Torque concentrated on catching a scent of the dragon. If she was still in the maze, then he should be able to find her.

Eventually…

He wasn’t sure how much time had passed when there was a flicker of movement in the ice beside him.

“Wait,” he said, coming to a halt as he studied the frozen wall. “I think I caught sight of her.”

Levet moved to join him, pressing his snout against the ice. There was another flicker, and the outline of a female appeared.

Torque felt a surge of hope, but giving a decisive shake of his head, Levet turned to face him.

"Non," he said. "It is an illusion."

Torque frowned, studying the shadowed silhouette. "You're sure?"

"It is my specialty to see through such magic," the gargoyle announced with his usual lack of humility. "I believe she is trying to lead us into a trap."

Torque made a sound of frustration. He was tired of walking in circles. And worse, Levet was right. It was too damned cold.

Soul-deep, to-the-bone cold.

"Why the hell would she lead us into a trap after she went to the effort of creating my lair?" he rasped.

Levet gave a lift of his hands. "That I cannot say."

Unfortunately, neither could Torque. He bit back a curse, instinctively wrapping his arm around Rya's shoulders as she moved to stand at his side.

"This place gives me the creeps," she muttered.

He placed a kiss on her temple. "When we get out of here I promise we'll go someplace very warm."

"Ah, *oui*." Levet clapped his hands together. "A perfect notion. I know of a demon bar in Fiji that serves the most delicious kava punch."

Torque shook his head, but before he could respond, a menacing pulse of energy flowed around them.

They all stiffened, unnerved by the unexplainable sense of dread.

"Do you feel that?" Rya at last demanded.

Torque nodded. "Yes."

She shivered. "What is it?"

"I don't know." He tightened his arm around her.

"Madness," Levet abruptly muttered, his wings twitching as he sent them a worried frown. "We must hurry."

Without further explanation, the gargoyle was scurrying forward. For once, Torque didn't argue, releasing Rya so they could keep pace with the small demon.

He had no idea where they were going, but he was sure it had to be better than remaining where they were.

Darting from one tunnel to another, Torque nearly missed the faint vibrations that warned of an enormous power not far away.

"Stop," he barked, coming to an abrupt halt.

Rya slammed into his back before she regained her balance and sent him an apprehensive glance. "What's wrong?"

"I feel her," he murmured, pressing his hand against the ice. Yep. Definite vibrations. "We need to go in this direction," he told the gargoyle.

Levet nodded, moving along the tunnel until he could press his hand through a seemingly solid wall.

"Here's an opening."

They moved together, entering a tunnel that was larger than the others.

Torque sucked in a deep breath, catching the scent of cinnamon. They were getting closer.

A flare of hope filled his heart. At least for a second. Then, without warning, there was a sharp sound of popping that made him wince.

Super-hearing wasn't always a bonus.

"What the hell?" he rasped.

Rya sucked in a sharp gasp. "Look."

Torque turned to see that she was pointing at the ice behind them. He frowned, not sure what had frightened her. Then he finally noticed the spiderweb of cracks spreading through the walls and along the ceiling.

The ice was splintering. Shit. The tunnel was going to collapse.

Or explode.

Neither option was something he wanted to experience.

"Follow me," Levet called, his wings flapping to

give him speed as he scurried forward.

Torque was directly behind him, the scent of cinnamon thickening as the gargoyle led them into a large cavern. Although made of ice, it felt denser…more real than the rest of the maze.

"I sense her," Torque muttered, slowing as he became distracted by the heavy weight pressing down on him. "She's stirring."

"Watch out," Rya cried, shoving her hands against the center of his back.

Torque stumbled forward, glancing over his shoulder to watch a large, lethal icicle drop from the ceiling to impale the floor. Precisely where he'd been standing a second before.

Levet gave a low whistle. "I do not think she wants company."

Shaken by the knowledge he'd nearly been skewered by the icicle, he parted his lips to thank the female who'd saved him from a nasty injury, only to snap them shut.

Instead he moved to wrap her in his arms as a shimmering mist suddenly filled the center of the cavern. The three of them watched in silence, no one certain what the hell was happening as the mist cleared to reveal two females.

One of them was the same, small creature with long red hair and pale eyes with flecks of color who had appeared earlier. This time, however, she wasn't alone. She had a young female with her with dark hair, although the same opal-like eyes.

A daughter?

Certainly they were both dragons. There was no missing the power that was now thundering through the cavern.

They were both wearing robes that shimmered with iridescent beads, as they stood facing one another, neither seeming to notice they were no longer alone.

"Torque." Rya pressed against his side, her gaze locked on the two dragons. "What's going on?"

Torque grimaced. That was the question. Although the two forms looked solid, and the power was very real, there was something about them that warned they weren't actually standing in front of them.

It was almost as if they were watching a projection of the females.

"I don't know. The older female is the dragon who I met earlier, but she doesn't feel the same," he muttered, glancing toward the gargoyle. "Is it an illusion?"

Levet slowly shook his head. "Not exactly. I believe it is…" He paused, as if trying to decide what he was seeing. "A memory."

"Yes," Torque abruptly agreed. That would explain why it felt like he was watching a movie. "The dragon is creating this."

***

Rya watched with a weird fascination as the last of the mist cleared around the females.

The older female was lovely, with hair that looked like a cascade of crimson silk, and pale, delicate features. And those eyes…glorious opals. And her power…good goddess, it made the floor pulse beneath her feet.

But looking closer, Rya thought she could see an expression of profound sadness on the dragon's face.

Something terrible was about to happen.

Rya could feel it in her bones.

Pressing against Torque's side, she watched in silence as the older dragon reached to touch her companion's face. At first Rya thought the younger female was a mere child. She had black hair pulled into a simple braid, with pale eyes flecked with the colors of a rainbow. Her features were delicate and she stood barely five foot.

Of course, a full dragon could take any form they wanted.

But as Rya continued to study the finely chiseled features, she sensed that the female was older than she first assumed.

"I think she's trying to show us something," she said, her gaze never wavering from the dragons.

"Yeah, I think so too," Torque muttered. "But what?"

Rya hunched a shoulder as she watched the older dragon step closer to the smaller female, her lips moving as if she was speaking. They could hear nothing, however, only emphasizing the realization this wasn't real.

Without warning, the young dragon suddenly slumped forward, as if she'd passed out.

Did dragons faint? Rya had never seen one appear less than indestructible.

Easily catching the female in her arms, the older dragon bent down, stretching the limp form on the ground. Then, with tender care, she straightened the female's beaded robe before she lifted her hand and started to wave it in an elegant pattern.

Rya frowned. Was she trying to wake the unconscious female?

The question drifted through her mind just as a thin layer of ice coated the form on the floor. The dragon gave another wave of her hand, and yet another layer of ice appeared.

"What the—" Torque bit off his words as the image began to fade, replaced by the sight of a massive dragon curled in the middle of the floor.

This time there was no sensation of an illusion.

The dragon was real.

Very, very real.

Even at a distance Rya could make out the iridescent shimmer in the crimson scales that covered the long, powerful body. The massive wings were folded tight to her back, but they would no doubt span over ten feet. Her legs were curled beneath her, but Rya caught a glimpse of hooked claws that could slice her in half. The female had a narrow snout with razor-sharp teeth, and even in her sleep there were puffs of smoke escaping her flared nostrils.

Rya's mouth went dry, her heart missing a painful beat. She'd grown up around dragons. Which meant she knew it was a bad idea to intrude into their private lair.

When she'd told Torque they needed to locate the female, she'd assumed they'd have plenty of warning before they stumbled across her. That way they could try and talk to her from a distance.

Now…

Hell, now all she wanted to do was turn and make a run for it.

"*Ma belle*, I am not so certain this is a wise notion," Levet muttered.

"No shit," Torque breathed, his arm tightening around her. As if he was having the same urge to flee.

But before any of them could actually get their frozen feet to move, the dragon abruptly lifted her head, white-hot fire burning in her eyes.

"What have you done?"

CHAPTER THIRTEEN

Torque swallowed a curse, instinctively moving to stand in front of Rya. Not that he could battle against a full-blooded dragon and survive. But he might be able to give his female time to escape.

Better yet, he hoped to soothe the annoyed creature before she decided to scorch them into crispy critters.

Or at least that was the thought before the tiny gargoyle waddled forward to perform a small bow.

"Forgive us, your Graciousness," he said, his wings spread wide. "We come in peace."

With a roll of his eyes, Torque moved to grab the creature by one horn, dragging him away from the angry dragon.

"Are you trying to get us killed?" he muttered.

Without warning there was a blast of magic. Torque recoiled as the sizzling power buffeted against him, nearly sending him to his knees. He cast a quick glance over his shoulder to make sure Rya hadn't been hurt before he was returning his attention to the female who was now standing in the place of the humongous leviathan.

Once again she was the beautiful female with bright red hair and opal eyes. On this occasion, however, her manner wasn't befuddled, or confused.

Belatedly he realized that when he'd met her before, she'd been in a deep, hibernating sleep. Only a tiny fraction of her mind had been awake enough to realize her lair had been invaded.

Now she was fully conscious and was even more dangerous.

"Who dares to—" She abruptly bit off her angry words, her brows drawing together. "Wait. I know you."

"Torque." He gave a cautious nod of his head. "We met earlier."

"Yes." She smoothed her hand down her beaded robe, her eyes still glowing with her inner fire. "And I told you to remain in the safety of the space I created for you."

He chose his words with care. "We received a warning that you were in danger. We tracked you down to try and keep you safe."

"Danger?" She glanced around the cavern, as if searching for any hidden enemy. "There's nothing that can harm me here."

Torque would normally agree. What the hell could hurt a dragon?

Still, he couldn't dismiss the gathering sense of doom that seemed to fill the air.

"I don't doubt your skills in protecting your lair," he said with careful respect for her powers. "But there's an enemy who managed to kidnap several frost sprites as well as a Shinto female and bring them here. We were following them when we became trapped," he reminded her.

The dragon tilted her head to the side, her eyes closing as she presumably used her powers to search through her lair for intruders.

"They are a nuisance, but they will eventually concede defeat and leave," she at last murmured.

Okay. If the big, bad dragon didn't think there was any reason to worry, Torque wasn't going to force the issue.

Instead he turned his attention to their most pressing problem.

"I'm happy to hear that," he said. "Unfortunately we don't have their skill with opening portals. We must ask for your assistance in allowing us to leave your lair."

The female's eyes snapped open. "That's not possible."

"But—"

She slashed her hand through the air, cutting off his protest. "This isn't my lair."

Torque paused. Was this some sort of quiz?

"Then what is it?" he asked.

Her features softened. "A refuge."

"A refuge for you?"

"No."

He felt a brush of heat along his arm as Rya moved to stand at his side.

"It's for the young dragon, isn't it?" she asked in soft tones.

"My daughter," the dragon revealed, her gaze suddenly locked on Rya. "And your sister."

Torque heard Rya suck in a startled breath. Without thought, he placed a comforting arm around her shoulders, tugging her close.

"Sister?" she breathed in baffled tones.

The dragon nodded, taking in Rya's confused expression with a hint of satisfaction.

"Blayze is also the daughter of Synge."

"Oh." Rya took a moment to consider the revelation. Then stunned disbelief was slowly replaced by a tentative smile. Clearly she was pleased by the thought of having a sister. "How wonderful."

"I am Ravel, mate to Synge," the dragon continued.

"Mate?" Rya blinked. Then blinked again. "I'm sorry, I had no idea. My father has never spoken of a consort or a full-blooded daughter."

"I left him a very, very long time ago," Ravel told her. "Before you were born."

Rya looked as amazed as Torque felt. When dragons mated it was for eternity.

"Were you driven away?"

"No. Synge has always been quite devoted to me," Ravel admitted. "I left to protect my daughter."

Her explanation only deepened Torque's confusion. Pureblooded dragons were exceedingly rare. And female offspring were…priceless. There was no worse sin than harming a child.

"Who would dare to hurt a baby dragon?" he demanded.

Ravel abruptly turned to pace across the barren cavern, her features tightening with a fierce emotion. "Synge has made enemies over the years," she muttered.

Torque rolled his eyes. Synge was a brutal, insatiable predator who ruled his vast kingdom with an iron fist. There was a good chance the bastard had made thousands and thousands of enemies. Torque was wise enough, however, to keep his thoughts to himself.

Turning back to face them, Ravel clenched her hands at her sides. "One of them managed to penetrate the lair shortly after the birth of Blayze and cursed her."

Torque hissed in horror. "What sort of curse?"

"Eternal madness."

"Oh dear goddess," Rya breathed. "That's horrible."

Torque shuddered. It was indeed horrible. He'd never actually met anyone who was cursed, but he knew they rarely survived.

But it wasn't his thought of Blayze's unfortunate fate that was making his skin crawl. It was the thickening malice that swirled through the air.

He desperately wanted to be out of the strange cavern, but he sensed that Rya wasn't going to budge until she heard the full story of her sister.

"What happened?" he pressed.

"The decision was made by the Dragon Council to kill her," Ravel said in stark tones.

Rya made a sound of distress. "So you left?"

The female nodded. "I pretended to accept the verdict, but I told them I couldn't live without my child. I promised I would destroy both of us." She shrugged. "It was the only way to get her out of the lair."

Torque arched a brow. It would have taken enormous courage to defy the ancient Council.

"How did you convince the dragons you were dead?" he asked.

She gave a wave of her hand, indicating the cavern around them. "I have a talent for illusion."

"*Oui*," Levet suddenly intruded. "Your skill is magnificent."

"Yes, it is," the female agreed.

Torque hid his smile. Clearly she had the customary humility of most dragons.

None.

He steered the conversation back on track. "So you convinced the dragons you were dead and brought your daughter here?"

"Not at first." Ravel's eyes grew distant, as if she was lost in memories. "I traveled to various worlds in the hopes of finding a cure. But every year that passed, the madness consumed more and more of Blayze." She heaved a deep, painful sigh, smoke curling from her nose. "Eventually it became too dangerous to travel with her."

"Is the curse physically hurting her?" Rya asked, her eyes glittering with unshed tears.

Clearly the thought of her sister in pain was troubling her.

"No, but the madness..." Ravel paused, wrapping her arms around her waist. "It doesn't just affect her. It spreads to everyone around her."

"Sacre bleu," Levet exclaimed. "That is why you were coating her in ice."

Ravel frowned, as if she hadn't intended for them to see the memory of her and her daughter. Had it been a part of her dream that they'd accidentally stumbled into?

It was hard to say.

Nothing had made sense in this crazy place.

"Yes," the dragon grudgingly admitted. "It is the only way to protect her until I can find a way to break the curse."

Torque nodded. "Have you had any luck?"

"Not so far," Ravel said, frustration smoldering in her pale eyes. "Blayze claims she can sense the creature responsible for cursing her, but I can't be sure it's not just a figment of her growing instability."

Torque was struck by a sudden thought. "Could Sylvermyst be involved?"

Ravel blinked in confusion. "Why would you believe the dark fey were connected?"

"We think they're the ones who brought the frost sprites here."

"Why would they do that?" she demanded.

Torque shrugged. "We don't know."

Looking more impatient than concerned, the dragon turned and gave a wave of her hand.

Instantly a shimmering circle appeared, hovering in

midair. The dragon gave another wave of her hand and the circle widened, revealing the image of an icy cavern.

Torque assumed Ravel had created a tiny portal to check on her daughter.

Like a magical nanny-cam.

Covertly inching his way to the side so he could see through the opening, Torque wasn't entirely surprised at the sight of the strange fey who were standing beside a large swell of ice. The three had varying shades of hair and eyes, but they looked enough alike to make Torque assume they were siblings.

They had to be the Sylvermyst responsible for opening the portals.

His gaze moved to study the motionless female form lying on the ground. It looked like another Sylvermyst, although the others weren't paying attention to her. Instead they were all focused on the huge mound of ice in the center of the floor.

There was a hiss from the female dragon, the air heating as she leaned toward the portal. "They've stolen my treasure."

Holy shit. Torque grimaced as his gaze caught sight of the cavities roughly gouged into the frozen floor. Were the dark fey truly stupid enough to try and steal a dragon's hoard?

Rya stepped to stand at his side. "Look." She pointed toward the male form almost hidden by the tallest of the Sylvermyst. "It's Finn."

The heat in the air intensified as Ravel growled low in her throat.

"The fool," she rasped as they watched Finn lift his hand and point it toward the mound of ice. "What is he doing?"

Torque felt a childish stab of pleasure at the female dragon's annoyance with the sprite.

Rya, however, was swift to rush to defend her friend.

"He came here to save his people. I think the Sylvermyst must be forcing him to use his powers," she murmured. "Is there more treasure under the ice?"

"No." The ground shook beneath their feet as Ravel's power caused a ripple of tiny quakes. "It's Blayze."

The dread pulsing in the air became a tangible threat.

Torque's stomach clenched at the potent sense of danger.

"Why would they want to release your daughter?"

"It doesn't matter," Ravel snapped. "They must be stopped."

Magic exploded through the room, the illusion of a cavern shattering to reveal they were standing in the middle of a swirling mist.

Torque stiffened, unnerved by the strange fog.

The ground beneath his feet was solid, but everything else felt…unsubstantial.

Before he could adjust, however, Ravel was pivoting to move away from them. Not about to be left behind in the haze, Torque grabbed Rya's hand and hurried after her.

"Hey," Levet called from behind them. "Wait for me."

***

Finn's powers faltered as a dense wave of evil crawled over him. The sensation made his hair stand on end and his skin feel too tight for his body.

Hell.

He didn't know what was under the mound, and he didn't want to know.

As if sensing Finn's less than enthusiastic participation in removing the ice, Micah turned his head to glare at him.

"Why are you stopping?" he growled.

Finn kept his hand extended, although his magic was a mere trickle.

"I'm doing the best I can," he muttered.

It wasn't entirely a lie.

He was exhausted and in need of food. His powers were running on empty.

"It's not good enough," Micah snapped, his eyes shimmering with a feverish hunger.

Finn took an instinctive step away. He suspected that whatever nastiness was floating in the air had already infected the Sylvermyst.

"This isn't natural ice," he reminded the male. "It's protected by a powerful magic."

"All I hear is excuses," Micah snarled.

"It's not an excuse—" Finn bit off his words as Micah turned around and violently slammed his foot against the side of Adair's face. The unconscious female jerked, but she didn't wake, thank the goddess. "Stop," he commanded.

Micah deliberately touched the bow that was strapped across his chest.

"If you care whether the bitch lives or dies, you'll try harder."

Finn hissed with frustration. "I can't perform miracles."

"Now." Micah leaned forward, the stench of rotting herbs wafting from him. The male had gone from greedy to full-throttle frantic.

The next step was no doubt batshit crazy.

"Dammit," Finn muttered, releasing the last dredges of his magic.

Small fractures began to form over the top layer of the ice. Like an eggshell being cracked.

Micah released a sharp laugh, stepping forward with his hand outstretched.

"It's working," he crowed in pleasure, seemingly unaware of the ominous glow of light that was spreading deep beneath the ice.

His joyous mood wasn't shared by the others in the cavern. Jarvis and Lila inched backward, their expressions reflecting a snowballing sense of dismay.

"Micah," the younger male Sylvermyst muttered. "Maybe we should—"

"Not now," Micah snarled, interrupting his brother even as he sent Finn a fierce glare. "Keep going," he ordered, turning back so he could step closer to the shattered ice. "I see something."

Finn could see something too. Something that had an iridescent shimmer. A brief sense of relief eased Finn's raw nerves.

Maybe it was just a pile of gems that'd been coated with an aversion spell. That would explain the thick dread that pulsed through the air.

But as the ice continued to break away, his premature relief was snatched from him.

The lustrous gleam wasn't coming from a priceless jewel. Instead he could see an inky blackness beneath the shimmer.

Was that a scale?

"It's not treasure," he muttered, his hand dropping as he continued to back away.

Lila cursed, pulling the bow over her head and grabbing an arrow.

"He's right, Micah," she warned.

"Keep your mouth shut," the male growled, his narrow face bathed in the light shining from the ice. "I won't be denied. Not when I'm so close."

"Idiot," Finn muttered, angling his retreat until he could lean down and scoop Adair in his arms.

Thankfully no one was paying attention to him. The Sylvermyst were fully consumed with the sight of the ice cracking and popping. Whatever was beneath was shedding the thick coating.

Which meant Finn had time to cradle Adair against his chest and duck into the hidden tunnel just before all hell broke loose.

CHAPTER FOURTEEN

Rya had a split second to reach for Levet's outstretched hand before Torque was dragging her through the weird fog. Hanging onto the tiny demon, she tried to ignore the mist that swirled around them.

Just seconds ago she would have been convinced there was nothing more unnerving than the ice that wasn't ice. The sensation of being trapped in the maze was something that was going to give her nightmares for weeks.

Now, however, she realized the fog was worse.

Much worse.

Not only did it hide any enemies that might be lurking nearby, but it gave her the sensation that they were running through clouds. As if the world wasn't quite solid.

"What is this place?" she muttered.

"It's a small pocket between dimensions," Ravel answered, her hectic pace never slowing.

Rya grimaced. She'd traveled through portals that were basically holes that burrowed through dimensions, but she'd never visited the space in between.

Now she knew why.

"How can you tell where we're going?" she demanded.

Ravel waved an impatient hand, her robe fluttering around her despite the lack of a breeze. In fact, the air was stifling. And eerily thick.

"We must hurry," the dragon warned. "Blayze is already awake."

Rya shivered, clutching Torque's fingers even as Levet clung to her other hand.

"I can feel her," she muttered, almost able to taste the darkness in the air. "It's…evil."

"It's not her," Ravel protested. "It's the curse."

Rya grimaced. She believed the dragon. The malevolent sensations that vibrated in the air were magical, not physical.

At last Ravel slowed her pace and came to a halt. Then, with a dramatic gesture, she gave a wave of her arms.

The fog moved aside, like a shroud being parted to reveal the cavern they'd glimpsed when they were still in Ravel's lair.

Or at least she thought it was. Only now the ice was gone and instead of a mound in the middle of the floor there was a very large, very angry dragon spewing fire at a tall, redheaded male.

"I think we might be too late," Torque muttered.

Rya grimaced, taking in the sight of the infuriated dragon.

She was lovely. In a lethal, melt-your-flesh and chomp-on-your-bones kind of way. Her scales were a deep ebony with a glossy sheen. Her eyes were pearly white and shimmering with a radiant light. Her snout was long and elegant, although at the moment it was widely parted to release her fire.

"Help," a female screamed from across the cavern. "You have to stop her."

Rya's attention moved toward the two fey who were huddled together, trying to inch away from the beast who'd finished with their companion and was turning her head in their direction.

"This is your fault," Ravel insisted, flames dancing over her skin at the sight of her daughter in full fury. "Why did you release her?"

"It wasn't us," the female babbled, her hand waving toward the crispy remains of the dead male. "It was Micah."

Rya grimaced. Nothing like throwing their companion under the bus. Or the angry dragon.

Then her gaze continued to sweep around the cavern as she searched for any sight of Finn. It took only a minute to accept that he wasn't there.

Refusing to believe that he might already be a dragon-snack, she instead convinced herself that the prince had somehow managed to disappear. Along with the unconscious female.

"Blayze," Ravel murmured in soothing tones, slowly walking forward.

She'd taken fewer than a half dozen steps when the two strangers lost the last of their nerves. With tiny squeals they scrambled away from the massive beast, no doubt hoping to get lost in the nearby mist.

"No," Ravel barked, holding up her hand in warning. "Don't move."

"Fuck that," the female rasped, knocking her

companion out of the way as she raced into the fog.

She was fast, but not fast enough as the dragon released a thunderous roar before she spewed a stream of white-hot fire that turned the two fey into piles of ash.

Yow.

Rya was half dragon, but she was smart enough to stand as still as a statue. No need to draw the attention of her pissy sister.

"Mon dieu," Levet breathed softly, for once doing nothing to try and create a scene.

Smart gargoyle.

Barely glancing toward the charred fey, Ravel continued forward, her movements deliberately slow. "Blayze."

The narrow head swiveled in Ravel's direction, the eyes still blazing with anger. Ignoring the danger, the older dragon continued toward her daughter, murmuring low words that Rya couldn't hear.

Seconds ticked past. The heat in the air eased, although the evil power continued to beat at Rya like a weapon.

Then, with a surprisingly gentle wave of magic, the infuriated dragon was surrounded by a swirl of sparkles. When they at last faded, a tall, slender female wearing a beaded robe stood in the center of the floor.

Wow. Rya blinked in shock. If Blayze's dragon was lovely, her human form was…breathtaking.

Her long black hair spilled down her back in a river of ebony, and her pale eyes were sprinkled with brilliant flecks of color. Her features were elegantly carved with full lips and a slender nose, and she had one charming dimple in her right cheek.

The last of the smothering heat dissipated, but a dark sense of doom remained.

Seemingly disoriented from her shift to human, Blayze gave a vague shake of her head. "Mother?" she murmured, warily watching the older female walk toward her.

Ravel held out her hand. "I'm here, darling."

The pale gaze moved in the direction of the black scorch marks that had once been three Sylvermyst.

"Intruders," she said, her pretty features hardening with anger.

"Yes, but you took care of them."

The pale gaze drifted toward Rya. "Not all of them."

Oh, damn. Rya stiffened even as Torque stepped to block her from the dragon's sight, his fire moving over his skin as he prepared to attack.

"These are friends," she heard Ravel assure her daughter. "They don't mean you any harm."

"No," the younger dragon breathed. "Stay back."

"Blayze, what's wrong?" Ravel demanded.

Inching to the side, Rya glanced around Torque's broad shoulder to see Blayze hold up a slender hand, her eyes beginning to glow with her dreadful power.

"I said to stay back," she hissed.

Ravel faltered, clearly torn between the need to reach her daughter and a fear she might push her over the edge of sanity. "Listen to me," she pleaded. "You're safe."

Blayze shook her head, the floor near her feet cracking beneath an unseen pressure.

Rya shivered. It wasn't the curse that was causing the ground to vibrate or the nearby mist to swirl.

Or at least it didn't feel evil.

Instead it held an edge of desperation as the young dragon backed from her mother.

"I won't be trapped again."

"Trapped?" Ravel shook her head, her expression heart-wrenchingly sad. "No one is going to trap you, my darling. But you must be protected."

The crooning words did nothing to ease Blayze's

spiraling panic.

"No more," she rasped, her ebony hair floating around her face as she created a white-hot ball of flames that danced in the palm of her hand. "I can't. I won't."

Ravel halted, glancing over her shoulder at Torque. "We can't let her escape."

Rya sucked in a horrified breath, but before she could protest, Torque was swiftly moving to stand on the other side of the increasingly desperate female.

Was the aggravating male intending to try and physically halt a full-blooded dragon?

"Torque." His name was wrenched from her lips as she took an impulsive step toward him.

Without warning, Levet reached to grab her hand, holding on with surprising strength.

"*Non, ma belle.*"

"Let me go," she commanded, trying to tug her hand free as she watched the female dragon head toward her betrothed, the fireball growing larger as she prepared to attack. "I have to do something. She's going to kill Torque."

The tiny creature wrinkled his nose. "Not much of a loss."

"Levet," she snapped.

"Forgive me. Now is not the time to discuss your mate's unpleasant manners." He wrinkled his snout. "Not when your mother is shouting so loudly."

Rya halted her attempts to break free, instead turning to gape at the gargoyle in disbelief.

"My mother?" she demanded, waiting for him to give a small nod. "She's here?"

Levet tapped the side of his head with a claw. "Here."

"Oh, thank the goddess." Rya pressed a hand over her heart. Her mother was still alive. And hopefully close enough that she could join them. Her magic was exactly what they needed at this moment. "Can she tell you how to find her?"

"There is no time," Levet muttered. "We must do it this way."

Rya frowned. "What way?"

The words had barely left her lips when the voice of her mother hammered into her brain.

Rya.

Holy shit.

She reeled, nearly falling to her knees as she absorbed the impact of the connection. "Mother?"

I'm here.

"Where are you?" Rya spoke out loud, unsure exactly how the magic worked.

It doesn't matter now, her mother said, her tone clipped with impatience.

Rya frowned. "But—"

She overrode Rya's protest. *You must open yourself to my powers.*

Rya struggled to clear her mind. She'd worry about locating her mother later. For now, they needed her magic.

"How?" she asked.

I'm using the gargoyle as a transmitter, her mother explained.

Levet made a sound of distress. "Hey, wait. I am no transformer."

Both women ignored him. Instead, Rya closed her eyes and concentrated on the feel of her mother that was nestled in the center of her brain.

Instantly she felt a sensation of peace flow through her, easing the raw fear.

Her mother had many gifts, but one of her greatest was spreading a sense of calm. She'd always thought that had been the reason Synge had been so fond of her mother. The older Shinto could offer a temporary relief from Synge's savage, sometimes downright aggressive instincts.

"Now what?" she asked.

Allow the magic to flow through you, her mother commanded.

Not exactly sure how she was supposed to let the 'magic flow through' her, Rya half expected to have to use her own powers to get things jump-started.

But even as she struggled to block out the sounds of Torque's curses and the stench of burnt flesh, a torrent of magic cascaded through her hand that Levet was still holding.

"Sacre bleu," the tiny demon rasped, his wings fluttering and his tail stuck straight out.

Rya understood his misery. She didn't have a tail, but her hair felt as if it was standing on end as she shuddered at the vast amount of power pouring into her.

She felt like a balloon about to burst.

Release it, Rya, her mother ordered, her sharp tone snapping Rya out of her stunned befuddlement.

Damn. She was wasting precious time.

Tugging away from Levet, she turned, her heart halting at the sight of Torque, who had inched his way toward the female dragon despite the burns on his chest and down his arm. Ravel didn't look much better. Her face was wounded and her robe charred in several places.

Worse, they were clearly in a losing battle as Blayze lifted her hands as she prepared to send another volley of fireballs.

Determined not to waste another second, she didn't bother to move toward the others. It didn't matter how close she was, so long as she could see where she wanted the magic to go.

Lifting her hand, she focused solely on her newly discovered sister, whispering a small thank you to her mother before she unleashed the power.

She gasped, not prepared for the sensation of the magic being wrenched out of her and hurtling across the room.

Damn. She'd thought it had been bad having the magic shoved into her. It was worse having it yanked out of her.

Gritting her teeth, Rya continued to concentrate on the female dragon who staggered backward as the power surrounded her with a golden glow. At first, nothing happened. Well, nothing beyond the fact that her fire was extinguished, which sent a flare of relief through Rya.

Then the glow began to spread and condense around Blayze, coating her in a thick layer of magic.

An eerie silence filled the cavern as they all watched the young dragon's eyes widen. Not with pain. No, it was just the opposite.

The pale eyes were filled with astonishment as the spell eased her panic, and soothed the fear that Rya sensed had been her sister's constant companion for as long as she'd been cursed.

Rya was briefly pleased at the thought that she'd managed to give the female a feeling of relief. Then a tragic expression of vulnerability touched Blayze's face, and with a tiny cry she pitched forward as her knees gave way. She was unconscious before she ever hit the ground.

Lowering her hand, Rya felt her connection to her mother being abruptly severed as Levet swayed and tumbled backward in exhaustion.

Rya just had time to see Torque turning to race toward her before she joined the others on the floor, her legs collapsing beneath her as she hit the ground with a jarring thud.

***

Torque ignored the raw burns that were seared over his chest and down his arm. It wasn't the first time he'd endured the agony of dragon-fire. And it probably wouldn't be the last.

Unfortunately.

Right now all that mattered was getting to Rya.

Reaching her just as she hit the floor, he grimaced as he crouched beside her. She'd clearly expended too much magic. Dammit. And while he was happy as hell not to be reduced to a pile of scorched bones by the crazed female dragon, he was aggravated that Rya had dangerously drained herself to complete exhaustion.

With gentle care, he gathered her in his arms, tugging her onto his lap.

"Are you okay?" he asked.

"I'm not sure." She wrinkled her nose, her body trembling as she reached up to touch his wounds. "What about you?"

"I'll survive," he assured her. Her touch was feather-light but it still sent a shiver of pleasure through him. "Thanks to you."

There was a sound of distress from across the cavern, warning Torque that the younger dragon might be magically catatonic, but the mother was very much awake, and not particularly happy.

"What have you done?" Ravel rasped, kneeling beside her unconscious daughter.

Torque tightened his arms protectively around Rya as Ravel glared at them with blatant suspicion.

The female had smoke curling from her nose and sparks of fire in her eyes. One wrong step and she would finish what her daughter started.

"I channeled my mother's magic," Rya explained, her voice weary as her attention turned toward her sister.

"It won't hurt Blayze, but it will keep her sedated."

A portion of the older dragon's smoldering frustration eased, but her power continued to prickle in the air, making the thick mist that surrounded them swirl in a dizzying pattern.

"For how long?" Ravel demanded.

Rya shook her head. "I'm not sure. I've seen grown orcs sleep for days."

Ravel glanced down at her daughter. The young dragon looked oddly peaceful as she lay on the ground, the darkness that had pulsed around her fully muted for the moment.

"A potent magic," she murmured.

"Yes," Rya readily agreed, her pride in her mother obvious.

"It gives me time to repair the damage the creatures did," she murmured, speaking to herself.

Without warning, Rya was pulling out of his grasp and trying to stand. Instantly he was on his feet, wrapping his arm around her shoulders.

"Lean on me. You're still weak," he murmured, not mentioning the fact he had a fierce need to feel her warmth pressed against him.

For a few terrible moments he'd thought they all might be killed by Blayze. He needed to reassure himself that she was alive and relatively unharmed.

"What about *moi*?" the gargoyle intruded, shoving himself upright with a pout on his ugly face. "I was the trans-meter maid. Look." He spun around, his tail twitching. "My wings are singed."

Torque scowled. He didn't know what the creature was babbling about, and he didn't care.

His attention was locked on the dragon as she rose gracefully to her feet and held a hand in their direction.

"You must go."

Torque parted his lips to agree. Rya, of course, had

to argue.

It was as predictable as the sun rising in the east.

"No. My mother is still here," she said. "I can't leave without her."

Ravel glanced toward her sleeping daughter. "Once I have Blayze fully protected by my magic I will attempt to send her to you."

"But—"

Torque overrode her protest. "Rya."

Ravel might not be as unstable as Torque had originally feared, but she was a full-blooded dragon with a volatile temperament. It wouldn't take much for her to decide she'd had enough.

Rya sent him a fierce glare. "My mother needs me."

He turned her to face him, gazing deep into her eyes. "*I* need you, Rya."

An elusive emotion rippled over her face, as if his words had touched her. Then she lifted her arm to place light fingers against his cheek.

"Please," she pleaded softly. "I can't abandon her."

He reached up, covering her fingers with his larger hand.

"Think, Rya. If your mother is as terrifying as the gargoyle seems to believe, she'll have me castrated if she learns I didn't take you to safety when I had the chance," he said with a rueful smile.

Her lips parted, but she couldn't argue. Which only emphasized Torque's belief he was going to have to walk on eggshells when he finally had the pleasure of meeting the formidable Kai.

A worry for another day.

A sudden heat rushed through the air, the swirling mist directly behind them parting to reveal a gaping portal.

Dragon-magic.

"I've opened a gateway," Ravel said, her tone stern.

"You must leave now."

"He is right, *ma belle*," Levet murmured, for once not making Torque want to choke him. "It is time to go."

She heaved a sigh. As if she was about to concede defeat. Then, without warning, the opening in the mist abruptly widened and the smell of sulfur filled the air.

"What's happening?" Rya demanded.

Ravel madc a sound of impatience. "Did you interfere with the gateway?"

Torque frowned at the accusation. "Rya can barely stand, let alone manipulate your magic."

"Someone is trying to…" Ravel hissed in shock, making Torque pull away from Rya. He wanted room to maneuver if they were about to be attacked.

"What is it?" he rasped, allowing his flames to flicker over his body.

Ravel abruptly dropped to her knees, wrapping her arms around her daughter.

"It's Synge. He's sensed the opening and he's using his power to drag us out of here."

"Shit." Torque smothered his flames and once again gathered Rya in his arms. "Stay close."

She shivered, her hair blowing back as a blast of searing energy wrapped around them.

"I don't think Father is very happy," she muttered.

He gave a sharp, humorless laugh, feeling as if his skin was about to be sucked off his body.

"You, my love, are a master of understatement," he managed between clenched teeth.

The magic thickened until there was no way to battle against the force yanking them through the opening.

A blinding heat seared over them, and still holding Rya tightly in his arms, he felt them cross from one dimension to another.

Once again he was reminded that traveling from world to world wasn't like a gentle stroll through the usual portal. No. It was like being roughly wrenched through the air by a giant hand.

Prepared for the awkward landing, Torque managed to remain upright. Beside him, Rya grunted, grabbing him around the waist to keep her balance. Torque grimaced, the pain from his wounds raw enough to yank the air from his lungs. And worse, the burns had been caused by a dragon, so they would take longer than usual to heal.

He had a brief second to glance around their new surroundings. A shudder of relief raced through him. He recognized the massive room that had golden tapestries hung on the walls that displayed violent battle scenes, and a crimson rug spread across the stone floor.

At the far end was an elaborately carved throne set on a high dais and surrounded by a number of half-naked females sprawled on large pillows. More servants and guards were spread throughout the chamber. Some half-breed dragons, some fey, and even a few vampires, but no matter their species, they were all dressed in green and gold uniforms with the emblem of a lightning bolt on their upper chest.

Synge.

Torque's gaze at last landed on Rya's father, who was standing in the center of the room.

The full-blooded dragon was a large, brutish man with black hair that was buzzed short, and eyes the color of polished silver. At the moment he was wearing leather pants and a matching vest that revealed the handful of tattoos that moved over his skin with a metallic beauty. They couldn't compare to his son's. Baine collected knowledge, while his father preferred a more tangible treasure.

There was a low growl behind him, and Torque turned his head to see Ravel slowly lowering her unconscious daughter to the ground. She obviously wasn't nearly as pleased as Torque was to be in the dragon's lair.

With a last glance to ensure her daughter hadn't been wakened by the violent transport between dimensions, Ravel straightened and headed across the lush rug with determined strides, not halting until she was standing directly in front of Synge.

Then, with what Torque could only assume was a death wish, she lifted a hand and slapped the male across the face.

"How dare you?" she rasped. "You've ruined everything."

The entire room gasped in horror, a few of the guards stepping forward as a halo of fire surrounded Synge. But even as Torque prepared to toss Rya over his shoulder and make a run for it, the flames faltered. And the most astonishing thing happened.

Synge's cruel features softened and his hand shook as he reached out to lightly touch his attacker's cheek.

"Ravel?" he breathed. "Is it truly you?"

Ravel's lips flattened, but she made no effort to pull away from his touch. "Obviously."

"But…" Synge's words trailed away as his gaze drifted toward the unconscious female who Ravel had laid on the floor. "Blayze?"

Disbelief and something oddly vulnerable darkened the male's silver eyes to smoke as Synge studied his daughter. But when he took an impulsive step toward the female, Ravel blocked his path.

"Stop," she commanded, her hand placed in the center of Synge's broad chest. "I won't let you hurt her."

With surprisingly gentle care, Synge grasped the female dragon by her shoulders and moved her out of his path. Then with measured steps he prowled to stand over his daughter.

"The curse is gone," he breathed in wonder, only to

give a slow shake of his head, his brows drawing together. "No. It's being contained by a Shinto spell." His head turned as he glanced toward Rya for the first time since their dramatic entrance. "Yours?"

Rya shook her head. "No. Mother's."

"Ah." The male's attention returned to Blayze as he crouched down beside her. He stretched out a hand to touch her hair that spilled over the carpet like a river of ebony. "Amazing."

Ravel made a sound of distress as she rushed forward. "No," she cried in a harsh voice. "Don't touch her."

The perpetual frown returned to Synge's brow as he watched Ravel lower herself next to their daughter, her body angled to block him from the sleeping female.

"I don't intend to hurt you or our daughter, Ravel," he muttered.

"You allowed her to be sentenced to death," Ravel reminded him in sharp tones.

Genuine pain twisted his blunt features. Torque arched his brows in shock. Until this moment he would have sworn that Synge was a hard-hearted, pitiless savage who had the emotional depth of a gnat.

Certainly he'd never shown any concern for Baine or his brothers.

But now it was obvious that Synge had bottled his feelings deep inside when he'd lost his mate and child.

"I truly thought it would be kinder to Blayze to allow her to die. How could I condemn her to an eternity of pain?" he asked, a raw guilt throbbing in his voice. "I loved her."

Ravel's ferocious expression slowly eased.

"I know," she conceded.

"But the moment you disappeared from my lair I regretted my decision." The two dragons shared a glance that spoke of a long, intimate relationship. "I desperately tried to find you, but my soldiers told me they'd witnessed your death." His shudder shook the entire lair. "I should have recalled your ability to create illusions."

Ravel leaned toward him so she could rest her hand on her mate's broad shoulder.

"Synge, let us go," she pleaded. "I'll disappear with our daughter and—"

"No. Not again."

His thunderous voice carried through the lair, making his servants back nervously away. Torque tried to tug Rya toward the nearby exit, only to have her dig in her heels. Typical.

And annoying as hell.

Ravel surged upright, her eyes glowing with power. "I'll fight," she warned.

Wriggling out of his arms, Rya took a half dozen steps toward her father before Torque could grasp her shoulders and yank her back.

"Stop," he commanded, fear clenching his stomach.

He didn't believe Synge would intentionally hurt Rya, but no one was truly safe around a pissed-off dragon.

She struggled against his firm hold. "I can't let him hurt my sister."

He muttered a curse. "We're going to have a long talk about your habit of rushing into danger."

She sent him a warning glare. "Or maybe we'll discuss your habit of trying to tell me what I can or can't do."

"Only a fool stands between angry dragons," he hissed, nodding toward Ravel, who had a shimmer of magic dancing around her as she prepared to shift. "Or mates."

"Dammit, I've told you," Synge snarled, straightening to face his furious consort without fear. "I'm not going to hurt you, Ravel." He pressed his hand to the center of his broad chest. "I swear."

Ravel shook her head. "I'm not worried about myself."

Synge glanced down at Blayze, a profound regret simmering in his eyes.

"Our daughter is safe in my lair," he swore.

"For now, perhaps," Ravel said, still prepared to fight for the safety of her child. "The spell that contains her curse won't last forever."

"Kai can help," Synge muttered, his head swiveling until he located Rya. "Where is your mother?"

Rya waved a hand toward the closed gateway. "She's still lost in the lair. We have to rescue her."

Synge glanced toward Ravel. "Can you make another opening?"

"No." The female dragon gave a firm shake of her head. "When you pulled us out my magic was no longer there to keep the space open. It's possible that it's already beginning to collapse."

Rya stiffened, her face draining of color. "Mother."

"She's still alive," Synge abruptly announced, clearly still possessing a bond with his former courtesan. He waved a beefy hand toward a clutch of nervous fey standing in a corner. "I'll have my servants find a way to reach her."

The fairies and imps moved to stand in front of the closed gateway, murmuring together as they discussed how to open it.

Ravel made a sound of impatience as they instantly started to argue at the best way to begin. Rya released an equally annoyed growl.

"I'm not sure we have time for her to be located and brought here before Blayze wakens," Ravel said.

"Call for Char," Torque abruptly suggested, sending out a silent apology to his friend.

He would do whatever necessary to end the family

drama so he could get Rya alone.

Char would understand.

Well, after he kicked Torque's ass a time or two.

Okay, maybe a dozen.

"Who?" Synge sent him an impatient glare before he recalled the half-breed dragon he'd given his son as a parting gift the day he left the lair. "Ah. Baine's personal servant. What could he do?"

Torque nodded his head toward the female on the ground.

"His mother is a Dalia demon," he explained. The demons were as rare as the Shinto and at one time had been worshipped as gods for their ability to manipulate the fate of humans. "He's capable of halting time in a small, confined space. It would give you a few days to find Rya's mother," he explained.

Synge nodded toward the nearest guard. "Call for him."

"At once, my lord." With a deep bow the guard spun on his heel and jogged out of the chamber.

Accepting his commands would be carried out, Synge turned back to his daughter. Then, bending down, he scooped his hands beneath her and lifted her off the ground with one smooth motion.

Ravel was swiftly at his side, her footprints leaving scorch marks on the crimson carpet.

"What are you doing?" the female dragon demanded.

Synge turned to head toward a nearby alcove that led to the private section of his lair.

"I'm taking my daughter to her rooms."

Ravel walked at his side, her anger replaced by an expression of wonder. "You still have them?"

"Of course." He sent his mate a brooding glance. "Just as your rooms are precisely like you left them."

Hoping to have a few moments alone with his

betrothed, Torque turned to Rya.

"We need to speak," he murmured in low tones. "In private."

Her lips parted, but before she could respond, the sound of Synge's voice interrupted.

"Torque, come here," he commanded.

Swallowing a growl of impatience, Torque smoothed his expression before he turned and reluctantly moved toward the dragon.

It wasn't like he could say no.

Not unless he had a sudden urge to become a smudge of soot.

Careful to halt far enough away that he couldn't be perceived as a threat to the unconscious female in Synge's arms, Torque offered a respectful nod of his head.

"Yes, my lord?"

"Kai promised that you and Rya would discover my lost treasure," he said. "I never dreamed…" He glanced down at his daughter, his body shaking with emotion before he was harshly clearing his throat in embarrassment. "You can consider Pyre's debt paid in full."

Torque reeled at the shocking words. Shit. Synge's missing mate and daughter were the treasure that Kai had foreshadowed? Not that he didn't agree that family was far more important than any shiny jewel. Still…

The mysterious treasure hunt wasn't supposed to happen yet. Not until he was formally mated to Rya.

Oddly disturbed by the pronouncement that only days ago would have made him leap for joy, Torque offered a stiff bow.

"Thank you, my lord."

Synge shrugged aside his thanks. "You can return to Baine or to your father's lair. Your future is your own."

"Yes, my lord," he murmured.

He already knew exactly what he wanted for his future and who he wanted to share it with.

Waiting for Synge and his unexpected family to leave the throne chamber, Torque turned back to locate his betrothed. The sooner they could get out of there, the sooner they could start planning their formal mating.

His brows drew together as he discovered the space where Rya had been standing was empty. Impatiently, his gaze skimmed over the servants and uniformed guards who continued to move through the room, a hollow fear settling in the pit of his stomach.

Suddenly he realized why he'd been so unnerved when Synge had made his startling announcement.

Not only had the dragon declared him free and clear of his father's debt. But he'd just publicly proclaimed the end of Torque's betrothal to his daughter.

After all, there was no need for Torque and Rya to mate if the treasure had been found.

And now she'd disappeared.

Along with the aggravating Levet.

Torque clenched his hands, a blast of fury making the nearby servants scurry away from the flames that moved over his body.

"Oh no, Rya," he growled. "You're not getting away from me that easily."

CHAPTER FIFTEEN

It was sheer exhaustion that at last halted Finn's desperate sprint through the thick, seemingly endless fog. Exhaustion and the terrible sensation he was running in circles.

With a low groan, he lowered himself to his knees and cradled the unconscious woman in his lap.

She'd remained so limp in his arms he'd briefly feared that she was more grievously injured than he first suspected. But as he ran a frantic glance over her pale face he was relieved to discover her wounds were beginning to heal and a hint of color was returning to her cheeks.

Thank the goddess.

With gentle care, he brushed her coppery curls over her shoulder.

"Adair, can you hear me?"

Her lashes fluttered, slowly lifting to reveal her

glorious platinum eyes. She blinked as she took in his face that was only inches away.

"Finn?" she murmured, confusion tightening her features as her gaze moved toward the grayish mist that surrounded them. "What's happened?"

"After you were knocked unconscious by Micah, I grabbed you and escaped through one of the tunnels," he said.

She frowned at his deliberately vague explanation. "What about my family? Are they still in the cavern?"

He grimaced. "The treasure they were so desperate to uncover turned out to be a very pissed-off dragon."

Adair's mouth fell open; clearly she was wondering if he'd lost his mind.

He didn't blame her.

It was the last thing any of them had expected.

"Dragon?" she repeated in disbelief.

"Yeah." He wrinkled his nose. Even though he'd managed to flee the cavern before the dragon had attacked, he'd caught the scent of charred flesh. Even after the weird ice had turned to fog, he'd been certain the stench was following him.

"It wasn't good," he muttered.

"Are they…" Her voice trailed away, as if she couldn't even say the words.

"I don't know, but it's doubtful they could have survived," he reluctantly confessed, unwilling to give her false hope.

He instantly regretted his decision as tears filled her eyes before sliding down her face.

"I knew their greed would eventually destroy them," she said, her voice unsteady.

Finn brushed his lips over her forehead, careful to avoid her healing bruises.

"I'm sorry," he murmured.

No doubt sensing that he regretted her pain, not so

much the death of the other Sylvermyst, she heaved a small sigh.

"I know they weren't much of a family, but they were all I had."

Finn allowed his lips to brush down the narrow line of her nose, relishing the earthy scent of rosemary that filled the air at his light caress.

"That's not true," he assured her. "You have me."

She stiffened. Almost as if she was frightened by his words.

"You?"

Lifting his head, Finn studied her wary expression. Was he pushing her too quickly?

He grimaced. Of course he was.

She'd just lost her family. Even if they were a bunch of bastards, it would take time for her to heal.

With an effort he forced a smile to his lips. "Well, I'll admit I'm not much at the moment," he teased lightly. "I'm weary, hungry, and in dire need of a hot bath, but I promise you'll never be enslaved or forced to do anything that doesn't make you happy."

Her gaze skimmed over his face, as if searching for some hidden truth.

"I don't understand what you're saying."

"I'm saying you have a home with me."

"But..." She slowly shook her head. "You're a prince."

He allowed his fingers to thread through her silky hair. "I don't think you should hold that against me."

She continued to study him with a heartbreaking vulnerability. Like a puppy expecting to be kicked even as she desperately hoped for a pat on the head.

Anger clenched Finn's heart. It was no doubt a good thing her family was already dead.

It would save him the effort of killing them himself.

"I'm a Sylvermyst," she abruptly blurted out.

His lips twisted. "Yeah, I figured that out."

"I helped my family kidnap your people," she pressed, as if she thought he might have forgotten.

He tugged her silky curl. "That's in the past."

Her chin jutted to a surprisingly stubborn angle. "They'll never forgive me."

He shrugged, even as he inwardly acknowledged that her arrival among his tribe wouldn't be without difficulties. But he had no intention of allowing that to stop him. Not when everything within him was convinced she belonged with him.

Forever.

"Who helped them escape?" he instead demanded.

She hunched her shoulder, wiggling in his lap. Finn swallowed a groan of pleasure.

They were stuck in the strange labyrinth, with an angry dragon on the rampage, not to mention the fact that Adair was healing from wounds caused by her recently dead brother, and suddenly all he could think about was getting her into his bed.

ASAP.

"I only opened the portal," she muttered.

Finn tried to control his stubborn cock that was determined to harden and press against her deliciously soft ass.

"Which I believe is the very definition of helping them escape," he told her, keeping his tone light.

Unable to convince him that she was unsuitable for his charity, she turned her attention to her next worry.

"You said you wanted me in your home." Her lashes lowered, hiding her expressive eyes. "What does that mean?"

Finn hooked a finger beneath her chin and tilted her head back.

"Look at me, Adair," he commanded in soft tones. He waited for her to grudgingly meet his gaze. "There you are."

Color touched her cheeks. Could she sense his hunger?

"Finn," she breathed.

"I'm not asking anything of you," he assured her in fierce tones. She'd already been at the mercy of her worthless family. The last thing he wanted was for her to feel indebted to him. "I merely want you to know that you are welcome to join my tribe."

"And that's all?"

He shrugged. "I would only ask that you be my friend."

"Friend?" Something that might have been disappointment flittered over her face. Had she hoped he would demand more? "I see." She pasted her lips into a smile. "Thank you. You're more forgiving than I deserve."

Finn cupped her face with his hand, brushing her lower lip with his thumb.

"And once you have become settled and no longer feel a sense of obligation toward me, then we can discuss if you might be interested in…"

Her eyes darkened as he deliberately allowed his words to trail away.

Either she would try to divert him, or she would offer him the encouragement he so desperately desired.

"In?" she breathed softly.

He smiled. *Oh yeah.* She tried to hide her response, but she was as acutely aware of their deepening bond as he was.

"More," he whispered, dipping his head down to claim her lips in a soft kiss that made no demands.

Until she was fully convinced that she had a home with his tribe that didn't depend on his generosity, he wasn't going to press for more.

He was just lifting his head when he caught the scent

of orchids. At the same time the sound of clapping broke the silence.

Already suspecting who had appeared out of the mist, Finn turned his head to watch the slender female wearing a scarlet silk robe strolling toward them.

Kai.

He took a swift inventory, reassuring himself she was unharmed.

She looked exactly like she did when she'd disappeared from his home in Iceland. Her pale face was perfectly composed, her long black hair was pulled into a complicated braid, and her dark eyes were glowing like polished ebony.

A surge of relief raced through him. Thank the goddess. Not only had the Shinto female worked tirelessly to try and help him locate his people, but Rya would be devastated if anything happened to her mother.

"Very charming," Kai murmured, glancing down at Adair. "My dear, I don't mean to tell you what to do. After all, a female must follow her own heart." She waved a slender hand toward Finn. "But I do believe he is a keeper."

Finn grinned, enjoying the flustered expression that skimmed over Adair's face. Then, with an effort, he turned his attention to their newest companion.

"I'm glad you're okay," he told her. "I feared the worst when I couldn't sense you."

Kai shrugged. As always, she appeared totally calm. Finn wasn't sure what it would take to ruffle the older woman, but he was pretty sure he didn't want to be around when it happened.

"After I was pulled through the portal I managed to disguise my presence so I could stay hidden from our captors," she murmured.

Adair made a small sound of distress, still punishing herself for her family's sin.

"Forgive me," she rasped.

"Never mind, my dear." Kai offered a faint smile. "It was fate."

Finn sent her a hopeful glance. "I don't suppose you've had a glimpse of the future that includes our rescue?"

Kai shook her head, her smile fading. "No, but I did sense that we need to move to the center of this space."

Finn's muscles tensed. "Why?"

"Without the dragon to maintain the magic, the"—she glanced toward the mist that surrounded them—"bubble she created between dimensions is beginning to shrink. In time it will vanish altogether." She paused, as if listening to something Finn couldn't hear. "If it doesn't collapse first."

Adair gasped as Finn muttered a curse.

Of course the damned place was going to collapse.

As if it wasn't enough he'd spent the past days desperately searching for his people, only to be sucked into this hellhole, tortured by a Sylvermyst, and then nearly toasted by a dragon.

"Perfect." Cradling Adair in his arms, he rose to his feet. Briefly he closed his eyes, concentrating on the magic that coursed through his blood. There was a brief sizzle of frost in the air before it was smothered by the thickening air. "I can't create a portal." He glanced down at Adair. "What about you?"

She sucked in a deep breath, her face tensing as she struggled to use her powers. At last she gave a frustrated shake of her head.

"No. I'm sorry," she uttered in a weary voice. "Maybe if I have time to recover my strength."

"It's okay." Finn brushed his lips over her damp brow. "We'll find a way to get out."

There was a shudder beneath their feet. As if the floor was about to buckle.

"We need to move," Kai warned, smoothly leading them into the silvery mist.

"We're going to be fine," Finn assured the woman shivering in his arms as they followed behind the Shinto.

He hoped like hell he wasn't lying.

***

Rya headed for the mosaic-tiled baths the minute she returned to her rooms in the harem at the far edge of her father's lair. She was in dire need of hot water and plenty of soap after being held captive for what felt like an eternity. And, just as importantly, she needed a private place to sob like a baby.

Not that she was willing to spend much time trying to decide why she was crying as she soaked in the scented water. She told herself it was concern for her mother, who was still lost, that caused her heavy sadness, but she wasn't convinced.

After all, she had no doubt Kai was going to be rescued.

She'd not only requested one of her father's servants to contact her the minute the gathered fey managed to open a portal, but she'd asked Levet to use his numerous contacts in the demon world to help. She'd even contacted her mother's family in Hong Kong.

It was only a matter of time.

And if she was being entirely honest, it wasn't the image of her mother that was making her heart ache.

No. It was the lingering memory of Torque that she couldn't banish no matter how hard she tried.

Who could have imagined that their mating could be ended before it ever began?

She'd gone from being resigned at the knowledge she was fated to become Torque's mate, to being filled with a glorious sense of anticipation.

And now…

Now she felt as if someone had sucker-punched her at the realization that it was over.

The treasure had been found, and Torque had been released from his duty. And she was back in the harem, in her rooms that had never felt so lonely.

As the last tear fell, Rya stepped out of the baths and wrapped a terrycloth towel around her naked body. Then, heading into her bedchamber, she considered whether or not she could force herself to eat.

She wasn't hungry despite the hours since her last meal, but she knew she had to keep her strength up if she wanted to join the mission to rescue her mother.

Still undecided, she stepped into the large room that was designed in a traditional Chinese style. The doors and windows were decorated with golden latticework motifs, each of them reflecting harmony between man and nature. There were several crimson-painted pillars and a door that led to an inner courtyard decorated with carved dragons and a koi pond with a tiny bridge built across it.

And in the center of the room was a large lacquer bed with a crimson satin cover and a matching armoire.

Lost in her thoughts, it took a second for Rya to recognize the heat that was pulsing through the air. With a frown she turned her head, her heart coming to a painful halt at the sight of Torque standing just a few feet away.

Dear goddess.

He was so gorgeous.

Not handsome like Baine, but his sternly chiseled features and brilliant sapphire eyes were so strikingly perfect Rya found that she couldn't look away.

Or maybe it was just the fact that she'd assumed she would never see him again.

Licking her dry lips, she was jerked out of her dazed

sense of disbelief as he broke the silence.

"Hello, Rya," he drawled, strolling forward. Like her, he'd recently bathed. She could catch the scent of soap on his warm skin. And he'd changed into a pair of jeans and soft blue sweater that matched his eyes. "Did you think you could hide from me?" he demanded as he came to a halt directly in front of her.

"Torque." She was forced to clear her throat. "How did you get in here?"

His lips twisted. "I threatened to have Baine turn this place into a barbeque joint if I wasn't allowed to speak with my betrothed."

She shook her head. Although the harem wasn't as fiercely protected as her father's inner lair, Torque must have terrified the guards to let him past the front doors.

"We're no longer betrothed," she reminded him in stiff tones.

Without warning he was prowling around her, his fingers lightly brushing over the tattoo that was exposed on her upper back.

"This marking says differently," he murmured.

She hissed, caught off guard by the shocking pleasure that jolted through her.

His touch wasn't supposed to make her gut clench or her pulse race. Not anymore.

"You heard my father," she muttered.

His fingers trailed over her shoulder as he continued to circle around her. Sparks and smoke rose from her bare skin, revealing her intense response to his touch.

"I did," he admitted.

She shivered, longing and pain churning through her. Why was he doing this to her?

"He's convinced that the treasure we were fated to discover has been found," she reminded him, as if he could have forgotten the staggering revelation. "You're free."

He stood in front of her once again, his fingers tracing the top edge of her towel.

"Good," he murmured.

The soft word felt like another sucker punch.

Rya clenched her teeth, wondering how her toes could be curling in bliss at the same time that her heart was breaking.

"Yes, it is good." She swatted away his hand. "Now if you don't mind, I'd like to get dressed."

His gaze lowered to the soft swell of her upper breasts that were revealed by the towel. Heat crackled through the air, sizzling over Rya's skin even as her inner dragon purred in anticipation.

A slow, wicked smile curved his lips, then at blinding speed, he bent down and swept her off her feet.

Rya made a choked sound of astonishment.

How had she once thought this male incapable of emotion?

Right now the entire room shuddered with the force of his desire.

"Torque, what are you doing?" she breathed.

Holding her wary gaze, he cradled her against his chest.

"Don't you want to know why I'm happy Synge decided my father's debt is paid?" he demanded.

She ignored the voice in the back of her head that warned she should struggle against his possessive hold. He didn't have the right to touch her as if she was his mate.

She didn't want to be released.

Not when her heart was thudding and her entire body was zinging with excitement at the feel of being wrapped so tightly in his arms.

Desire, white-hot and intoxicating, flowed like lava through her veins.

"You don't need to. You never wanted to mate with

me," she forced herself to mutter. "Now you can return to your life as a warrior and I don't have to worry about being a burden—"

Her words were cut short as he lowered his head to press a silencing kiss to her lips.

"Hush," he commanded against her mouth.

She stiffened. Okay, Torque might be surprisingly good at sweeping a female off her feet, but that didn't give him the right to interrupt her. "Hey."

He nibbled at the corner of her mouth before brushing feather-light kisses over her cheek.

"I'm happy because I want it to be crystal clear that our mating has nothing to do with visions," he murmured, his lips tracing the line of her jaw. "Or obligations." He once again found her mouth, kissing her with a tender yearning that she felt to her very soul. "Or duty."

She tilted back her head, groaning when his lips took advantage of the new angle to skim down her throat.

"There is no mating," she reminded him.

Or maybe she was trying to remind herself.

With a slow movement, Torque lifted his head, his dragon smoldering in his eyes as he gazed down at her.

"Is that what you want?" he asked. "Would you like the betrothal to be broken?"

"I—" The words stuck in her throat.

He studied her with a brooding intensity. "I'll accept what makes you happy, Rya, but I hope very much you'll give me the opportunity to prove that I can be the sort of consort you desire."

Rya's breath caught in her throat. Was he saying that he actually *wanted* to be her mate?

"You do?"

"Yes," he said, a rueful smile curving his lips at her disbelieving tone. "I do."

"But you said—"

"Please don't remind me of anything I might have said," he pleaded. "I was an ass."

She grimaced, the memory of his stoic speech about duty still capable of making her cringe in revulsion.

"I can't argue with that," she told him.

"Ouch." He winced, as if she'd truly struck a raw nerve. "If I'm being honest, there was a part of me that resented the idea that my future had been decided for me," he admitted. Rya's lips parted, but before she could tell him to take his future and shove it, he stole her words with a fierce kiss. "Wait."

She tried to hold on to her brief spurt of annoyance. Something that would have been easier if his lips weren't nibbling a path of destruction from her mouth to her jaw and down the curve of her neck.

"Bossy," she muttered as delicious tingles raced through her, tightening her nipples and creating an aching void between her legs.

"Which was why I told myself that it was duty that made me so easily accept the betrothal," he said, his lips finding a tender spot just behind her ear before his mouth continued its slow, glorious exploration. Rya swallowed a moan of approval. "Of course, that didn't explain why you haunted my dreams," he continued. "Or why I couldn't so much as glance at another female."

"Not even a glance?"

"I couldn't see them," he insisted, licking a rough tongue over the pulse that hammered at the base of her throat. "Not when my heart was set on a dark-haired beauty with amber eyes and the intoxicating scent of lotus blossoms."

It was increasingly difficult to concentrate. How was she supposed to have a reasonable conversation when her mind was filled with images of stripping Torque naked so she could kiss every hot, granite-hard inch of him?

"Pretty words," she managed to grumble.

He lifted his head, his eyes luminous with a sapphire fire. "You don't trust me?"

"I trust you with my life," she slowly admitted. "I'm not sure that I trust you with my heart."

His jaw tightened at her blunt words, but he offered a slow nod, accepting he deserved her lack of faith.

"Just answer one question, Rya," he said.

"What?"

"Do you want to end our betrothal?"

Oddly, she wasn't prepared for his direct attack.

Her first instinct was to deny her fierce desire to become his mate. She didn't want to make herself vulnerable only to have her heart crushed.

But one glance at his wary expression warned her that she would regret the lie for all of eternity.

He'd said he would walk away. She sensed he would keep his promise.

Did she truly want to spend the next century alone, crying in her private baths?

"No," she breathed, holding his gaze. "I don't want it to end."

Heat blasted through the room as her soft words fell from her lips. But unexpectedly, Torque froze, doing a mannequin routine for what seemed to be an eternity.

Okay.

Was he pleased? Excited?

Feeling like she'd just put a noose around his neck?

At last he smiled.

And it wasn't just a regular, things-are-good smile.

It was a stunning, I-just-won-the-lottery smile.

"Thank the goddess," he breathed, turning so he could carry her toward the nearby bed.

Her heart soared with excitement. How many nights had she dreamed of this moment? Even when she'd tried to convince herself that she didn't want a mate, her dreams had been filled with vivid fantasies of lying in Torque's strong arms.

And now that it was here, she wanted to savor each and every moment.

Her gaze drifted over his stark features, committing each one to her memory. The noble brow. The aquiline nose. The high cheekbones and finely sculpted lips.

And most compelling of all, the sapphire eyes that held the awesome power of his inner dragon.

"So we're staying betrothed?" she breathed, suddenly needing to know that this was forever.

"That depends on you," he murmured, gently laying her in the center of the bed.

Her breath caught at his words. "Me?"

Leaning forward, he planted his hands on either side of her shoulders, gazing down at her with a burning intensity.

"As far as I'm concerned we can formalize the mating today," he said, instantly easing her fears. Then, allowing his gaze to move down the length of her slender body, he gave a slow shake of his head. "Well, maybe not today," he corrected in husky tones. "I already have plans for the next few hours."

She released a low chuckle as her beast roared in approval. In this moment, she was feeling much more dragon than fey.

"I think I can guess your plans," she assured him.

"Can you?" He lowered his head until they were nose to nose. "Tell me."

She shivered, her usual shyness seared away as she basked in the heat of Torque's desire.

"I think you intend to kiss me," she told him.

"A good guess," he agreed in throaty tones. "Where?"

"Here." She placed a finger against her cheek, enjoying the sensual game as his lips instantly pressed a soft kiss to where she pointed. She moved her finger to the tip of her nose. "And here." Another lingering kiss. She trembled, pointing toward her lips. "And here."

With a low growl, Torque released his pent-up passion, kissing her with a fierce intensity that sent shockwaves of pleasure jolting through her.

Oh, hell yeah.

His tongue pierced between her lips, sweeping through the moist heat of her mouth. Her hands lifted to fist in his hair, her body instinctively arching upward as his kiss deepened.

Sweet and tender were great. More than great.

But she was ready and willing for the full blast of his hunger.

Tasting her over and over, he moved his hand to skim over her shoulder before lightly tracing the line of her collarbone.

She made a sound of approval as his roaming fingers moved downward, giving a firm tug at the towel wrapped around her. Instantly the thick material fell away, offering him full access to her naked body.

Swift to take advantage, Torque allowed his mouth to ease from her lips so he could blaze a path of kisses down her neck and over the upper curve of her breasts.

"What about here?" he teased in soft tones.

"Yes," she breathed, her flames making a rare appearance as his lips at last found the aching peaks of her breasts.

Rya squirmed against the bedcover beneath her, the intensity of her pleasure almost overwhelming.

Seriously. Had anything ever felt so good?

Cupping the breast in his hand, Torque used his tongue, and even his teeth, to pleasure her tightly budded nipple.

Her fingers tangled in the satin strands of his hair, her breath a ragged rasp as a tight knot of need formed in the pit of her stomach.

"Lotus blossoms," he murmured, giving her nipple a last lick before he was rubbing his face against the flames that formed between her breasts. "And fire." He lifted his head to gaze down at her with eyes darkened with restless hunger. "A potent combination."

"You're all fire," she murmured, trailing her hand down his nape before exploring the hard muscles of his back.

"I feel like it," he said in a harsh voice. "I'm burning up."

"Maybe you should take off some of those clothes," she suggested, shockingly comfortable in the role of Torque's lover.

No doubt because he made no effort to disguise just how much he wanted her.

She felt sexy and confident and well-desired.

A cascade of heat rippled through the air as he slowly smiled. Then, straightening, he deliberately held out his arms.

"Help me."

Rya didn't need a second invitation. Rising up to her knees, she reached for the hem of his sweater and pulled it up and over his head. She paused long enough to run her hands over his bare chest as he kicked off his shoes.

His skin was silky smooth and as her fingers trailed over his hard muscles, tiny flames sparked to life. He sucked in a breath as she traced his washboard abs before awkwardly unsnapping his jeans and pulling down the zipper.

Instantly the hard length of his cock sprang free and with a small smile she circled the thickness with her fingers.

"So beautiful," she murmured, stroking down to the soft sack at the base.

"Not me," he rasped, stepping away from her touch

to shove his jeans down his legs and kick them aside. "You're the beautiful one," he insisted, his gaze sweeping over her flushed face. "Lush lips that beg for my kisses. A neck that was created for this."

He reached out to draw a pattern along her upper chest. Rya felt a whisper of magic, and glancing down in surprise she watched in astonishment at the sight of the delicate gold necklace that now hung around her neck.

It was exquisite.

But more importantly, it was created out of pure dragon-magic.

"I didn't know you could create a dragon marque," she breathed, her fingers stroking over the rare gift with pleasure.

His eyes danced with wicked anticipation. "I have several hidden talents that I intend to reveal now that I finally have you naked."

Yum. Rya had already had a taste of a few of his talents. She was ready and eager for more.

"Promises, promises," she teased, the words barely leaving her lips before she found herself tumbled back onto the satin cover with Torque perched on top of her.

Her eyes widened in surprise as he braced his hands on either side of her head and wiggled his lower body until he was firmly cradled between her spread legs.

"Now," he murmured, "where was I?" Holding her wide gaze, he lowered his head, slowly licking his tongue over her sensitive nipple. "Here?" He watched her eyes dilate and the flames return to her skin. "Yes, definitely here," he said with a chuckle.

"Oh." Her head tilted backward, her heels digging into the mattress as he tugged the tip of her breast between his lips. Scalding bliss seared through her, wrenching a groan from her lips. "This is…"

Her words trailed away. Even after endless nights of dreaming about having Torque make love to her, nothing she imagined could come close to the reality.

The heat. The excitement.

The raw intimacy of naked flesh pressed together.

"Paradise," he finished for her.

She released a shaky sigh, drowning in the sapphire beauty of his eyes. "Yes, paradise."

Swirling his tongue around the tip of her nipple, Torque moved his head to kiss the underside of her breast. Then, as she moaned in pleasure, he continued downward. Licking and nibbling, he paused to explore the tense muscles of her stomach even as his hands slid beneath her thighs to tug her legs farther apart.

"Torque?" she murmured, glancing down the length of her body to watch as he kissed over the curve of her hip.

At the sound of his name, Torque lifted his head, revealing eyes that had gone fully dragon.

"I want to taste you," he said, his voice a deep growl. Before she could respond, he settled on the edge of the mattress, still holding her gaze as he dipped down his head and licked through her damp cleft.

Rya jerked, feeling like she'd been struck by lightning.

Yow.

Her hands clutched at the cover beneath her as he feasted on her, his tongue teasing over her clit before sinking into the slick heat of her body.

Absently she was aware that her skin was coated in golden flame, but she didn't have the ability to marvel at her intense response. Not when a sensual pressure was building with every lick.

Over and over, he stroked his tongue over her tender bud, grasping her hips as she arched upward. The force of her looming climax wrenched soft groans from her throat.

It was too much. Too much.

Her eyes squeezed shut as she hovered on the edge of bliss…and then it happened.

The orgasm blasted through her, shattering her with the sheer intensity of the sensations.

Damn.

She briefly floated in the melting pleasure before she reached down to thread her fingers through Torque's hair.

"That was amazing," she breathed.

"Mmm," Torque murmured, seeming to enjoy the taste of her climax on his tongue. "Sweet." Another slow lick. "And spicy."

"It's my turn," she commanded in husky tones.

"Later."

"I—" Her words broke off with a small squeak as Torque suddenly tightened his hold on her hips and with one smooth motion rolled her onto her stomach. Puzzled by her new position, she glanced over her shoulder to see Torque straddling her legs, the proud thrust of his cock brushing her lower back. "What are you doing?"

In answer, he reached to brush his fingers over the elaborate tattoo that shimmered across her skin.

"I love this," he said, smug satisfaction laced through his voice. "It proves that you belong to me."

She shivered, her inner beast delighting in the feel of his fingers against the betrothal marking.

"That's a little…" Her words faltered as his lips replaced his fingers. With blazing kisses he traced the wings that spread from shoulder blade to shoulder blade. "Territorial," she at last managed to choke out, shocked to discover her body responding to his erotic caresses.

A thunderous heat pulsed through the air.

"Not a little territorial," he assured her in dark tones. "A lot territorial. Any other man comes near you and I'll destroy him."

She chuckled. It was the response of a predatory

male.

"How did I ever think you didn't have emotions?" she murmured.

Once again Rya found herself being spun around, this time landing flat on her back with Torque looming over her.

"They're all for you," he rasped, his eyes burning with need. "Every one."

She released a soft sigh, love for this male spreading like wildfire through her. He might not be flashy or overly romantic. But he was loyal and kind and utterly faithful. Precisely what she desired in her mate.

Reaching up, she wrapped her fingers around his thick cock, sliding them down and back up with a slow, ruthless motion.

"Rya," he choked out, his skin heating as his flames sparked at her touch.

Squirming until she was in a seated position, she bent forward.

"It's my turn to taste," she told him, wrapping her lips around the blunt tip and drawing his length into her mouth.

"Oh…shit," he growled, his fingers grasping her hair as she sucked him deeper, her hand gently cupping his soft sack as she scraped her teeth back up his throbbing length.

The taste of raw male power sizzled against her tongue, stirring her passions like an aphrodisiac. They groaned in unison as she pressed down, her tongue teasing at the tip of his cock.

His erection swelled, becoming impossibly large as his body bowed beneath the pleasure.

"Enough," he at last rasped, turning until he was seated on the mattress and leaning his back against the lacquer headboard. "I need to be inside you."

Grasping her hand, he tugged her toward him,

draping her legs over his waist. Then, holding on to the backs of her thighs, he arranged her above his erection.

Rya grasped his shoulders, quivering as she lowered herself to allow the tip of his cock to slide into her body.

Delicious. She hissed in pleasure as she pressed down, aroused by the sweet sting as she was stretched to accommodate him.

"Are you okay?" he rasped, his hands skimming up to cup her breasts, his thumbs stroking her nipples into tingling peaks.

"Better than okay," she assured him, leaning forward to press a kiss to his lips.

"Put your arms around me," he murmured, waiting for her to wrap her arms around his neck. "Now hold on tight."

Lifting his hips off the bed, he slammed upward, fully impaling her.

Rya's eyes closed, her head falling backward as their flames surrounded them in a blaze of white-hot passion.

CHAPTER SIXTEEN

Snuggled in the middle of the bed with Rya wrapped in his arms, Torque was fairly certain he was a complete and total idiot.

How could he have ever have imagined that his mating with Rya would be nothing more than duty?

Not only had he just experienced the most stunningly life-altering sex a male could ever hope to enjoy, but now he had an entire future to share with this rare, courageous, beautiful female.

He'd been offered nirvana, and he'd very nearly allowed his pride to destroy it all.

Shuddering at the mere thought of an existence that didn't revolve around Rya, he lifted himself on his elbow to gaze down at her.

An odd ache clenched his heart.

Dear goddess. She was so lovely with her glossy black hair spread over the crimson cover, and her amber eyes still smoldering with the heat that had combusted between them.

He would never, ever grow tired of looking at her.

"So about our mating," he murmured, suddenly anxious to have their relationship formally recognized. And not only by the dragons. He wanted to make sure that no one and nothing could try and claim it was anything but an eternal bond.

She arched a brow. "What about it?"

"I thought you might prefer to follow the traditions of your mother," he murmured.

"Oh." A smile of pleasure curved her lips. "Yes. That would be lovely."

He released a breath he hadn't even known he was holding.

"Good." He blinked in surprise when she suddenly giggled. "What's so funny?"

"Shouldn't you ask what the traditions are?" she teased. "You might have to crawl through lava. Or perform circus tricks."

Did she truly think there was any demand that would be too great for him to claim her as his consort?

"Whatever makes you happy," he assured her.

Her eyes glowed with an emotion that made his entire body warm with pleasure.

"*You* make me happy," she murmured, lifting her hand to press it to his cheek.

He covered her hand with his own, turning his head so he could press his lips to the center of her palm.

"Thank the goddess. You're stuck with me for a very long time." He paused, his lips twitching. "There aren't any circus acts, are there?"

Her laughter rang through the air, a sound that resonated deep within him like the striking of a bell.

Yep. Nirvana.

"Not one," she assured him, her thumb brushing the

line of his jaw. “I promise it’s a very simple ceremony where the elders bless our union and my mother offers a vision of our future—”

He abruptly interrupted her soft words. “No.”

She studied him in confusion. “No?”

He shook his head. As happy as he was that Kai’s initial vision had prompted Synge to insist that Rya become his mate, it had also swayed the way he’d approached his life. And not in a good way.

“Visions never turn out like you imagine they will,” he muttered, bending his head down so he could brush his lips over her furrowed brow. “Besides, I don’t need magic to know what our future holds.”

Her fingers trailed down the side of his neck. “What’s that?”

“An eternity of happiness.”

“Mmm.” She stirred against him. “I’ll take that.”

He skimmed his hand down her naked back. He loved feeling the betrothal tattoo that was spread across her skin. Just as he loved the glint of gold from the delicate dragon marque that hung around her neck.

A primitive male need to lay claim to his mate?

Damn straight.

And he wasn’t even a little ashamed.

He cleared his throat, trying to look casual. “And perhaps a hatchling or two.”

Rya froze, as if shocked by his words. “You want children?”

“I never thought about it until now,” he said with blunt honesty. Warriors rarely mated, let alone had families. It was a distraction that could get them killed. Now he was far more interested in an existence that included more than killing things. “But I’m suddenly anxious to hold a tiny daughter with amber eyes in my arms.”

An unexpected yearning rippled over her face. As if

she'd suddenly been struck with a maternal urge.

"Or a little boy who is always serious and loyal and as gorgeous as his father," Rya suggested.

He kissed the tip of her nose. Her words didn't scare him at all.

Hell, he'd be happy if she wanted a dozen children.

"Maybe one of each to start with," he murmured.

Her hands smoothed over his shoulders, her foot brushing down his calf.

"First we'll need a lair of our own."

Torque shuddered at the light caress. How the hell was he supposed to think when his mind was filled with wicked images of having Rya flat on her back with his cock pressed deep inside her?

"We could use mine," he at last managed to offer, pressing a kiss to her lips that instantly parted in horror. Okay. He was beginning to understand why everyone thought his rooms were…barren. Certainly they didn't have the same sort of gracious comfort that Rya's offered. "Before you say no, I promise you'll be given full authority to decorate it however you want," he assured her.

She pulled back to study him with a curious expression. "Do you intend to remain in Baine's service?"

He considered for a long minute. A part of him wanted to take this female and disappear where no one could ever find them. But he knew that wasn't possible.

Not only did he truly enjoy his role as Baine's guard, but he knew there was no place in this world, or any other, that was safer than Baine's lair.

Nothing and no one could get in.

"I'll admit that I will feel safer if we are living within the magical protection of a full-blooded dragon," he told her. "Especially if we have children. Besides, you'll have a fey near when you decide you're tired of my company and want to socialize with another female."

"Who?" It took a second before her confusion cleared. "Oh, you mean Baine's mate."

He nodded. "I think you'll like Tayla. She's very…" He searched for a word to describe the lovely, effervescent imp who Baine had chosen as his mate. "Feyish."

"Hey." She pressed her hands against his chest, her eyes narrowed. "What's that supposed to mean?"

He smiled. His inner dragon was certainly addicted to her passionate beast, and the fire they created between them. But there was a large part of him that enjoyed the sparkling fey side of her nature.

"Flighty, charming, and enjoys talking. A lot," he said. There were times when he wondered if the chatty imp was ever quiet. "You'll never feel lonely when she's around."

"I'm not flighty," she protested, although she couldn't hide the twitch of her lips.

He continued to stroke his hand over her back, savoring the growing sense of intimacy being woven between them.

There was a glorious joy in lying next to his female and discussing their future together.

"Not always," he admitted. "When we met for our betrothal ceremony you were very zen."

She wrinkled her nose. "My mother's training. She was afraid I hadn't entirely grown out of my…feisty stage."

"Feisty stage? I'm afraid to ask," Torque murmured, not entirely teasing.

While his first impression of Rya might have been one of a calm, passive creature, he'd swiftly learned that beneath her façade was an impulsive, loving, courageous female who didn't understand the word 'fear.'

"I wasn't that bad," she retorted. "Like any child, I

enjoyed playing pranks on my father's servants. They were usually forgiving." She released a rueful chuckle. "Except for the time when I used my shadow to slip into the war room when my father was planning an attack on another dragon. Things got a bit testy when I was spotted."

"Good god," he muttered. "You were lucky you weren't thrown in the dungeons."

She gave a small shrug, revealing her confidence in her father's love. Synge would have destroyed anyone else who had dared to spy on his war council.

"That's when my mother began to train me in controlling my powers," she said. "Along with my emotions."

"When you're with me you don't ever have to control your emotions," he murmured, his voice husky as he allowed his hand to trace the lush curve of her ass. "I like when you're feisty."

She snorted, even as her eyes darkened with a ready passion. "Not always."

"True." He traced her lower lip with the tip of his tongue before giving it a small nip. "Not when you're putting yourself in danger."

Without warning she stiffened, almost as if his words had touched a nerve.

"Speaking of putting myself in danger, there's something I need to tell you," she muttered in a strained voice.

Torque lifted his head. Was she teasing him?

On the point of demanding an explanation, Torque was distracted by a voice that echoed sharply through his brain.

He didn't have the gargoyle's telepathic powers, but all of Baine's guards were capable of mental communications. And at the moment, Char was impatiently demanding his attention.

"Hold that thought," he murmured, pressing a frustrated kiss to her lips before reluctantly crawling out of bed.

Although Char couldn't see him or Rya, it seemed creepy to talk to his fellow warrior while he was sprawled next to his naked female.

Rya hastily wrapped the blanket around her slender body, watching as Torque pulled on his jeans and sweater.

"What is it?" she demanded.

"Char." He grimaced and reached down to pull on his boots. "He's arrived from Baine's lair and is demanding to see me." Once he was finished, he moved back to perch on the edge of the mattress. If he hadn't been the one responsible for Char being ordered to Synge's lair he would have ignored the summons.

"Ah." She forced a smile to her lips. "Then you have to go."

He reached to run his fingers through the tangled silk of her hair.

"I don't want to leave you." He wasn't ashamed to admit it.

"It won't be for long."

She was right about that. He intended to tell Char why he'd called for him, listen to him bitch, and then he was out of there.

He gave her a last kiss. "Don't move," he commanded softly. "I intend to finish this as soon as I can get back."

"Torque," she breathed as he rose to his feet.

He glanced down at her with a lift of his brow. "Yes, my love?"

"I…" She gave a shake of her head. "We'll talk later."

He felt a brief stab of unease, but before he could determine what was bothering him, Char was once again demanding that he join him.

With a sigh, he turned to leave the harem. He took a minute to speak with the guards, ensuring that no one was allowed to enter Rya's rooms. Then, with long strides he hurried to join Char in Synge's public chamber.

The large room looked the same as when he left. Except it had thankfully been emptied of servants. Well, except for two uniformed guards who stood near the opening to Synge's private quarters.

At his entrance, Char turned with a narrowed gaze to watch him cross the floor.

The half-breed dragon was currently dressed in black slacks and a crisp white shirt, his gray eyes darkened to smoke.

Then, without warning, the older male was striding forward and wrapping his arms around Torque.

"Damn, dude, I thought we'd lost you," Char growled in rough tones.

Astonished by his friend's obvious concern, Torque returned the man-hug. "I tried to reach out to Baine, but the dragon's magic blocked me."

"Don't scare me like that again."

There was a shared moment of mutual relief that Torque had survived. Then, belatedly unnerved by his rare display of affection, Torque pushed Char away to send him a faux scowl.

"Enough mushy stuff," he commanded, his voice husky. "Let's get this over with."

"As charming as ever, old friend," Char drawled, his lips twitching.

Torque folded his arms over his chest, well aware he wasn't fooling his companion.

"You interrupted my private time alone with my mate."

"And why would that bother you?" The eyebrow

inched even higher. "When you left Baine's lair you made it clear that the last thing you wanted was to be stuck with your betrothed. Surely you should be happy to get away from the female?"

"Careful, old friend. Her name is Rya," he growled, not entirely teasing. "And of course I don't want to be parted from her."

Char folded his arms over his chest. "How was I supposed to know? You acted like you were being sent to your own funeral the last time I saw you."

Torque felt a burst of embarrassment. Did the male have to remind him that he'd behaved like an arrogant jerk?

Thankfully, Rya was willing to forgive him for being an ass.

"I've had the opportunity to truly discover Rya's value," he told his friend.

"Her value?" Char rolled his eyes. "You mean her beauty?"

"Her beauty." Torque readily agreed. Of course he admired her lovely features and sexy body, but that wasn't what made him desire her as his mate. "And more so, her courage. Her heart." He smiled, just the thought of Rya making him happy. "They all combine to make her special."

Char recoiled, as if he'd been punched. "Hell. You're as sappy as Baine," he rasped.

"There are worse things."

"Not as far as I'm concerned."

Torque shrugged. Unlike him, Char had always had a full, robust appreciation for the fairer sex. But he was adamant that it was his duty to spread his charm far and wide.

More than once the male had claimed it would be a sin against nature for him to mate and deny the females of the world the opportunity to capture his attention.

"That's what you say now," Torque murmured. It'd taken only a few hours for his entire world to be turned upside down.

Char held up a hand. "Don't curse me."

"Curses," Torque muttered, suddenly reminded of why he'd asked for Char to be called to the lair. "That's why you're here."

Char looked confused. "Are you joking?"

"Do I ever joke?"

Char's lips twisted. "Fine. What's going on?"

With a crisp efficiency, Torque gave a brief rundown of the past hours, including the revelation that Synge had a mate and a full-blooded daughter.

Char furrowed his brow, taking several minutes to sort through the most pertinent parts of the story. "So she's really cursed?"

Torque shuddered. He was going to have nightmares about the dark pulses of energy that had surrounded the young dragon.

"Yeah, she's really cursed," he muttered.

"Great." Char's eyes swirled with thunderclouds. "And you want me to be trapped in time with her?"

Torque frowned. He'd assumed Char could cast the spell and walk away.

"All I know of your powers is that you can halt time," he said.

Char shook his head, his hand dropping. "I don't actually halt it," he said. "My powers can slow it for a limited time."

"And you have to be wrapped in the magic?"

"The powers alter my place in time. With an effort I can spread it to include whoever is near me. Which means that the closer they are, the longer I can maintain the magic."

Torque grimaced with guilt. "Dammit. I shouldn't have suggested that you help." He reached out to put his hand on Char's shoulders. The older male could be a pain in the ass, but he was like a brother to him. "I didn't know it would put you in danger."

"As long as she's unconscious I should be fine," Char muttered.

Was he trying to convince Torque or himself?

Torque parted his lips to demand that Char return to Baine's lair when there was a roar of scalding power and Synge stepped into the chamber.

Too late.

The older dragon scowled at the two of them. "Finally," he snapped. "Follow me."

Pivoting on his heel, Synge was marching back into his private quarters, confident the two males would follow.

Char and Torque were swiftly trailing behind him.

Only an idiot ignored an order from a dragon.

A dead idiot.

"It's nice to know not everyone has changed," Char muttered in a low voice.

Torque abruptly recalled Synge's expression when he'd discovered his mate and daughter were alive. The brutish predator had revealed a shocking vulnerability. Not that he was about to share that particular revelation. Not when the old dragon might overhear him.

He preferred not to have his flesh seared off his bones, thank you very much.

"Actually, you might be surprised," he instead breathed.

Char sent him a curious glance before they were coming to an abrupt halt as Synge stopped in the middle of a doorway.

Glancing over his shoulder, the dragon sent Char a warning glare.

"We are about to enter the room of my daughter," he growled. "She is precious beyond all measure and if something were to happen to her…"

Char held up his hands in a gesture of peace. "I promise I'll do everything in my power to keep her safe."

The male gave a grudging nod before he turned to lead them into a room shaped like an octagon, with a domed ceiling that was covered with tiles made from pure gold. On the windows were lattice coverings and at one end of the marble floor a small fountain shimmered in the light from the numerous candelabras.

In the far corner was a wide bed where a slender female was lying on a white satin cover. Her long black hair had been brushed until it glowed with an ebony luster and her skin had the sheen of a pearl in the candlelight.

Moving to stand at the edge of the mattress Char glanced down, an odd, thunderstruck expression on his face.

"Tell me what you need," Synge commanded, his hands on his hips.

"Need?" Char muttered, his gaze never leaving Blayze's face that was softened with peace as she slept.

The dragon scowled at him and Torque covertly kicked his friend in the shin.

"Char," he muttered.

"Have you taken a blow to the head, or are you just slow?" Synge snapped, waiting for Char to send him a wary glance. "What do you need?"

"Nothing," Char muttered, still looking as if he'd seen a ghost. Could he sense Blayze's curse? Being trapped with the evil sensation would be unnerving for anyone. "I mean…" Char stopped and cleared his voice. "I can spread my powers to include this room, but the door needs to remain locked to ensure the magic isn't disturbed."

Synge clenched his hands. "How long can you keep

the spell in place?"

"A day," Char said. "Maybe two."

"Do it," Synge commanded before he was heading toward an opening on the opposite side of the room.

Stepping forward, Torque studied his friend's tense profile with a frown.

There was definitely something off. But what?

"Are you okay?" he at last demanded.

"Yeah." The male stepped closer to the bed, his hand reaching out as if he was battling an urge to touch the beautiful dragon female. "You need to go."

Torque hesitated. "Char—"

"I got this," Char snapped.

"Are you sure?" Torque pressed, only to grimace in defeat when Char turned his head to glare at him with eyes as dark as thunderclouds.

"Go."

"Okay, okay. Do your thing," Torque muttered, backing toward the doorway. "Call me if you need me."

Char ignored him, his attention already centered back on Blayze.

Leaving the room with a vague sense of concern, Torque entered the public chamber. Maybe he should contact Baine. The dragon considered Char more a friend than a servant. He would want to know if the male might be in danger.

Torque's lips twitched. It would also give Baine the opportunity to annoy his father. Pissing off Synge was something that gave the younger dragon great joy.

On the point of leaving the lair, Torque was halted by the sound of his name being called.

"Torque."

He stiffened. Shit. He'd been so close to escape.

For a crazed moment his muscles clenched as he actually considered bolting. He wanted to be with Rya. Now.

Not to mention the fact he needed to contact Baine.

Thankfully, he clung to enough sanity to squash the suicidal urge.

Forcing himself to turn, he offered Synge a low bow. "My lord," he murmured.

The dragon moved from the shadowed alcove where he'd obviously been waiting for Torque. His nose flared as he folded his arms over his massive chest. "You smell like Rya."

Torque met the accusing gaze. If he had to fight for his right to be with Rya…then so be it.

"She's my betrothed," he said.

"You intend to complete the mating?" Synge demanded.

"As soon as her mother returns," Torque said, waiting for the male to protest his right to claim Rya. When the dragon gave a slow nod, Torque decided to press his luck. "Have your servants been able to create an opening?"

"No, but they assure me it's only a matter of time," Synge said, his brow furrowed with concern. After all, he was depending on Kai's rescue to protect his beloved daughter from her curse. "They've gathered outside the lair. They were afraid my magic was interfering in their efforts."

Torque swallowed a frustrated curse. He'd hoped they were actually making progress.

"Rya won't wait long," he muttered.

Synge released a sharp laugh. "You know my headstrong daughter well."

"Well enough to suspect she's going to take matters in her own hands if she believes we aren't doing enough to rescue her mother," he said.

Synge sent him a warning frown. "Then you'd better convince her."

Torque resisted the urge to roll his eyes. "Thanks."

CHAPTER SEVENTEEN

Rya felt like she was going to jump out of her skin.

As time passed, she became increasingly worried about her mother. About Torque. About Finn, who, she'd just discovered, had yet to return to his tribe.

In an effort to ease her tension she'd taken yet another bath and pulled on a pair of jeans and a bright yellow sweater. She didn't know what she intended to do, but it didn't include twiddling her thumbs while she waited for something to happen.

She'd just finished braiding her hair when she caught the unmistakable scent of granite floating on the faint breeze.

Oh, thank the goddess.

Hurrying down the corridor that led to the outer

courtyard, she found her guards holding a tiny gargoyle with bright, lacy wings.

"Release me, you buffoon," Levet was commanding, squirming as he tried to break free of the guard's ruthless grip. Then, catching sight of Rya as she stepped into the garden that was cloaked in darkness, his tiny face brightened with relief. "Ah, *ma belle*. At last. These"—his tail twitched with agitation—"*imbéciles* have forbidden me to enter."

Rya scowled. Her servants were there to protect her. They had, after all, been trained by her father's own warriors.

But she wasn't a prisoner. If someone arrived to visit her, the guards should have contacted her right away.

"What's going on?" she demanded.

The two guards exchanged uneasy glances before they were meeting her impatient glare.

"We were told not to let anyone pass," the guard holding Levet informed her.

"Told by whom?" she asked, even though she knew the answer.

"Your mate."

She pointed toward the gargoyle. "Release him immediately."

"But…"

The servant's words trailed away as Rya planted her hands on her hips and allowed her eyes to glow with the power of her dragon. "Yes?"

"Your consort said that no one was allowed inside," the poor male stammered, his face pale.

Rya ground her teeth. Clearly she was going to have to remind her betrothed that they weren't yet mated. And that even when they did formalize their relationship, becoming her consort didn't equal becoming her boss.

"Is this my lair or Torque's?" she snapped.

The guard licked his lips. "Yours."

"Then release my guest."

The male grudgingly loosened his hold, allowing Levet to drop to the ground.

"Bully," Levet sniffed, waddling toward Rya with his snout in the air.

"Return to your duties," Rya ordered the befuddled guards before she reached down to pat Levet between his stunted horns. "Come with me."

Sending the guards a loud raspberry, Levet followed her down the corridor and into her private rooms.

His gray eyes widened as he made a slow circle of the round room that had ivory and gold tiles on the floor and delicate tapestries hung on the walls.

"A most charming lair," he murmured, carefully touching a rare jade statue that had been carved in the shape of a dragon in full flight.

"Thank you." Moving to stand in the center of the room, Rya studied her companion with a barely leashed impatience. "Have you found a way to reach my mother?"

"Ah." The gargoyle turned to face her, his head tilted to the side. "I see you intend to get straight to the pointy end."

Rya wrinkled her nose. "Forgive me. I'm just anxious to get her out of that place."

Levet waved aside her apology. "Perfectly understandable that you are in no mood for chitty chit, *ma belle*."

A small smile tugged at her lips. The creature could make her chuckle no matter what was going on.

"Can you help?" she asked.

"Oui," he said. "I believe I have found someone who can help us create a portal."

Rya released a shaky sigh. "Who is it?"

"Laylah," Levet said. "She is a half-Jinn."

Rya's eyes widened in shock. Jinn were incredibly

powerful, but they were also cunning, evil demons who created chaos wherever they went.

Sort of like dragons. Without the whole fire-breathing thing.

"A Jinn?" she said, unable to disguise her disappointment.

How could she possibly trust her mother's rescue to a creature who might decide it was more fun to slaughter them all?

Clearly sensing her unease, Levet moved forward, reaching out to lightly pat her leg.

"Do not fear. Laylah is not like other Jinn. She is quite civilized," he promised. "And despite her incomprehensible decision to mate with a vampire, you can trust her."

Rya gave a slow nod. She didn't trust any Jinn, but she did trust this gargoyle.

He wouldn't have suggested Laylah help them if she was dangerous.

"Is she going to meet us here?" she asked, ignoring her instinctive aversion to the treacherous demons.

"Non." Levet wrinkled his snout, as if he'd just caught a bad smell. "Her mate refuses to allow her to travel to the harem of a dragon," he told her. "Tane is a savage, and like most vampires is annoyingly unreasonable, I fear."

"Oh." Rya felt a stab of disappointment although she couldn't really blame the vampire.

No demon would be happy to have their female mate anywhere near a dragon harem.

Not only because they were known to be heavily guarded, but because a full-blooded dragon could alter his or her appearance to please any lover.

A potent talent.

Levet gave her leg another pat. "He has, however, agreed to allow you to meet with her at my home," he assured her.

"Now?"

"Oui."

A fierce urgency to run out the door beat through her. She was acutely aware of the passage of time since her mother had been trapped between dimensions. And that each tick of the clock put her in more danger.

But even as she pivoted toward the door, she abruptly remembered that she couldn't just leave.

"Give me a second to write a note for Torque and then we'll go," she muttered, crossing toward a low table.

She'd taken less than a dozen steps when a tingle of heat raced over her skin.

Uh oh.

Coming to a halt, she slowly turned to discover Torque standing in the doorway, his hands planted on his hips.

"Go where?"

She cleared her throat. *Crap.* She hadn't deliberately tried to leave before he returned to her lair, but she hadn't been opposed to avoiding the looming argument.

"Torque." She managed a stiff smile.

The glorious sapphire eyes narrowed with suspicion.

"You said something about leaving," he growled.

Rya squared her shoulders. She wasn't going to feel guilty for doing whatever necessary to rescue her mother.

"Levet has found someone who can open a portal into Ravel's lair."

His gaze took in her defiant expression before moving toward the gargoyle. "Who?"

Levet gave a flick of his wings. "A friend. She will meet us at my house."

"We have to hurry," Rya said, walking forward.

Predictably, Torque moved to stand directly in front

of her.

The only surprise would have been if he hadn't tried to block her path.

"No," he growled.

Her eyes narrowed to tiny slits as flames erupted to swirl around her feet. "Excuse me?"

There was a sudden scrape of claws against the tiled floor as Levet scurried toward the door.

"Perhaps I should wait outside," he muttered.

Smart gargoyle.

Torque lowered his head until they were nose to nose.

"You're not going to risk your life with some unknown demon who might or might not have the ability to reach your mother," he growled.

She met his glare without flinching. This sort of behavior was going to have to be nipped in the bud.

Or something a bit more tender on the male anatomy was going to get nipped.

"Do you assume becoming my consort gives you the right to tell me what I can or can't do?"

His jaw clenched, but he wasn't stupid.

"It gives me the right to protect you," he cautiously corrected.

She pressed her finger to the center of his chest.

"Protecting and controlling are two different things," she informed him.

"If something happened—" His words broke off, a soul-deep vulnerability darkening his eyes as he grabbed her hand to give it a gentle squeeze. "I couldn't survive, Rya," he rasped. "Not without you."

Her annoyance instantly faded, but she refused to back down. This was too important.

Torque was a predatory male who would walk all over her if she didn't take a stand.

"Just as I couldn't survive without you," she said,

her voice softening. "But what if Baine was attacked? Would you be willing to step aside because it might put you in danger?"

His brows snapped together. "It's not the same."

"Because I'm a female?"

"Because I don't want to be reasonable," he muttered.

Threading her fingers through his, she tugged his hand to her lips.

"You know I have to do this," she murmured, pressing a kiss on his knuckles.

He heaved a harsh sigh. "Then I'm coming with you."

It was her turn to frown. It was one thing for her to risk everything to save her mother. But it wasn't Torque's responsibility.

"But—"

"End of discussion," he interrupted in tones that didn't offer any room for argument.

Rya rolled her eyes in defeat. It was a waste of breath to try to convince him to return to his lair.

"We're going to have an interesting future together," she muttered, stepping around him to head out of her rooms.

"We are indeed," he said from behind her.

In silence they joined Levet who was pacing the corridor.

"We're ready," she announced.

Levet glanced toward Torque who was standing in brooding silence before returning his attention to her.

"Can you take us to my house?" he demanded.

She reached out to lightly touch the upper curve of his wing. She'd never visited the teahouse just south of Chicago that had once belonged to Baine's mate, Tayla, but she could use the mental bond that Levet had forged between them to locate it.

Closing her eyes, she allowed her fey magic to flow through her blood. It wasn't like her dragon powers. This was light and bubbly and oddly intoxicating.

"There," she muttered in satisfaction, feeling the portal form.

Torque instantly moved to stand at the entrance of the opening. "I go first," he said.

His expression revealed that he was just waiting for her to argue.

"Whatever makes you happy." Going onto her tiptoes, she planted a soft kiss on his cheek before stepping back to let him enter ahead of her.

He blinked, as if unsure how to react. Beside him, Levet heaved a rueful sigh.

"They learn quickly, do they not?" the gargoyle murmured.

"They do, indeed," Torque breathed, giving her one last lingering glance before turning back toward the portal.

Then, taking the necessary time to slip into his warrior mode, he at last stepped forward and disappeared from view.

Levet entered behind him, and Rya swiftly followed.

There was a momentary ripple of darkness as they moved through the portal and stepped into a garden bathed in a silvery moonlight.

Beyond the well-tended yard were empty fields and a rolling vineyard. And directly in front of her was a large Victorian home with a wraparound porch. It had a gabled roof and gingerbread wood trim. The outside was painted a pretty pink with white shutters that she adored, although she could see Torque grimace.

Clearly she would have to avoid pink and froufrou when she decorated their lair.

There was a faint sound of footsteps before a lovely female stepped out of a wooden grotto built in the center of the garden.

Her hair was a brilliant red and cut in a short, spiky style that gave her the look of a pixie. Her eyes were a pure black, although they were missing the malicious cunning she expected of a Jinn.

In fact, they were filled with a gentle kindness that instantly melted the last of Rya's lingering concern.

"Ah," the female murmured, stepping next to Levet. "You must be Rya. You're just as beautiful as Levet said," she said.

Rya smiled. "And you're Laylah," she murmured. "I've never met a half-Jinn before."

"Then we're even," Laylah admitted with a dimpled smile. "I've never met a half-dragon."

"You see, *ma belle*, I told you that you would adore her, did I not?" Levet asked Rya with a smug smile.

"Yes. And I hope very much that we'll have time later to get to know one another. But for now…"

She allowed her words to trail away, thankful when Laylah instantly took the hint.

"I get it," the pretty Jinn murmured. "You're concerned for your mother."

Rya nodded. "The space where she's trapped is unstable. I don't know how long she has left." She swallowed the lump that threatened to form in her throat. "Can you open a gateway?"

"I can try," Laylah assured her, a hint of warning in her voice. "But to find her I'll need something that can connect me to her."

Rya grimaced. Levet hadn't mentioned that she would need to bring something with her that belonged to her mother.

"Like a personal possession?" she demanded, her mind already trying to sort through various items that she might have in her lair that had once belonged to Kai.

Laylah brought a swift end to her musings. "It has to

be more intimate than that." With a rueful smile, the female reached into the pocket of the light jacket she was wearing to reveal a small ceremonial knife with a gold handle and what looked like a bone blade. "I'll need your blood."

Accepting the cost to find her mother, Rya was holding out her arm when she was abruptly shoved aside so Torque could stand in front of her. At the same time there was a blur of movement from the grotto and a male was standing next to Laylah, his lips pulled back to reveal his elongated fangs.

A vampire.

Rya studied the elegant features that hinted at Polynesian ancestors. His eyes were a rich shade of honey and his inky black hair had been shaved on the sides, leaving the top to form a mohawk that fell past his broad shoulders.

This had to be Tane. Laylah's vampire mate.

Distracted by her brief interest in the male who had the courage to mate with a Jinn, even a half-breed Jinn, it took Rya a second to recognize the danger brewing in the air.

As if the flames suddenly dancing over Torque's body and the blast of icy power that came from the vampire weren't warning enough.

The two male predators were ready to fight.

To the death, if necessary.

"Sacre bleu." Levet lifted his arms, his tail twitching. "Someone stop them."

Laylah sent her snarling vampire a small glare before glancing toward Rya with a rueful smile. "I just need a drop or two, I swear."

With a nod, Rya moved to stand directly in front of Torque, her hand lightly touching his chest despite the flames that seared over her fingers.

Thank the goddess she was part dragon.

"Torque, she's not going to hurt me."

He narrowed his gaze that remained sharply focused on the vampire. "You're damned straight she's not going to hurt you. And neither is anyone else."

She shook her head. "She just needs a drop or two."

"No—"

"Please," she interrupted in soft tones. "This is for my mother."

Tension continued to sizzle in the air, but with a low curse, Torque shoved out his hand. "I'll do it," he said, waiting for Laylah to offer him the knife.

Then, with blatant reluctance, he used the very end of the blade to prick her finger. Blood instantly welled, and Laylah reached out to brush her palm against the tiny wound.

Once her skin was stained with the blood, the Jinn turned toward the side of the garden, holding her arm straight out in front of her.

There was a rush of wind circling around them like a cyclone as Laylah released her power. Rya felt Torque wrap an arm around her waist as her hair was tugged from its braid.

Yow.

The female packed some serious mojo.

At last the wind eased and Laylah stepped back, revealing the narrow portal she'd just created.

"This should lead you to her," she murmured, a hint of weariness in her voice. Instantly her mate was at her side, his honey gaze regarding them with impatience. He was clearly eager to take his mate back to the safety of their lair.

Rya sent the pretty female a smile of gratitude. "I don't know how to thank you."

Laylah waved aside her thanks, her expression troubled. "Be careful," she warned. "It's very close to collapse."

Rya nodded before she was darting forward and entering the portal. She didn't need her mother's visions to know that Torque was going to try and convince her this was a bad idea.

The sooner she could get in and start the search, the better.

There was a blast of heat behind her and Torque followed her through the opening.

"Shit," he muttered. "I have a very bad sense of déjà vu."

CHAPTER EIGHTEEN

Finn shivered as he came to a halt. He was a frost sprite, but even he wasn't immune to the brutal cold that would kill many demons. Holding Adair tightly in his arms, he was thankful the young Sylvermyst had passed out.

Not just because she would have been in misery from the chill. But he could actually feel the space shrinking around them.

"Kai," he muttered, watching the Shinto female come to a stop a few feet away.

She grimaced. "I know." She lifted her hand, as if pressing against the walls that were closing in. "We don't have long."

He felt a bitter stab of frustration.

He'd had always understood that death could happen, even for an immortal. And that his role as prince meant he had to be willing to sacrifice himself for his people.

But the thought of the fragile woman in his arms dying was impossible to accept.

"You still can't make contact with anyone?" he demanded.

A stupid question. If Kai could have found a way to reach out for help, she would have.

The older demon shook her head. "The dimension is beginning to drift in time," she said. "It's impossible to make a telepathic connection."

The ground trembled. At the same time the pressure in the air crushed against them.

"It's not only drifting," he muttered.

Kai's serene expression tightened with an unease she couldn't entirely disguise.

"Without the dragon it will soon disappear completely," she muttered.

Adair stirred in his arms. Had she heard the Shinto's dire prediction?

"Finn?" she breathed, her face tinted blue as a thin layer of frost covered her skin.

"Shh." He bent his head to press his lips to her forehead. "It's going to be fine."

Her lashes fluttered, as if she was struggling to regain consciousness. Then, with a faint sigh, she thankfully sank back into her protective sleep.

"Is there anything we can do?" he asked in a low voice.

Kai gave a regretful shake of her head. "No. I'm sorry." The older fey suddenly jerked her head to the side. Had a noise startled her? "Did you feel that?"

Finn frowned. Had the stress at last gotten to the female? There was nothing to feel but the increasingly painful pressure.

Wait.

There was something.

A tiny surge of hope raced through him as he

belatedly sensed the…breeze? There was no other way to explain the stir in the frigid air.

"What's happening?" he demanded.

"Someone's trying to open a portal."

Relief pounded through him. They hadn't been abandoned. *Thank the goddess.*

He tried to reach out with his magic, only to be thwarted by the mist. "Is it the dragon?"

She gave a slow shake of her head, something that might have been surprise rippling over her face. "Jinn."

Finn's relief dimmed. What was that old saying? 'From the frying pan into the fire?'

It wasn't something a frost sprite usually had to worry about.

"Oh hell," he rasped. "Is it hunting us?"

Kai tilted her head to the side. "I don't think so. It's not entering the portal," she said in distracted tones. Then a brilliant smile curved her lips. "Oh. It's Rya."

"Rya?" He would have jumped for joy if it wouldn't have disturbed the female in his arms. "She found us."

"Yes." The word barely had time to leave her lips before there was a shudder beneath their feet and the mist closed in even tighter. Kai hissed in pain. "Let's hope it's not too late."

"Shit," Finn muttered, refusing to believe they could be squashed when they were so close to escape.

Kai glanced around. "We need to stabilize the space. Do you have any ideas?"

Did he? Finn sucked in a deep breath, trying to use his magic to reach out to Rya. He could feel the portal. He could even latch onto it for a brief moment. But the rippling movement of the dimension made it impossible for him to breach an opening.

Which meant he couldn't get them closer to Rya.

He had to keep them alive until she could reach them.

Easier said than done.

He glanced toward his companion. "Can you clear the mist around us?"

The female gave a slow nod, her brow furrowed. "Yes, but that won't help us."

"Do it," he commanded. He didn't have time to explain that the mist was a distraction.

She lifted her hand, discharging a burst of magic. "Do you have a plan?"

Continuing to hold Adair in his arms, he lowered himself to his knees.

"I can use my magic to create a bubble of ice," he said.

Pushing back the mist so they were standing in a circular clearing, Kai lowered herself next to him. "It won't last for long."

"Hopefully we'll only need a few minutes," he muttered. "Hold still."

Releasing his magic in a fierce burst, he created a dome of thick ice to surround them. For a second there was a blissful respite from the crushing pressure. But even as Finn took in a deep breath, there was a series of pops as the ice began to fracture.

They would have only moments before it collapsed.

"Let's hope they hurry," Kai muttered.

Finn glanced down at the unconscious Adair. "No shit."

***

Rya grimaced. Any hope that they could step into the portal and discover her mother standing directly in front of them was instantly destroyed.

Instead they walked straight back into the unnerving mist.

Crap.

With an effort, she tried to ignore the voice in the back of her head that screamed at her to run out of the portal and never look back.

It was even worse than when they'd been lost in the creepy fog the first time.

Now the squeezing heaviness was nearly unbearable.

No. Not nearly. It *was* unbearable.

And cold. Soul-crushingly cold.

"Rya," Torque rasped from behind her. "We can't bear this for long."

"I know," she muttered, her heart giving a tiny jump as she caught the scent of her mother. "She's this way."

"Are you sure?" he demanded as she darted at an angle through the fog.

"Yes," she assured him. "She's not far."

Torque moved until he was at her side, wrapping them both in the heat of his dragon.

"I smell a sprite," he said, his eyes glowing.

She gave an absent nod. "Finn," she said, her pace never slowing.

"And…" Torque sucked in a harsh breath. "Sylvermyst. Be careful." He reached to touch her arm. "They already released a crazed dragon. Who knows what else they might do."

Rya shivered. The fear of the dimension collapsing was bad enough without adding in the fear that there were dangerous Sylvermyst lurking in the mist.

Trying to distract herself, she concentrated on the only good thing that had come out of their first trip into this miserable space.

"She wasn't actually crazed," she said.

"What?"

"The dragon. Blayze wasn't crazy."

Realizing he'd just insulted her sister, Torque sent her a rueful glance.

"You're right. I'm sorry."

She shrugged. She couldn't blame Torque for his less than stellar opinion of Blayze.

Trying to kill someone didn't make the best first impression.

"It's still hard to believe that my father had a true mate." She altered her course as the ground moved beneath them, keeping her senses fixed on her mother's scent. They were getting closer. Even if it did feel as if they were struggling through molasses. "It seems so out of character."

Perhaps realizing that she needed to keep her mind off the danger that surrounded them, Torque gave a short laugh.

"Yeah, he's not really a romantic sort of male."

Her lips twitched. She'd heard her father described as a beast and a savage and a ruthless predator.

But never, ever as a romantic.

Then her amusement faded as she remembered the achingly terrible loss he'd suffered. Was it any wonder he'd become so vicious?

"It must have devastated him to lose his mate and daughter," she said.

"True." The sapphire eyes darkened. "I never thought I would say this, but I actually feel sorry for the ill-tempered brute. I don't know how he endured the pain."

Neither did Rya. And worse, she hadn't even realized the burden he carried.

"Hopefully my mother can keep Blayze asleep long enough for them to find a way to break her curse."

"It doesn't bother you?"

She turned her head to meet Torque's curious gaze. "The curse?"

"Your father's happiness in discovering his full-blooded daughter," he clarified.

She was baffled by the question. How could she be

anything but overjoyed for Synge?

"Of course not," she breathed. "I'm delighted he has Ravel and Blayze back in his life. Plus, I have a new sister." She wrinkled her nose. "Or at least I will once the curse is broken."

Torque reached to run a finger down her cheek. "You're an amazing female."

She shook her head. As a half-breed she'd been treated with far more care than most.

In truth, she'd been pampered and adored her entire life.

"Not really. I accept that Blayze will hold a special place in Synge's heart, but that doesn't mean he doesn't love me," she said, sending Torque a smile. "And now I have you. That's all I need."

Fire smoldered in his eyes. "True."

She turned back toward the swirling mist. It was becoming almost impossible to breathe as the compression nearly took her to her knees.

Time for another distraction.

"Do you have any siblings?"

"Hundreds." He shrugged. "Possibly thousands."

The number wasn't shocking. Dragons were capable of impregnating a wide variety of demons. And most males kept vast harems filled with willing females.

But she hadn't missed the disdain in Torque's voice when he spoke of his father.

"Pyre wasn't very paternal?"

Torque snorted. "As far as Pyre is concerned, his children are nothing more than assets to be bartered to the highest bidder."

She reached to grasp his hand. Instantly his warmth jolted up her arm, arrowing straight for her heart.

"I'm sorry," she murmured.

Anger simmered deep inside her. Torque had been shortchanged when it came to family. His mother had done a disappearing act, and his father was a typical dragon.

But that was all about to change. She intended to offer him all the love he could possibly need.

Clearly reading her mind, he sent her a rare smile. "I'm not. If my father wasn't a greedy bastard, he wouldn't have given me to Synge and your mother might not have had her vision." He squeezed her fingers. "We would never have become betrothed."

Rya shook her head. She'd wasted so much time resenting her mother's vision. Now she couldn't imagine a future without Torque.

"Fate works in mysterious ways," she murmured.

Torque's smile faded to a grimace as he gave a low grunt of pain. Every step was a misery.

"Rya." He tried to pull her to a halt. "We have to go back."

"No." She pointed toward the thinning mist. "They're right there."

Yanking free of his grasp, she stepped through the edge of the mist to discover Kai bending near the ground along with Finn and an unknown female cradled in his arms. The three of them were covered by a thin dome of ice. Or at least they were until it abruptly shattered in a spray of frost.

Rya rushed forward, wrapping her arms around her mother as soon as the older woman managed to rise to her feet. "Oh, thank the goddess," she breathed.

"Rya." Her mother fiercely returned her hug.

"I was so worried," Rya muttered, pulling back to study her mother's pale face.

She couldn't see any visual injuries, but that didn't mean she wasn't hurt.

Kai reached up to pat her cheek. "I'm fine, but we need to get out of here."

"My thought exactly," Torque muttered.

Kai glanced toward the prince of frost sprites as he straightened, the pretty young fey tightly clutched in his arms. “Finn, you go first with Adair.”

Torque scowled. “You’re taking the Sylvermyst?”

Finn instantly bristled, a fine cloud of frost swirling through the air. “Do you have a problem with that?”

Rya arched a startled brow. *Hmm.* She’d seen Finn flirt with every female in his vicinity. Including herself. It was never serious.

But this time…

He was clearly territorial when it came to his Sylvermyst.

“Did you forget it was the dark fey who trapped us here in the first place?” Torque demanded.

Finn stepped forward, and Rya swiftly moved to stand between the two males. *Yeesh.* Could two alphas ever be in the same space without trying to start a fight?

She laid her hand on Torque’s chest. “Later,” she murmured softly.

Fire smoldered in his eyes, but he gave a grudging nod of his head. “Fine.”

Thankfully, the frost sprite was smart enough not to press the issue, and with a nod toward Rya, he darted through the mist, following the trail they’d created to the waiting portal.

“Mother, you next,” she said.

The older woman briefly hesitated, but no doubt sensed that Rya wasn’t going to budge. With a kiss on Rya’s cheek she disappeared into the mist.

“Let’s go,” Torque muttered, grabbing her hand to follow the others.

Moving as fast as the thick fog would allow, they concentrated on putting one foot in front of the other. A task that was becoming increasingly difficult.

Up ahead she could sense when Finn managed to escape through the portal. And then her mother.

They were only steps away when there was a violent quake that sent them both sprawling onto the spongy ground. Torque cursed, jumping back to his feet and pulling her up beside him.

But the momentary delay was too much.

Even as they stepped forward, the portal collapsed with explosive force.

CHAPTER NINETEEN

Torque cursed, wrapping his arms around Rya as the floor shuddered and the mist tightened around them like a vise.

The air was being crushed from his lungs, even as his bones began to throb. Soon they would begin to snap beneath the pressure.

It was agonizing.

And promised to get worse.

"We're trapped," Rya choked out, burying her face against his chest.

He absently ran his hand over her hair. "I've got you," he muttered in distracted tones. He was desperately trying to come up with a plan of escape.

"I'm sorry." She wound her arms around his waist, tears trickling down her cheek. "I should have insisted on coming here alone."

He surrounded them in his fire. He couldn't halt the

crushing compression, but he could damned well battle back the lethal cold.

"Yeah, like that was ever going to happen," he muttered.

She sniffed. "This was my duty, not yours."

He kept his expression stoic even as pain sliced through his heart.

She was already blaming herself. He wasn't about to add to her misery.

"We're partners now." He insisted. "Right?"

She shivered, her fiery spirit muted by the mist. "I don't want you hurt."

"Rya." He cupped her chin in his hand, tilting back her head so he could capture her gaze. "I would rather die holding you in my arms than live an eternity without you."

The amber eyes darkened, and with a choked sound she pressed her head back against his chest. With a sigh, Torque rested his cheek on top of her head.

He hadn't lied. If he had to face death, he wanted to do it with Rya in his arms.

And if he had any true regret, it was the fact that he'd never found his mother.

He should never have allowed his hurt pride to keep him from searching for her.

So much time wasted…

Lost in his dark thoughts, he absently noticed the tiny sparks that suddenly began to dance in the air.

Was the ruthless pain making him hallucinate?

Lifting his head, he tried to think past the sensation of being flattened into a pancake.

More sparks gathered, moving to whirl directly in front of his face before dancing away.

What the hell?

"Torque," Rya muttered, her gaze locked on the tiny bits of fire.

"I see them," he assured her.

"Are you doing that?"

Torque frowned. Was he?

It was possible he was losing control of his magic.

"Not intentionally," he said, then gave a shake of his head as the sparks danced away. If it was his power, they wouldn't be traveling farther into the mist. He barely had enough strength left to stand upright. "No, it's not mine."

She pulled back, her face strained from the torturous pressure.

"I think they want us to follow."

Torque was getting the same feeling. Still, he wasn't super excited to be led deeper into the fog that was killing them.

"I'm not sure we should trust strange sparks of light that appear out of nowhere."

She sent him a startled glance. "What's the option?"

Okay. She had a point.

"Fine," he muttered, "but stay—"

"I know," she interrupted. "Stay behind you."

"You're learning," he said, savoring the heat that warmed her amber eyes.

He hated the sight of her defeated. This was the fiery mate he loved.

"Careful, dragon," she warned.

Brushing a soft kiss across her furrowed brow, he grabbed her hand. Then, turning, he forced his heavy feet to follow the sparks that looked like they were quivering with impatience.

One step. Two. Each more difficult than the next. Only the refusal to allow Rya to give up kept him battling through the pain.

He didn't know how far they traveled. The mist and the pain clouded his senses. But he did have enough awareness to feel when the mist began to part, and the brutal pain eased.

"It feels different," Rya said, her voice shaky with relief.

On cue the fog disappeared, leaving them in a thick darkness.

"Stop," Torque muttered.

They were out of the collapsing dimension, but as the sparks swirled around them faster and faster, he sensed them being pulled into an opening portal.

Shit. Holding Rya's hand in a tight grip, Torque felt them being ripped out of the darkness. Seconds later they dropped through the air to land on a rough stone floor.

Jolted by the impact, Torque fell to his knees, barely managing to catch Rya in his arms.

Holding her against his chest, he cast a swift glance around.

Not that there was much to see.

Stone floor. Stone walls. A low ceiling. And a steel door with a small slit.

"Where are we?" Rya asked, pulling out of his arms to study their cramped surroundings.

"I don't know," Torque admitted, slowly rising. A stab of relief shot through him as the stone beneath his feet remained stationary. "At least it feels solid."

"And warm," Rya muttered, pushing herself upright.

Torque slowly nodded. He'd been so focused on the fact they were no longer about to be squashed like bugs, he hadn't really paid attention to the heat that radiated through the stone.

"Really warm," he muttered, his inner dragon purring in pleasure, along with…

Hmm. He wasn't sure.

But a part of him tingled with a glorious sense of power he'd never felt before.

Baffled by the sensation, he crossed the short

distance to grab the doorknob. They needed to discover where they were. And just as importantly, who'd brought them there.

Giving the handle a turn, he wasn't at all surprised when it wouldn't budge.

"Locked?" Rya demanded.

He rolled his eyes. "Of course it is." Debating whether or not to risk pissing off their captors by trying to break down the door, he stiffened. "Someone's coming," he said in harsh tones.

Rya moved to stand at his side. "I smell…" She wrinkled her nose. "Lava?"

Torque blinked in surprise. She was right. It was lava.

So. Was the scent coming from a nearby volcano or the approaching stranger?

Maybe both.

Leaning forward, Torque peered through the small slit in the door. Outside their cramped cell he could see more stone. Floor. Walls. Ceiling. As if a tunnel had been carved into a mountain.

His attention, however, was captured by the sight of a short female with her dark hair pulled into a knot at the nape of her neck and her broad form covered by a simple brown robe.

Torque stepped back, ensuring that he was standing between the door and Rya. The female looked harmless enough, but he wasn't taking any chances.

Not after all they'd managed to survive.

There was the scrape of metal against metal. As if the female was sliding a key into the lock. Then, slowly, the door opened.

Torque winced at the loud creak. Hell, how long had it been since the door had been used?

Stepping into the cell, the female regarded them with a pleased smile.

"Ah, you're awake," she murmured.

Torque exchanged a puzzled glance with Rya. The stranger was fey, although he wasn't sure if she was fairy or sprite or imp. And old enough to have gained a look of maturity in her round face.

It was the seemingly genuine joy in her dark eyes that was confusing.

Usually people who were happy to see you didn't lock you in a cell.

"Why have you imprisoned us?"

The female blinked, as if startled by the question. "It was for your own protection."

Torque scowled. "Protection?"

"Truly." The fey waved a hand toward the open door. "This lair is shielded by runes that would have killed the Shinto," she explained. "This is the only place we could bring her that she wouldn't be injured."

There was a sincerity in the female's voice that was hard to dismiss.

Instead, Torque sent a suspicious glance toward the tunnel outside the cell. "What is this place?"

"Tofua," the female answered without hesitation. "The primary home of the fire imps."

"Fire imps," Rya breathed. "You're home."

Torque released a slow breath. Home. Was that why he felt the tingle of power?

He gave a faint shake of his head. Until he was certain they were safe, he wasn't going to be distracted.

"Who are you?"

"I am Dasi." The female pressed her hands together and offered him a deep bow. "One of your mother's handmaidens."

The breath was yanked from his lungs.

Being told this was the lair of his people was one thing.

To think his missing mother was nearby was…

Hell, he didn't know what it was.

"She's here?" he rasped.

As if sensing he was struggling against the unexpected flood of emotion, Rya moved to wrap her arm around his waist. Her touch instantly grounded him.

"Yes, indeed." The female gave a bob of her head. "She would have come to speak with you herself but she collapsed after she released her spell to bring you to this lair."

"Oh," Rya breathed, instantly concerned. Sometimes it was hard for Torque to believe his betrothed could be half dragon. Her heart was far too tender. "She isn't hurt, is she?"

"No, just weary," the servant assured them, her glance resting on Torque's face. "She is already asking to see you."

Torque hesitated. He wasn't entirely sure he was ready for the meeting. After so many years of convincing himself he didn't need or want a mother, it was instinctive to deny any desire to meet her.

Then sanity returned and he was fiercely shoving aside his cowardly reluctance.

Dammit. Just moments ago he'd thought he might die without ever knowing his mother.

Now he wasn't sure it was the right time?

Stress was truly making him nutty.

"Very well."

Placing his arm around Rya's shoulders, he stepped forward only to halt when the servant held up a slender hand.

"I'm afraid the Shinto can't come."

Torque's brows snapped together. "Why?"

Dasi gave a helpless lift of her hands. "As I said, the runes would kill her."

Torque's suspicion wasn't entirely eased. They were in a strange place, surrounded by strange people. The last thing he wanted was to be separated from Rya.

"I'm not leaving her alone."

"I assure you that she is quite safe," Dasi said, her expression pleading.

"No."

"Torque." Rya moved until she was standing directly in front of him. Lifting her hand, she placed it over his heart. "I'll be fine."

"You don't know that."

She narrowed her eyes. "I believe we've already had this discussion."

"What discussion?"

"Whether or not I'm capable of protecting myself."

Torque snorted. He didn't remember a discussion.

More of an ongoing 'agree to disagree' sort of thing.

Glancing toward the waiting servant, he returned his gaze to Rya's upturned face. "We don't know why we've been brought here."

"Obviously your mother saved our lives and now she wants to speak with her son." She gave him a small push toward the door. "Go."

He wasn't nearly so confident it was that simple.

They'd been in constant danger since going in search of Kai. Why would his mother choose that particular moment to save them?

Still, they were currently trapped in the cell.

Did he really have any choice?

"I won't be gone long," he promised, lowering his head to plant a soft, lingering kiss on her mouth. Then, reluctantly stepping away from his betrothed, he turned toward the handmaiden. "Take me to her."

Dasi nodded before glancing at Rya. "I'll leave the door open, but please don't try to leave this room," she murmured. "I'll send a tray of food."

With a swish of her robes against the stone floor, the female led him into the long tunnel.

The heat increased as they climbed down a narrow flight of stairs. They paused as Dasi opened another steel door, then they were stepping into a massive cave that was bustling with people.

Torque arched his brows as they moved across the floor that'd been worn smooth by centuries of footsteps. The ceiling of the cave was high enough to be lost in the shadows while the edges were lined with shallow alcoves that had been dug into the stone walls. Inside the alcoves were a wide variety of items.

Food. Delicate ornaments. Clothing. Even small pieces of furniture.

A market?

His attention turned toward the slender creatures who were dressed in loose linen clothing that blended into the gray stone. Their hair was dark and their skin pale. Torque was betting they didn't get a lot of sunlight.

And clearly they didn't have a lot of visitors.

Probably because they had the damned place covered with runes that would kill strangers.

Trying to ignore the blatant stares and deep bows as he passed, he kept pace next to Dasi.

"How many fire imps live here?" he asked in low tones.

"Fewer than one hundred now," the female said, leading him toward an opening on the other side of the market. "Over the past centuries it has become increasingly rare to produce children. Which is why your mother—"

Torque glanced toward his companion as she bit off her words.

"What about my mother?"

She gave a sharp shake of her head, looking annoyed with herself.

"I'm sorry. That is her story to tell."

There was more bowing as they passed a long table

where several males were eating what looked like a hearty stew.

“Is everyone always so polite?”

Dasi shrugged. “They’ve waited a very long time to catch a glimpse of you.”

Growingly confused, Torque gave a faint shake of his head. Before he could continue his questions, however, they left the open space and headed down another flight of stairs carved in the stone.

A smothering heat wrapped around him even as the scent of lava became more pronounced.

They were definitely in a volcano. And they were nearing the center.

Stepping into a small space, Dasi waved a hand toward the opening just ahead of them.

“She’s through there.”

He offered her a small dip of his head. “Thanks.”

Taking a step forward, he was abruptly halted by the sound of his name.

“Torque.”

He glanced back at Dasi. “Yes?”

“She’s sacrificed a great deal for our people,” the handmaiden told him, her expression pleading. “Be kind to her.”

Before he could demand to know what she was talking about, Dasi turned to scurry back up the stairs. Torque heaved a sigh.

He felt like he was walking into the middle of a drama he knew nothing about. Ironic, considering he’d spent most of his life avoiding messy emotions.

Squaring his shoulders, he moved to enter the connected cave.

He hated being parted from Rya.

He needed to convince his mother to release them so they could return to the safety of his lair.

Stepping through the arched entrance, he glanced

around the walls that were painted with pretty murals of sunlit meadows. On the floor was a woven rug and above was a heavy chandelier where a dozen candles were burning.

The furniture was delicately carved from wood, with bright yellow cushions tossed on the chairs and low couch.

It looked like whoever lived there had tried to create an impression of sunshine despite the fact they were buried beneath tons of earth.

"Torque," a female voice called from an attached chamber.

Torque crossed the carpet and cautiously stepped through the arched opening into the smaller but just as brightly decorated room.

Even the ceiling was covered in vibrant murals of dew fairies dancing beneath a clear blue sky.

At last his gaze moved to the huge bed in the center of the space. His heart missed a beat as he took in the slender female who was settled among a pile of pillows in the center of the mattress.

Like the other fire imps he'd seen, she had glossy black hair that she had pulled into a complicated knot on top of her head. Her skin was pale and her features delicately carved. Her eyes, however, were a startling blue.

Just like his.

The realization made the floor tilt beneath his feet.

Not an earthquake. Just a stunning acceptance that this was the woman who'd given birth to him.

He cleared his throat of the strange lump that was threatening to form.

"I assume you must be my mother?"

A smile curled her lips as she lifted a shaky hand to wave him closer to the bed. "Yes. I'm Nalani."

He frowned, belatedly noting the shadows beneath

her eyes.

"Are you unwell?"

"Just exhausted from the spell," she assured him even as her hand dropped back to the yellow blanket that covered her. "I haven't had to use that much magic in a very long time."

Torque felt a pang of guilt. Whatever his complicated feelings toward this female, she had rescued them from a very painful death.

He gave a low bow. "I should thank you for saving us," he murmured.

She waited for him to straighten, her shrewd gaze easily reading his wariness.

"But you don't trust my motives for doing so?"

Torque shrugged. There was no point in lying.

"Not really."

She gave a slow nod, a hint of yearning in her brilliant blue eyes.

"You can't imagine how many years I've longed for this moment," she murmured.

He flinched. Her words touched a raw nerve. Well, maybe 'touched' wasn't the right word.

More like yanked off a scab and poured salt into the wound.

"You're right," he said, his voice harsh. "I can't imagine how you've longed to see me, considering that you've never made the slightest effort to acknowledge me as your son."

She gasped, as if he'd physically struck her. Then a dark flush stained her cheeks.

"Damn that dragon," she growled.

CHAPTER TWENTY

Torque blinked, catching the unmistakable scent of lava as tiny sparks danced in the air.

Clearly he wasn't the only one with raw nerves.

He studied her angry expression with a small frown. "Excuse me?"

She sucked in a deep breath, visibly attempting to control her burst of temper. "Would you sit down?"

"Why?"

"It's difficult to see your face," she explained. "You're quite large for a fire imp."

He lifted his shoulder. He still hadn't really processed the fact that he now knew his heritage. Hell, he didn't even know what it meant to be a fire imp.

"That's because I'm a dragon," he stubbornly muttered.

"Not entirely." She sent him a pleading glance. "Please, my son. I can explain everything."

He released his breath with a low hiss. Rya would tell him that he was being ridiculous.

And he was.

Slowly he moved forward, perching on the edge of the mattress. "Is this better?"

"Much better." She reached out, as if she wanted to touch him. Then with a grimace she hastily pulled her hand back. He felt a stab of regret that he was making her feel wary, but he couldn't lower his barriers until he knew why she'd abandoned him. "Thank you."

"You said you would explain," he reminded her.

She nodded, resting back against the pillows. "First I should tell you a bit of our history."

"Keep it short," Torque commanded, grimacing as he watched her eyes darken with pain. *Dammit.* He was a warrior. He was good at killing things. But the emotional crap? Not so good. "I'm worried about Rya," he forced himself to explain.

"Ah." Her expression instantly brightened. "The Shinto who was with you."

"My betrothed," he revealed with pride.

"Then I understand your impatience," she murmured. "In short, the fire imps have always depended on volcanoes to provide us protection, warmth, and magic." She grimaced, glancing around the room. "Unfortunately, that means we're unable to travel from our lairs for more than few weeks. At least not without severe anguish."

Torque studied her, recalling Dasi's warning that his mother had been forced to sacrifice for her people.

"Like you suffered?" he demanded.

"Yes."

He felt a surprising pang of distress at the thought of this woman being in pain.

"Then why leave your lair?"

"I had no choice," she said. "Over the past few

centuries our tribe has found it increasingly difficult to produce offspring. And the few that were born have all been females."

"Why?"

"We're not entirely sure, although it could be a product of centuries of inbreeding."

Torque nodded. It was a problem with those fey who demanded 'purity' in their bloodlines, as well as those tribes who were too isolated to encourage mating with outsiders.

"We desperately needed a male, so it was decided we must seek help to revive our fading magic," his mother continued.

Torque wrinkled his nose. He didn't have to ask his mother to explain. By 'help' she meant 'sperm donor.'

"Why dragons?" he instead demanded.

"They're known to produce more male children than female."

"True," he said. That was one of the reasons Synge had to have been so overjoyed to have Blayze returned. She was quite likely his only pureblooded daughter.

"Plus we hoped the dragon-magic would give our future children the advantage of not being so dependent on the magic of the volcanoes," she continued.

His lips twisted. His father had used him to pay a debt. Synge had used him to reclaim his lost treasure. And now it seemed the fire imps hoped to use him as a breeding machine.

"I suppose that makes sense," he muttered.

"It did, but I foolishly didn't take into account the treachery of dragons." The blue eyes widened as his mother belatedly remembered he was half dragon. "Oh. Sorry."

"Don't apologize. It's a fair assessment of most dragons," he said wryly. "How did you end up with my father?"

"I sent out my offer to several dragons, but only Pyre responded."

Hmm. If his father responded, it was because he'd already figured out a way to take advantage of the fire imps.

"What was the offer?"

"A treasure chest of diamonds for impregnating me with a son."

He flinched at her blunt words. "That's very…"

"I know, but we had to do something," she said as his words trailed away. Then, gathering her courage, she reached out to place her hand lightly against his arm. "And please don't think for even a second that I just wanted a child to help my people. I truly, truly ached for my own baby." Tears glistened in her eyes. "I loved you from the moment I felt you spark to life."

An unwanted emotion tugged at his heart. Her regret felt so sincere.

"So why leave me?" He asked the question that had haunted him for centuries.

"It wasn't my decision." The sparks returned, swirling around the bed as his mother clenched her hands into tight fists. "The contract stated that you were to leave with me as soon as you were born, but Pyre refused to let you go." An aching sadness softened her features. "By that time, I was too weak to fight. I had no choice but to return to this lair."

Torque ground his teeth together. He should have suspected that his father was responsible. The cunning old bastard had devoted endless centuries to taking advantage of gullible demons.

That's when he wasn't using his brute strength to get his way.

"He lied," he said in flat tones.

"Yes." His mother shook her head in self-disgust. "I should have suspected he intended to break his promise when he demanded that I remain at his lair during my pregnancy."

Torque glanced down at the slender hand that was lying on his arm, and tried to shuffle through his various emotions.

Relief that this female hadn't purposely walked away from him. Anger that Pyre was such a greedy beast. And a lingering hurt that refused to be dismissed.

"I find it easy to believe my father would have cheated you. I was a valuable addition to his hoard," he said in dry tones. "I even understand your need to return to your lair…" His words faltered as he belatedly realized he was revealing a vulnerability he'd kept hidden since he'd been bartered to Synge. He forced himself to continue. "But I've been away from my father for a very long time." He had to know the truth. "Why didn't you try to contact me?"

Her eyes widened in confusion. "I did."

Torque shook his head. "I wasn't hard to find."

She gave his arm a light squeeze. "I swear, I tried to reach out, but you always blocked me," she told him. "Eventually I realized it wasn't fair to keep troubling you if you were so reluctant to make contact."

"I—" Torque snapped his lips together. As much as he wanted to deny her claim that she'd tried to reach out to him, he suddenly remembered all the times the thought of his mother would pop into his mind, only to have him firmly shove it aside. Now he felt a stab of remorse. "I didn't realize that was what I was doing."

She waved aside his apology. "It wasn't until you reached out to me when you were in danger that I was able to make a connection."

He allowed his hand to gently cover her fingers that rested on his arm, holding her gaze.

"I'm glad you did," he murmured softly.

"Me too." She blinked back tears. "More than you'll

ever know."

***

Rya was trying to be patient.

Not her best talent.

Okay, it was at the very bottom of the list of her talents.

Still, she did her best not to let her imagination run away as she paced the stone floor and counted the passing minutes.

Even when she found it impossible to send a telepathic message to her mother. Or even Torque.

Everything was fine. More than fine.

She'd escaped near-death. Her betrothed was about to formally mate with her. And she was going to have the family she always desired.

Even more important, Torque had the opportunity to heal the wounds of his past.

What could be better?

Clinging to her optimistic thoughts, she was caught off guard when she felt a sudden tingle of magic.

Coming to a halt in the center of the cell, she turned in a slow circle.

"Hello?" She held out her hand, trying to pinpoint the source of the magic. "Is someone there?"

There was another tingle before the scent of granite filled the cell. Then, seeming to step out of midair, a tiny gargoyle suddenly appeared.

Giving a flap of his fairy wings, the demon offered her a broad smile.

"Ah, *ma belle*," he murmured. "There you are."

Rya blinked in surprise. "Levet?"

The gargoyle took a step toward her, his claws scraping against the stone floor.

"You cannot imagine how difficult it has been to

locate you."

She gave a faint shake of her head. "How did you do it?"

"Your mother."

"Oh, she made it," Rya breathed, relief cascading through her. She'd refused to dwell on the fact that the portal might have collapsed while her mother was still inside, but she couldn't deny that there'd been a sliver of concern she couldn't entirely dismiss. "How is she?"

"She is fine," Levet assured her.

Wrapping her arms around her waist, Rya released a shaky breath.

"What about Finn?"

"Who?" Levet furrowed his brow before he gave a dismissive flap of his wings. "Ah. The frost sprite." He shrugged. "I believe he is well enough, although his tribe has not yet accepted his houseguest.

She lifted her brows. "He intends to keep the Sylvermyst?"

"It appears so," Levet said in bored tones. He clearly hadn't developed a warm and fuzzy relationship with the prince. "He claims she was a victim of her family. I believe she also helped to rescue his people."

Rya chuckled. She truly liked Finn, but she couldn't deny that she relished the thought of him having to fight for his female.

It would make him appreciate her.

"I hope she makes him happy," she said with complete sincerity.

"She no doubt will." Levet tilted his head to the side, as if considering the prince's future with his Sylvermyst. "So long as she does not kill him in his sleep."

Rya made a choked sound of shock. "Levet."

"She is a dark fey," he said with a faux innocence. "It is what they do."

Rya rolled her eyes. Finn's future wasn't her

concern. Instead, she turned her attention to more important matters.

"Did mother help Blayze yet?"

Levet surprisingly shook his head. *"Non."*

Rya stiffened, concern clenching her heart. "Is something wrong?"

Levet widened his gray eyes. "You were missing."

"I don't understand."

"Obviously, your mother has devoted her energy to locating you. She has not had the time or strength to concern herself with the dragon."

"Oh." Rya bit her lip.

"It took us a great deal of power to discover that you had managed to escape that nasty mist," Levet explained.

"Yes. That was…" She grimaced, the memory of how close they'd come to being squished by the hideous fog still capable of sending chills through her body. "Terrifying."

"And even more power to track you to this lair," he continued.

"I tried to reach out, but the area is protected by runes."

"Very potent ones." The gargoyle glanced toward the tunnel outside the open door. "I'm impressed."

Rya wasn't. She might logically comprehend the need to protect their lair, but it was aggravating that she was trapped in this cell.

"Where is Mother now?" she demanded, needing a distraction.

Levet gave an airy wave of his hand. "She collapsed after opening this portal."

Rya gasped. "Oh no," she breathed. "You said she was fine."

He continued to look remarkably unconcerned. Although it was hard to tell with his lumpy little features.

"It was just exhaustion," he said in soothing tones. "I promise she will soon recover, but she did not have the strength to come and find you." He puffed out his chest as he spread his wings. "So, of course, I volunteered. I am, after all, the official KISA."

Reassured, Rya allowed her lips to twitch with rueful humor. She'd never met an official Knight In Shining Armor before, but she was fairly certain this one was the most unique.

"Thank you," she murmured.

"It is what I do." Suitably pleased by Rya's gratitude, the gargoyle waved a hand toward the opening of the portal. "We should go. Your mother is waiting."

Rya gave a sharp shake of her head. "I can't leave without Torque."

"Why not?"

She rolled her eyes. "Because he's my betrothed."

"If he is your betrothed then should he not be here to protect you?"

"He's visiting with his mother."

Levet blinked in surprise. "He has a mother?"

"Everyone has a mother," she said, ignoring the fact that there were a few demons, including vampires, that didn't have mothers in the traditional sense.

Levet gave a flick of his tail. "I assumed he crawled from beneath a rock."

Rya sent her companion a chiding frown. "Be nice."

"I do not know why I should." Levet deliberately glanced around the empty space. "He has left you trapped in a cell while he is enjoying his resurrection."

She was briefly confused. *Resurrection?*

Then she realized what he meant.

"Reunion," she corrected before giving a small shake of her head. "Never mind. I can't leave the cell because of the runes."

Levet's lips parted, but before he could speak he was tilting back his head to sniff the air.

"Fire imps," he murmured.

"Yes."

He waddled toward the door, still sniffing the air. "I have never met one before," he muttered, his wings fluttering. "Oh la, la."

Rya frowned in confusion. "What is it?"

Levet moved to one side, and the reason for his sudden distraction strolled into the room carrying a tray.

The young female had dark hair that was pulled into a knot on top of her head. Her face was thin, with pale, delicate features, and she had eyes that were nearly as blue as Torque's.

A pretty young creature who had clearly bedazzled the gargoyle.

"I have brought your dinner." Her gaze shyly moved toward Levet. "I did not know that you had company or I would have brought another plate of food."

"Mon dieu," Levet breathed, his tail standing straight out behind him like he'd been struck by lightning. "Who are you?"

The female flushed, moving to set the tray on a shelf that was chiseled in the stone wall.

Then, slowly turning, she offered a tentative smile. "I am called Charda."

"Charda." Levet heaved a rasping sigh. "Beautiful."

The female's blush deepened. "Are you a gargoyle?"

"I am, indeed." Levet moved to stand directly in front of the imp. "Levet." He performed a bow. "At your service."

She blinked, either bemused or fascinated by the silly creature. It was tough to know which.

"Pretty wings," she at last murmured.

Levet turned to the side. "You may touch them if you wish."

"Levet," Rya chastised, watching as the young female began to inch her way toward the door.

He sent her a startled glance. "What?"

"Behave yourself."

With a tiny giggle, the imp abruptly dashed out of the cell. Of course, she did manage to send a glance of invitation over her shoulder before she disappeared down the tunnel.

Levet gave a click of his tongue. "See what you have done?"

"Me?"

"You frightened away the lovely imp," he said in reproaching tones, heading toward the door.

Rya conjured a mock frown. "Hey. I thought you were here to rescue me?"

The miniature demon shrugged. "I can multi-axe."

"Task," she corrected. "Multi-task."

His pace never slowed. "The portal is open. You are rescued."

Rya's amusement abruptly faded as she realized that Levet truly intended to leave the cell.

"Wait," she called out.

Levet came to a sharp halt, glancing over his shoulder to study her concerned expression. "What is wrong?"

"You can't go out there."

A wounded expression twisted his ugly features. "I will not harm the imps. I merely wish to become better acquainted with sweet Charda."

"I'm not afraid for the imps," she swiftly assured him. "I'm afraid for you. The runes are too dangerous."

"Ah." He waved aside her warning. "Do not fear, *ma belle*. I am a gargoyle. We are impervious to runes. Enjoy your dragon." With a last smile he was hurrying away, clearly on the hunt for his pretty imp.

Rya shook her head as she moved to inspect the tray.

There were several bowls of fresh fruit and vegetables, as well as a plate of roasted meat. Her mouth watered. No sense in letting the food go to waste.

Polishing off a bowl of pineapple as well as several slices of meat, she was nibbling on a carrot when a tidal wave of heat rushed through the air.

Torque.

Turning away from the tray, she watched as the gorgeous male stepped into the cell.

Instantly her dragon roared in satisfaction. Although she'd been pleased with the thought of Torque becoming acquainted with his mother, there'd been a part of her that had been unnerved to be parted from this male.

As if he felt the same sense of emptiness, Torque instantly crossed the floor to wrap her in his arms and brush a kiss over her welcoming lips.

"I thought I caught the scent of granite," he murmured as he lifted his head. "Is the gargoyle here?"

"Yes."

He gazed down at her upturned face, his expression baffled. "How did he get here?"

"My mother was concerned so she created a portal," she explained. "Levet came through to rescue us."

He grimaced. "Does your mother hate us?"

Her lips twitched. "He *is* a KISA."

Torque muttered his uncomplimentary opinion of the tiny gargoyle in his role as a hero. "Where was he going?"

"He was chasing after a young fire imp."

"I hope she singes him," he muttered.

Rya wrapped her arms around his neck. She didn't want to talk about Levet.

She was far more interested in her delicious soon-to-be mate.

"What about you?" she murmured.

He arched a brow. "Me?"

“Were there any pretty fire imps who caught your attention?” she teased, not really concerned.

The one thing she could trust in this world was Torque. He was utterly and completely loyal.

“None,” he said without hesitation, his arms tightening around her. “I am addicted to the scent of lotus blossoms.”

She went on her tiptoes to place a light kiss on his jaw.

“Did you see your mother?”

His eyes darkened, but it wasn’t pain. Instead it was a bittersweet regret.

“Yes.”

Her hand moved to cup his lean cheek. “And?”

“We can discuss it once we’re in my lair—” He gave a sudden shake of his head. “Not my lair. *Our* lair.”

She tried to read his expression. “At least tell me you listened to what she had to say.”

“I listened.” He flashed a teasing smile. “And even learned.”

She widened her eyes. “A miracle.”

He pressed his lips to her forehead before they skimmed down her cheek to the corner of her mouth.

“You are the miracle, my love,” he murmured in husky tones. “My mother is preparing a portal for us to leave. Let’s go home.”

“Oh.” Rya stiffened at the mention of a portal.

Torque narrowed his eyes, studying her apologetic expression.

“Hell. I’m not going to like this, am I?”

“I have to see my mother.” She gave a small shrug. “She used the last of her strength to create the portal.”

He heaved a resigned sigh. “Perhaps my father wasn’t completely wrong to barter off his family.”

She skimmed her hands down his neck and over his broad shoulders. Torque wasn’t the only one anxious to return to the privacy of his lair.

"Thankfully, you will be a much better father," she assured him in husky tones.

His eyes flared with sapphire fire. "I'm more interested in being a mate."

Pulling out of his arms, she grabbed his hand and tugged him toward the waiting portal.

"We have a whole eternity ahead of us."

He stroked a finger down the curve of her back, sending sparks of fire through her blood.

"Not long enough."

CHAPTER TWENTY-ONE

Torque had been a very good dragon.

Not only had he patiently escorted Rya to her mother's lair so she could assure herself that Kai was properly resting, but he'd actually waited until they were in the privacy of his lair before he'd torn off her clothes and ravished her.

Then, as a reward for his excellent behavior, he'd carried her to his bed, and allowed her to ravish him.

Now he held her tightly in his arms and nuzzled at her throat.

Eventually he would get up and make them something to eat, but for now he intended to enjoy a slow, thorough seduction that might very well take the entire day.

Nibbling a path of kisses down the curve of her neck, he pretended he didn't hear the sharp knock that echoed through the lair.

Beneath him, Rya stiffened. "Torque."

His lips traced the dragon marque that draped over the luscious curve of her breasts.

"Hmm?"

"There's someone at the door."

He released a small burst of fire that made her squirm with pleasure.

"Ignore them and they'll go away," he told her.

She gave a throaty laugh, her fingers combing through his hair.

"You always say that."

"Because it's true," he said.

Then the knocking stopped, only to be replaced by an explosive burst of power that rattled the bed and sucked the air out of the room.

Which meant that either a nuclear bomb had just been planted in his lair, or it was Baine on the other side of the door.

"Not when it's a pissed-off dragon," she muttered.

No shit.

Muttering beneath his breath, Torque reluctantly climbed out of bed and pulled on a pair of faded jeans.

"I've changed my mind," he said, his gaze captivated by the sight of Rya spread across his bed.

Her dark satin hair was spread over the pillows, her eyes smoldering with amber fire. She was sensual female temptation wrapped in glorious beauty.

Was it any wonder that he wanted to toss her over his shoulder and disappear in a puff of smoke?

"About what?" she demanded, covering her slender body with the sheet.

He barely resisted the urge to reach down and yank it back off.

Dammit. He'd just gotten her alone and naked.

He didn't want to be interrupted.

"I no longer want to live in this lair," he told her.

She lifted her brows. "You want to move into my rooms in the harem?"

"Hell, no," he growled with a shudder. "I was thinking about our own island." There was another blast of power. This one shattered his mirror. "Far, far away," he continued with a grimace.

"First you need to answer the door," she warned.

Accepting he'd pushed his master far enough, Torque leaned down to press a swift kiss against Rya's mouth.

"Don't move," he commanded.

Forcing himself to straighten, he headed out of the bedroom and across the open living space. Then, not bothering with a shirt or shoes, he pulled open the door.

He found Baine in his usual human shape. Narrow face, Asian features, and almond-shaped eyes that burned with the same amber fire as Rya's.

Today his black hair was pulled into a tail at his nape and he was wearing a loose pair of dojo pants that revealed the metallic tattoos that swirled over his chest with vibrant color.

"What?" Torque demanded.

Baine planted his hands on his hips, his brows lifted.

"That's not a very nice way to greet me."

Belatedly realizing that being rude to a dragon was a good way to end up toast, quite literally, he gave a stiff bow of his head.

"Forgive me, master," he murmured. "I was hoping for some time alone with my mate."

Baine glanced over his shoulder, noting the overturned furniture that had happened during their frenzied arrival in the lair.

"Have you completed the ceremony?"

"Not yet. We're waiting for Kai to recover her strength." His lips twisted in a rueful smile. "And now I suppose we'll have to include my mother," he added. From the short amount of time he'd spent with Nalani, he was fairly certain she would be overjoyed to be asked to assist with his formal mating. "Not that I need a ceremony. As far as I'm concerned, Rya is mine."

"Yes." The floor beneath their fcct abruptly shuddered. A sure sign that Baine was trying to control his emotions. Not his greatest skill. "Kai is the reason I'm here."

Torque hissed. Damn. He'd been so caught up in his annoyance at being interrupted during his time alone with Rya, he hadn't considered that Baine might be there to deliver bad news.

"Has something happened?"

"Not to her."

"Thank the goddess." He released a breath he didn't even know he was holding. Rya would be destroyed if her mother had been hurt. "What is it?"

"Kai traveled to Synge's lair to use her magic to keep Blayze unconscious," Baine said.

Torque nodded. "Yeah, she promised to help while Ravel seeks a way to end the curse." He studied his companion's grim expression. "It didn't work?"

"She didn't have a chance to try."

Torque felt a stab of surprise. When they'd left Synge's lair he'd been desperate to locate Kai so she could help his daughter. "Why not?"

"Blayze is missing."

Missing? Torque blinked. And then blinked again.

The words didn't make any sense. Nothing and no one could get into a dragon's lair. Well, except Baine's mate, Tayla.

Which meant she couldn't have been kidnapped.

And since she was knocked unconscious, she

couldn't have walked out.

So that left…? What?

"How's that possible?" he at last muttered.

Baine shook his head. "No one knows, but my father is on a full-out rampage trying to discover what happened."

Torque shuddered. He didn't doubt for a second that Synge's fury was epic. He'd just had his daughter returned to him. Now to have her snatched away…

Yeah. He was going to make sure Rya stayed away from her father until Blayze was returned.

Already considering the best means of convincing his stubborn mate to avoid Synge's lair, Torque was struck by a sudden thought.

"Wait," he said. "What about Char?"

Flames danced in Baine's amber eyes. "He's missing too."

"Oh, shit," he breathed.

Baine gave a slow nod. "Yeah, that pretty much sums it up."

KILL WITHOUT MERCY (ARES SECURITY)

BY ALEXANDRA IVY

PROLOGUE

Few people truly understood the meaning of 'hell on earth.'

The five soldiers who had been held in the Taliban prison in southern Afghanistan, however, possessed an agonizingly intimate knowledge of the phrase.

There was nothing like five weeks of brutal torture to teach a man that there are worse things than death.

It should have broken them. Even the most hardened soldiers could shatter beneath the acute psychological and physical punishment. Instead the torment only honed their ruthless determination to escape their captors.

In the dark nights they pooled their individual resources.

Rafe Vargas, a covert ops specialist. Max Grayson, trained in forensics. Hauk Laurensen, a sniper who was an expert with weapons. Teagan Moore, a computer wizard. And Lucas St. Clair, the smooth-talking hostage negotiator.

Together they forged a bond that went beyond friendship. They were a family bound by the grim determination to survive.

CHAPTER ONE

Friday nights in Houston meant crowded bars, loud music and ice-cold beer. It was a tradition that Rafe and his friends had quickly adapted to suit their own tastes when they moved to Texas five months ago.

After all, none of them were into the dance scene. They were too old for half-naked coeds and casual hookups. And none of them wanted to have to scream over pounding music to have a decent conversation.

Instead, they'd found The Saloon, a small, cozy bar with lots of polished wood, a jazz band that played softly in the background, and a handful of locals who knew better than to bother the other customers. Oh, and the finest tequila in the city.

They even had their own table that was reserved for them every Friday night.

Tucked in a back corner, it was shrouded in shadows and well away from the long bar that ran the length of one wall. A perfect spot to observe without being observed.

And best of all, situated so no one could sneak up from behind.

It might have been almost two years since they'd returned from the war, but none of them had forgotten.

Lowering your guard, even for a second, could mean death.

Lesson. Fucking. Learned.

Tonight, however, it was only Rafe and Hauk at the table, both of them sipping tequila and eating peanuts from a small bucket.

Lucas was still in Washington D.C., working his contacts to help drum up business for their new security business, ARES. Max had remained at their new offices, putting the final touches on his precious forensics lab, and Teagan was on his way to the bar after installing a computer system that would give Homeland Security a hemorrhage if they knew what he was doing.

Leaning back in his chair, Rafe intended to spend the night relaxing after a long week of hassling with the red tape and bullshit regulations that went into opening a new business, when he made the mistake of checking his messages.

"Shit."

He tossed his cellphone on the polished surface of the wooden table, a tangled ball of emotions lodged in the pit of his stomach.

Across the table Hauk sipped his tequila and studied Rafe with a lift of his brows.

At a glance, the two men couldn't be more different.

Rafe had dark hair that had grown long enough to touch the collar of his white button-down shirt along with dark eyes that were lushly framed by long, black lashes. His skin remained tanned dark bronze despite the fact it was late September, and his body was honed with muscles that came from working on the small ranch he'd just purchased, not the gym.

Hauk, on the other hand, had inherited his Scandinavian father's pale blond hair that he kept cut short, and brilliant blue eyes that held a cunning intelligence. He had a narrow face with sculpted features that were usually set in a stern expression.

And it wasn't just their outward appearance that made them so different.

Rafe was hot tempered, passionate and willing to trust his gut instincts.

Hauk was aloof, calculating, and mind-numbingly anal. Not that Hauk would admit he was OCD. He preferred to call himself detail-oriented.

Which was exactly why he was a successful sniper. Rafe, on the other hand, had been trained in combat rescue. He was capable of making quick decisions, and ready to change strategies on the fly.

"Trouble?" Hauk demanded.

Rafe grimaced. "The real estate agent left a message saying she has a buyer for my grandfather's house."

Hauk looked predictably confused. Rafe had been bitching about the need to get rid of his grandfather's house since the old man's death a year ago.

"Shouldn't that be good news?"

"It would be if I didn't have to travel to Newton to clean it out," Rafe said.

"Aren't there people you can hire to pack up the shit and send it to you?"

"Not in the middle of fucking nowhere."

Hauk's lips twisted into a humorless smile. "I've been in the middle of fucking nowhere, amigo, and it ain't Kansas," he said, the shadows from the past darkening his eyes.

"Newton's in Iowa, but I get your point," Rafe conceded. He did his best to keep the memories in the past where they belonged. Most of the time he was successful. Other times the demons refused to be leashed. "Okay, it's not the hell hole we crawled out of, but the town might as well be living in another century.

I'll have to go deal with my grandfather's belongings myself."

Hauk reached to pour himself another shot of tequila from the bottle that had been waiting for them in the center of the table.

Like Rafe, he was dressed in an Oxford shirt, although his was blue instead of white, and he was wearing black dress pants instead of jeans.

"I know you think it's a pain, but it's probably for the best."

Rafe glared at his friend. The last thing he wanted was to drive a thousand miles to pack up the belongings of a cantankerous old man who'd never forgiven Rafe's father for walking away from Iowa. "Already trying to get rid of me?"

"Hell no. Of the five of us, you're the..."

"I'm afraid to ask," Rafe muttered as Hauk hesitated.

"The glue," he at last said.

Rafe gave a bark of laughter. He'd been called a lot of things over the years. Most of them unrepeatable. But glue was a new one. "What the hell does that mean?"

Hauk settled back in his seat. "Lucas is the smooth-talker, Max is the heart, Teagan is the brains and I'm the organizer." The older man shrugged. "You're the one who holds us all together. ARES would never have happened without you."

Rafe couldn't argue. After returning to the States, the five of them had been transferred to separate hospitals to treat their numerous injuries. It would have been easy to drift apart. The natural instinct was to avoid anything that could remind them of the horror they'd endured.

But Rafe had quickly discovered that returning to civilian life wasn't a simple matter of buying a home and getting a 9-to-5 job.

He couldn't bear the thought of being trapped in a small cubicle eight hours a day, or returning to an empty condo that would never be a home.

It felt way too much like the prison he'd barely escaped.

Besides, he found himself actually missing the bastards.

Who else could understand his frustrations? His inability to relate to the tedious, everyday problems of civilians? His lingering nightmares?

So giving into his impulse, he'd phoned Lucas, knowing he'd need the man's deep pockets to finance his crazy scheme. Astonishingly, Lucas hadn't even hesitated before saying 'yes.' It'd been the same for Hauk and Max and Teagan.

All of them had been searching for something that would not only use their considerable skills, but would make them feel as if they hadn't been put out to pasture like bulls that were past their prime.

And that was how ARES had been born.

Now he frowned at the mere idea of abandoning his friends when they were on the cusp of realizing their dream.

"Then why are you encouraging me to leave town when we're just getting ready to open for business?"

"Because he was your family."

"Bull. Shit." Rafe growled. "The jackass turned his back on my father when he joined the army. "He never did a damned thing for us."

"And that's why you need to go," Hauk insisted. "You need—"

"You say the word closure and I'll put my fist down your throat," Rafe interrupted, grabbing his glass and tossing back the shot of tequila.

Hauk ignored the threat with his usual arrogance. "Call it what you want, but until you forgive the old man for hurting your father it's going to stay a burr in your ass."

Rafe shrugged. "It matches my other burrs."

Without warning, Hauk leaned forward, his expression somber. "Rafe, it's going to take a couple of weeks before we're up and running. Finish your business and come back when you're ready."

Rafe narrowed his gaze. There was no surprise that Hauk was pressing him to deal with his past. Deep in his heart, Rafe knew his friend was right.

But he could hear the edge in Hauk's voice that made him suspect this was more than just a desire to see Rafe dealing with his resentment toward his grandfather. "There's something you're not telling me."

"Hell, I have a thousand things I don't tell you," Hauk mocked, lifting his glass with a mocking smile. "I am a vast, boundless reservoir of knowledge."

A classic deflection. Rafe laid his palms on the table, leaning forward. "You're also full of shit." His voice was hard with warning. "Now spill."

"Pushy bastard." Hauk's smile disappeared. "Fine. There was another note left on my desk."

Rafe hissed in frustration.

The first note had appeared just days after they'd first arrived in Houston.

It'd been left in Hauk's car with a vague warning that he was being watched.

They'd dismissed it as a prank. Then a month later a second note had been taped to the front door of the office building they'd just rented.

This one had said the clock was ticking.

Once again Hauk had tried to pretend it was nothing, but Teagan had instantly installed a state of the art alarm system, while Lucas had used his charm to make personal friends among the local authorities and encouraged them to keep a close eye on the building.

“What the fuck?” Rafe clenched his teeth as a chill inched down his spine. He had a really, really bad feeling about the notes. “Did you check the security footage?”

“Well gosh, darn,” Hauk drawled. “Why didn’t I think of that?”

“No need to be a smartass.”

Hauk drained his glass of tequila. “But I’m so good at it.”

“No shit.”

Hauk pushed aside his empty glass and met Rafe’s worried gaze.

“Look, everything that can be done is being done. Teagan has tapped into the traffic cameras. Unless our visitor is a ghost he’ll eventually be spotted arriving or leaving. Max is working his forensic magic on the note, and Lucas has asked the local cops to contact the neighboring businesses to see if they’ve noticed anything unusual.”

“I don’t like this, Hauk.”

“It’s probably some whackadoodle I’ve pissed off,” the older man assured him. “Not everyone finds me as charming as you do.”

Rafe gave a short, humorless laugh. Hauk was intelligent, fiercely loyal, and a natural leader. He could also be cold, arrogant, and inclined to assume he was always right. “Hard to believe.”

“I know, right?” Hauk batted his lashes. “I’m a doll.”

“You’re a pain in the ass, but no one gets to threaten you but me,” Rafe said. “These notes feel...off.”

Hauk reached to pour himself another shot, his features hardening into an expression that warned he was done with the discussion.

“We’ve got it covered, Rafe. Go to Kansas.”

“Iowa.”

"Wherever." Hauk grabbed the cellphone on the table and pressed it into Rafe's hand. "Take care of the house."

Rafe reluctantly rose to his feet. He could argue until he was blue in the face, but Hauk would deal with the threat in his own way.

"Call if you need me."

"Yes, mother."

With a roll of his eyes, Rafe made his way through the crowd that filled the bar, ignoring the inviting glances from the women who deliberately stepped into his path.

He was man enough to fully appreciate what was on offer. But since his return stateside he'd discovered the promise of a fleeting hookup left him cold.

He didn't know what he wanted, but he hadn't found it yet.

He'd just reached the door when he met Teagan entering the bar.

The large, heavily muscled man with dark caramel skin, golden eyes and his hair shaved close to his skull didn't look like a computer wizard. Hell, he looked like he should be riding with the local motorcycle gang. And it wasn't just that his arms were covered with tattoos or that he was wearing fatigues and leather shit-kickers.

It was in the air of violence that surrounded him and his don't-screw-with-me expression.

Of course, he'd been thrown in jail at the age of thirteen for hacking into a bank to make his mother's car loan disappear. So he'd never been the traditional nerd.

"I'm headed out."

"So early?" Teagan glanced toward the crowd that was growing progressively louder. "The party's just getting started."

"I'll take a rain check." Rafe said. "I'm leaving town for a few days."

"Business?"

"Family."

"Fuck," Teagan muttered.

The man rarely discussed his past, but he'd never made a secret of the fact he deeply resented the father who'd beaten his mother nearly to death before abandoning both of them.

"Exactly," Rafe agreed before leaning forward to keep anyone from overhearing his words. "Keep an eye on Hauk. I don't think he's taking the threats seriously enough."

"Got a hunch?" Teagan demanded.

Rafe nodded, as always surprised at how easily his friends accepted his gut instincts. "If someone wanted to hurt him, they wouldn't send a warning," he pointed out. "Especially not when he's surrounded by friends who are experts in tracking down and destroying enemies."

Teagan nodded. "True."

"So either the bastard has a death-wish. Or he's playing a game of cat and mouse."

"What would be the point?"

Rafe didn't have a clue. But people didn't taunt a man as dangerous as Hauk unless they were prepared for the inevitable conclusion.

One of them would die.

Rafe gave a sharp shake of his head. "Let's hope we have culprit in custody when we find out. Otherwise..."

"Nothing's going to happen to him, my man." Teagan grabbed Rafe's shoulder. "Not on my watch."

ABOUT THE AUTHOR

Alexandra Ivy is a New York Times and USA Today bestselling author of the Guardians of Eternity, as well as the Sentinels, Dragons of Eternity and ARES series. After majoring in theatre she decided she prefers to bring her characters to life on paper rather than stage. She lives in Missouri with her family. Visit her website at alexandraivy.com

Other Books by Alexandra Ivy

DRAGONS OF ETERNITY

BURNED BY DARKNESS
KINDLE: http://amzn.to/1JUmwA1
AMAZON PRINT: http://amzn.to/1G4cpVy
NOOK: http://bit.ly/1JglFtK
KOBO: http://bit.ly/1Jfrd6D
IBOOKS: http://apple.co/1zUPABn
GOOGLE PLAY: http://bit.ly/1dsR54D

ARES SERIES

KILL WITHOUT MERCY
KINDLE: http://amzn.to/1NZm7Nj
AMAZON PRINT: http://amzn.to/1Cq8K3d
NOOK: http://bit.ly/1JqAGui
B&N PRINT: http://bit.ly/1JRzMVV
ITUNES: http://apple.co/1HZe1T8
KOBO: http://bit.ly/1D2I4YO
BOOKSAMILLION: http://bit.ly/1yc7Ef0

GOOGLE PLAY: http://bit.ly/1z210TI

SENTINELS:

BLOOD LUST:
KINDLE: http://amzn.to/1KoE41O
AMAZON PRINT: http://amzn.to/1OyQaiu
KOBO: http://bit.ly/1FPmJkW
BOOKSAMIILION: http://bit.ly/1FPmSVH
BOOKSAMILLION PRINT: http://bit.ly/1FiSnfP
NOOK: http://bit.ly/1MwvhzB
B&N PRINT: http://bit.ly/1keNUkW

ON THE HUNT:
KINDLE: http://amzn.to/1ZlnA85
NOOK: http://bit.ly/1In9jUr
KOBO: http://bit.ly/1ZnewzB

RAPTURE SERIES BUNDLE:

KINDLE: http://amzn.to/1Piu2WU
NOOK: http://bit.ly/1Q1ES33
KOBO: http://bit.ly/1mggh2N

GUARDIANS OF ETERNITY

WHEN DARKNESS ENDS
B&N: http://bit.ly/1ExPYc9
AMAZON: http://amzn.to/1EKROZ9
KOBO: http://bit.ly/1FA1rbA
ITUNES: http://apple.co/1NZnQIB
GOOGLE: http://bit.ly/1JvJU6K
BOOKSAMILLION: http://bit.ly/1yc8Dvr

DARKNESS ETERNAL
AMAZON: http://amzn.to/1ACFHOk

B&N: http://bit.ly/1Emy8IQ
KOBO: http://bit.ly/1FXprFu
IBOOKS: http://apple.co/1BSRE31

HUNT THE DARKNESS
KINDLE: http://amzn.to/1euRlxQ
NOOK: http://bit.ly/1dxG9wz
KOBO: http://bit.ly/1UslA9R
IBOOKS: http://apple.co/1EgIyN7

EMBRACE THE DARKNESS:
Amazon: http://amzn.to/1vJIcWW
Barnes and Noble: http://bit.ly/1j8qRqz
ITUNES: http://apple.co/1FJ7spi
KOBO: http://bit.ly/1GJ7d9L

WHEN DARKNESS COMES:
AMAZON: http://amzn.to/1z5UVYu
B&N: http://bit.ly/1kbospL
KOBO: http://bit.ly/1N8JUg3
ITUNES: http://apple.co/1EFSsqZ
GOOGLE: http://bit.ly/1GHo3rI

Made in the USA
Lexington, KY
18 April 2016